That is when he appeared.

He stepped out of the darkness into the waning firelight, as if materializing out of nowhere.

For a second, Lyssa thought her eyes deceived her. No man could be so tall, so broad of shoulders. Smoke from the fire swirled around his hard-muscled legs. His leather breeches had seen better days and molded themselves to his thighs. A pistol was stuck in his belt and his eyes beneath the brim of his hat were those of a man who had witnessed too much.

Here was her Knight come to life.

He spoke. "Miss Harrell?" His voice rumbled from a source deep within. It was the voice of command.

Lyssa lifted her chin, all too aware that her knees were shaking. "What do you want?"

The stranger smiled, the expression one of grim satisfaction. "I'm from your father. He wants you home."

CATHY MAXWELL

Adventures of a
SCOTTISH HEIRESS

AVON BOOKS

An Imprint of HarperCollinsPublishers

This is a work of fiction. Names, characters, places, and incidents are products of the author's imagination or are used fictitiously and are not to be construed as real. Any resemblance to actual events, locales, organizations, or persons, living or dead, is entirely coincidental.

AVON BOOKS
An Imprint of HarperCollins*Publishers*
10 East 53rd Street
New York, New York 10022-5299

Copyright © 2003 by Cathy Maxwell
Excerpts from *Adventures of a Scottish Heiress* copyright © 2003 by Cathy Maxwell; *Flowers from the Storm* copyright © 1992 by Amanda Moor Jay; *And Then He Kissed Me* copyright © 2003 by Patti Berg; *Fool for Love* copyright © 2003 by Eloisa James
ISBN: 0-06-009296-3
www.avonromance.com

First Avon Books paperback printing: May 2003

Avon Trademark Reg. U.S. Pat. Off. and in Other Countries, Marca Registrada, Hecho en U.S.A.
HarperCollins® is a registered trademark of HarperCollins Publishers Inc.

Printed in the U.S.A.

10 9 8 7 6 5 4 3 2 1

For Trinity Jude Sencindiver
Welcome to the world!

Chapter One

August, 1816

IAN Campion was bloody tired of being poor.

Making his way through the foul and narrow streets of the rookery known as the Holy Land for the Irish inhabitants who lived one on top of another there in unrelenting poverty, he wondered how he could have ever believed he could create a better life for his family here than the one they'd had in Ireland. He hated the closeness of the buildings, the crushed spirit of the people, and the soot in the air from the hundreds, no, thousands of smoking chimneys.

Of course, the last time he'd lived in London, he'd been on his way to becoming a man of means as a student of the law at Lincoln's Inn. The streets he'd walked had been vastly different then. His future had been full of promise until he'd returned to Dublin and destroyed everything with his pride and arrogance.

His dark thoughts were interrupted when a half

dozen children in ragged clothes dashed past him
on the chase for a rat one of them had spied. Their
mothers sat on the front stoop sucking down gin
and laughing wildly at some joke one of them had
shared. The women fell silent, their expressions
speculative, when a party of barefoot, unkempt
sailors newly off their ship swaggered by on their
way to one of the area's many brothels. Meanwhile,
in the entrance of a supposed butcher's shop, pick-
pockets, lazy and in good humor from working
richer areas, haggled with the "butcher" over fenc-
ing their stolen goods.

Ian walked through the party of sailors. They
had the good sense to move out of his way, as he
knew they would.

He was a big man, a hard one, and willing to
use his size to his advantage. The wide brim of the
hat he wore low over his eyes added to his dangerous air. His hand rested on the strap of the
leather knapsack he'd stolen off the body of a
dead French soldier during the war over a year
ago. In it was everything he owned, including the
flintlock pistol that could get him transported if it
was found on his person. The English weren't
comfortable with the idea of an Irishman walking
their streets with a gun.

Not that they would need the gun as a reason to
see Ian gone.

A whore sitting in a window across the street
called in greeting, "Well, look who has finally returned home." She leaned forward, her breasts

practically tumbling out of her bodice. "Hey, Campion, are you going to give me a go this time?"

Ducking into the narrow, open doorway of a corner building, Ian ignored her, as he always did. He didn't consort with whores. There was no time in his life for women or other pleasurable pursuits—not while he had a family to support.

The rickety stairs groaned under his booted tread. Sound carried through the thin walls. A baby cried for milk. A man and woman argued, an argument that came to an abrupt end with the sound of a fist hitting flesh. A door slammed and there was silence, then crying. Ian stepped out of the way as a heavy-jowled man, his eyes red from drinking, barreled past him down the stairs.

Three more flights up and Ian reached home to the flat he shared with his two sisters and their children. But what he saw made his heart stop.

The door to the flat had been broken off its hinges. It hung cockeyed and loose, the wood splintered.

Alarmed, he charged in, his fists clenched and ready to do battle. However, instead of a deadly crime, he ran in on the sight of the little ones, Johnny and Maeve, at the table saying their grace before supper. His sudden, angry entrance startled his sister Janet, who stood over them. With a startled cry, she dropped the wooden platter she was holding. The supper sausages hit the floor, but the children didn't care. They leaped from their chairs, their arms wide.

"Uncle Ian!" they shouted in unison. Johnny tackled Ian's knees while Maeve stretched her arms for him to take her up, which he did.

"You're prickly," Maeve laughingly complained, rubbing her fist against his beard stubble. "And you have a cut, too." Maeve, no older than five but a sweet, gentle soul, traced the line above his eye where Tommy Harrigan's beefy knuckles had split the skin open.

"It's nothing but a nuisance," he assured her and then addressed his nephew, "Johnny, you're growing so fast you're about to knock me over." He'd been gone less than a month, but children change rapidly at this age.

His words only served to make the lad determined to do more damage. There was nothing for Ian to do but set Maeve down and give her brother the quick wrestle he so dearly wanted.

Janet broke them up. "Here now, that is enough. Welcome home, brother." She gave him a kiss on the cheek at about the same time Ian's other sister Fiona, the oldest of the three of them, walked in the door. They were all dark-headed, the girls with eyes so blue they sparkled like jewels, while Ian had the sharp, silvery gray ones of his father.

"Ian," Fiona greeted him with undisguised relief. "I am so glad to see you home."

"What happened to the door?" he asked.

"Later," she whispered as she gave him a sisterly kiss. "After the children have eaten."

He pulled out the cloth pouch he wore on a cord around his neck. Taking it off over his head, he tossed it to Janet. "There's not as much as I'd hoped there. At the fair in Birmingham I ran into a lad who was half a head taller and had a punch like a mule's. I ended up having to give him half of what I had planned to bring home."

"Someone beat you?" Johnny asked incredulously.

"There's always someone that can beat you, lad. A wise man chooses his fights carefully," Ian advised him.

"Then you shouldn't have fought him," Maeve said.

The common sense of her words startled a laugh out of Ian and he agreed. "Aye, and, Johnny, I have no desire to see you using your fists for a living."

"I want to be like you."

"And I want you to be a *better* man than I." His words echoed those that his father had once said to him, words he'd not fulfilled. "Now sit up at the table and eat your dinner."

Janet had picked up the sausages and settled the children down to their meal. A hungry child didn't waste food, even if it had been on the floor. Besides, in spite of the squalor around them, Janet's floor was so clean a duchess could have eaten off of it and been satisfied.

"Here." Fiona motioned him over to the table. "We've some cheese and a slice of that good bread you like so much. It tastes almost the way Mother used to bake it." At the mention of the word *cheese*, both children looked up longingly.

"Share it," Ian told Janet as he tossed his hat on a nail in the wall. He took his shaving kit from his knapsack and dropped the bag on the floor by a table leg. After washing the dust of travel off his hands and face in a chipped washbasin, taking extra care with the soap to get his nails clean, he shaved. The shadow of his beard gave him a disreputable air, an air that embarrassed him, especially around the children.

Finishing the last stroke of his razor, he noticed there was one sausage left in the pan. "Where is Liam?" he asked, drying his hands on a rag. Liam was the son of Fiona and the man who had been his best friend in the world.

"Out," Fiona said but there was a brightness in her eyes and a wariness in Janet's Ian didn't trust.

Something was not right, and it clearly had to do with the broken door.

Not touching the meager meal before him, he waited impatiently until the children were excused from the table to go play in the corner with their prized toys—a doll and lead soldiers he had brought back from France.

"What happened to the door?" he demanded in a low voice, once Maeve and Johnny were well occupied.

Janet shot an anxious look at Fiona. But her sister answered calmly, "Things have changed in the weeks since you've been gone. Liam is running with a bad crowd. I was out looking for him before you arrived."

"He's only nine," Ian said. "He shouldn't be running the streets."

"Try and stop him," Janet said, cleaning the table. "We have and naught has come of it." She leaned close to Ian to say very softly, "And I worry about Johnny. Until you returned it was Liam he wanted to ape. Glad I am that you are back."

Back to do what? Ian wanted to ask in frustration. For the past ten months, he'd been living by his wits to make money. Every time they seemed to get a bit ahead, some disaster struck, like the croup that had almost claimed Maeve's life or a hike in the bloody rent.

Lately, he'd taken to traveling to village fairs looking for bare-fisted fights. The money was good and he hoped to make a name for himself and fight in London where the money was better. However, the giant in Birmingham had been a setback to his plans.

Still, he was determined to get his sisters and their children out of London. Their husbands had been soldiers like himself. They'd given their lives in England's war against Napoleon, and their families had nothing to show for it save for widows and hungry children.

All he needed was one bit of luck, one opportunity to rise above all of this and free them from the nightmare of what their lives had become. He owed it to his sisters because he was responsible for where they were now. It had been his rash actions, his foolish defiance that had cost his family their land and their fortune.

"It's not your fault," Fiona said quietly, reading his mind.

"It isn't?" he asked bitterly. "If I hadn't been such a fool—"

Janet hushed him with a pointed gaze at the children. "It's past. Done. If it hadn't been you, then the Humphries and the English would have found another reason for stealing our land. Even Father said so."

Ian had his doubts.

"Recriminations are a waste of time," Janet said firmly.

He nodded. She was right. It was their future that should concern him. "What of the door?"

Johnny, whom they had thought wasn't listening, was the one who answered, proving Janet's concerns right. "A man came looking for Liam. A big, ugly man. Mama wouldn't open the door and he broke it in. He woke me up. Maeve, too. She cried, but I didn't."

"You cried, too," his sister answered. Janet crossed to her children.

Anger made Ian dangerous. "Did he find Liam?"

"Not that I know," Fiona said. The tight clasp of her hands in her lap belied her external air of composure. "But, Ian, I can't find him."

"He didn't come home at all?"

"No." The word cut the air. Her jaw tightened as she said, "The landlord wants to charge the price of five doors for the damage."

The money in the cloth purse now seemed a pittance. "I'll take care of it," Ian promised, his temper rising. He'd shake the bastard by his neck until he came to his senses.

Suddenly, there was the sound of footsteps running up the stairs, and a pale-faced Liam appeared in the doorway. In his expression, Ian recognized the signs of a boy being forced to grow up too fast.

Fiona was up from her chair and ready to throw her arms around him but Ian demanded, "Where have you been?"

Liam shrugged off a reply and his mother, something he wouldn't have done several weeks ago. Instead, he said, "There is a gent here in the neighborhood to see you, Ian. He's been asking for you at Boney's." Boney's was the pub around the corner and not a place for young boys. Liam's voice was also losing the soft lilt of their native country and in its place was the edge of the streets.

Ian rose to his good six feet and more. "Didn't I tell you to stay away from the pubs?"

Liam's chin came up before he hesitated and then bowed his head slightly, an acceptance of his uncle's authority—but for how much longer?

"What does the man want?" Ian asked.

"I don't know," Liam answered. "He's on his

way here right now. He's driving a big coach and his horses—! Gawd, Ian, you ought to see them. Matched grays. They are the handsomest I've ever seen."

There was a movement, a shadow in the hallway. His reflexes honed by years of war, Ian pulled Liam and Fiona behind him and faced the door just as a gentleman dressed in a green striped coat with a cherry vest moved with the silence of a cat to stand in the doorway. He wore his impossibly black hair combed forward into curls fringing his forehead. His hat was a green silk to match his coat. "The boy is a good messenger," the gentleman said. "They told me at the pub if I were to follow him, I would find you."

"What do you want me for?" he asked the man coldly.

" 'Tis not I who want you, but my employer, Dunmore Harrell. You have heard of him?"

Who hadn't heard of "Pirate" Harrell, the Scotsman who had made a fortune for himself in trade through hard work and unorthodox investing and was now accepted in the highest circles? Harrell had even married the widow of a duke. There was not a man who wanted to make something better of himself who did not admire him.

"What does he want with me?" Ian asked.

"My name is Parker and we have a job for you, Mr. Campion. We've heard you are a man with a talent for doing what is necessary."

"And how did you hear that?" Ian asked, wary

and all too conscious of Liam listening. There were things he'd had to do to earn money he'd rather not have his family know.

Parker sensed his reticence. He looked Ian right in the eye and said, "From your satisfied employers of course."

Ian weighed the risk. It would do no harm to listen to what the man had to say. "My service doesn't come cheap and I'll not do anything illegal," he lied.

The foppish Parker smiled. "We didn't think you would, sir. As to the particulars, perhaps you will be kind enough to step downstairs with me? A coach awaits to take us to see Mr. Harrell."

Fiona placed her hand on Ian's arm. "Be careful, brother," she whispered. She claimed she had the gift of the sight and although Ian often had his doubts concerning her supposed powers, he was not one to ignore good advice.

"Should I not go?"

"*You must.*"

Her sudden urgency made him pause. She squeezed his arm. "Go. You must go."

Ian didn't like his sudden doubts but he forced them aside. What harm was there in hearing what a man like Harrell had to offer? Had he not just been wishing for a piece of luck?

He covered her hand with his. "I'll be back shortly. Hand me my knapsack." Reaching for his hat, he turned to Liam. "Watch the family—and that means you don't go out."

The lad nodded solemnly.

Satisfied, Ian said, "I'll fix the door when I return."

Downstairs, a handsome, black-enameled carriage took up the width of the street, its bright brass fittings and driver dressed in gold-trimmed livery commanding everyone's attention. Liam had been right. The grays were prime bloodstock. Horses were in the Campions' blood and they knew fine cattle when they saw them.

Parker waved a perfumed kerchief in front of his nose. "The streets stink. Climb in."

Conscious that everyone gaped at him, including the whore in the window, Ian did as ordered. He had never been inside such a large coach or one as luxuriously decked out as this, with its velvet cushions and burled wood paneling. The fop jumped in behind him, a footman closed the door, and in moments they were on their way, the footman shouting at people, "Make way for the horses."

"What is this about?" Ian asked Parker.

"You'll find out soon enough," was the cryptic answer.

Ian grunted his response. He hated surprises.

They drove fifteen minutes to a new, fashionable section of the city. Here the roads were less crowded and far wider. Harrell's man set aside his perfumed cloth and drummed his fingers on the door.

The coach turned into the paved drive of an opulent mansion. The driver reined the horses to a stop. A butler in stark black, a marked contrast to the gold trimmings of the other servants and to Parker's flamboyant jacket and vest, came down the front steps to open the coach door himself. "Mr. Parker, you are to go to the master immediately. He is most impatient."

Parker didn't respond but jumped down, signaling Ian to follow. As Ian stepped out of the coach and walked up the front steps, he was all too conscious of the shabbiness of his appearance. His tanned leather breeches and cobalt coat with its frayed edges were definitely out of place. Ill at ease, he touched his neck cloth, which he wore wrapped around his neck once and loose. The devil-may-care style suited him but it was far too casual for these surroundings.

The main hall was as big and open as a banker's lobby. The black onyx and white marble squares on the floor were polished to such a degree they reflected the worn heels of Ian's boots, and a statue of some ancient Greek with a missing arm and leg stared down at him with unseeing disapproval. Two maids had lowered a chandelier that held at least a hundred candles. They were too busy cleaning off the wax to notice the likes of him.

"Your hat, sir?" the butler asked.

Ian handed it to the man, who passed it to another footman. Harrell apparently had servants for his servants.

Parker walked down a long, thickly carpeted hallway. The air smelled of beeswax and lemon oil. Ian followed, noticing the lavish wealth—the paintings by old masters, the carved scroll work in the wainscoting, the shining brass wall sconces—surrounding him. At the end of the hall, Parker opened a set of double doors without knocking.

"Mr. Campion," he announced and stepped back. Ian had no choice but to walk forward and found himself in a walnut-paneled study. The walls were lined with books and statuary. The carpet was an Indian rug woven of reds and blues. Leather upholstered chairs created seating areas in front of the windows and the huge, ornate desk that dominated the center of the room.

Dunmore Harrell, the richest man in London, rose from a chair behind the desk. Ledger books were stacked in multiple, neat piles in front of him. He took off the glasses perched on the end of his nose and came around to greet Ian.

He was of medium height and whipcord thin with hair that had once been as red as a brick but had faded to a graying muddy brown. Like his butler, he wore austere black, but there was the twinkle of diamonds in the studs he wore in his neckcloth and on the buttons adorning his coat.

If Ian had been sizing Harrell up for a bout in the ring, he'd have considered the man a threat. Harrell obviously knew his strengths and his weaknesses and would use both to his advantage.

He scrutinized Ian with a stare that was discomfiting. Ian challenged him by staring back, opening and closing one fist, a sign to the older man that he was no green lad either.

Harrell's astute green gaze darted to Ian's clenched hand. His lips curved into a half smile, an acknowledgement. "You'll do." He motioned to a chair in front of the desk. "Please sit." Ian noted a small hint of a Scottish burr in his speech, but it was so carefully hidden, however, Harrell could have passed for one of the king's courtiers.

There was another man in the room, but Ian had been so intent on Harrell, he'd not registered the other's presence until he took his seat. Now he looked to the gentleman who had remained sitting in the high-backed winged chair opposite the one Ian was to take. The man was built like a small bull, with a receding hairline and a pompous attitude. Ian decided that here was a man who was more bluster than bite, one who lacked Parker's flamboyant presence.

"This is my daughter's betrothed," Harrell said offhandedly, "*Viscount* Grossett." By the emphasis he placed on "Viscount," Ian knew Harrell was well pleased with his daughter's choice. "My lord, Ian Campion, soldier, mercenary, devil's own henchman when he has the mind to be."

Ian didn't know how to react to such an introduction, and was embarrassed to realize all the titles were accurate.

The viscount leaned back in his chair as if not

wanting to be any closer to Ian than he had to, and he certainly didn't offer his hand. Parker, pulling up a leather-backed chair for himself, stifled a smile—whether over his employer's wit or the viscount's fastidiousness, Ian didn't know, but he didn't like it. And so, he paid extra attention to the viscount.

"Congratulations on your betrothal, my lord," Ian said smoothly, his King's English as good as anyone's in the room . . . and his nails were clean, which the viscount's were not. "When is the happy occasion?" he asked as if the two of them were members of the same club.

A dull red stole up the viscount's neck. Apparently, Ian had touched upon a sensitive subject.

However, it was Harrell who answered. "We hope you can help us with that, Campion." He handed a miniature to Ian. "I have a job for you. I want you to find the young woman in the picture."

Ian took a moment to study the portrait, taking in the pouty lower lip and the long, dark lashes the artist had given her. There was no mistaking her green eyes. This was Harrell's daughter, the much-touted heiress. The viscount's intended. It was a pity to waste beauty and money on a bore. "A redhead," he murmured.

"Very much so," Harrell agreed proudly. "Her hair is the color of the finest garnets and she has a passion for life to match. There is no in between with my daughter, and I want her back."

"Who has her?" Ian asked.

"I don't know," came the curt reply. "There has been no ransom note, no letter, nothing." Harrell leaned across his desk. "But when you find them, *whomever they are*, I want you to make them pay. No one crosses me without receiving like for like. *No one.*"

His words echoed in the stillness of the room and Ian felt his guard go up. Something was not right. "Why ask me? Why not go to Bow Street?"

"I have been to them. They have been incompetent. They want me to tell them where she is—if I knew, I'd go fetch her myself. I am a man who expects results . . . and am willing to pay for them."

Outwardly, Ian was calm, but inside he recognized opportunity. "Do you have any suspicions concerning who might have her?"

"None. There's been no clue." Harrell was not a man who liked to admit defeat. He sank into his chair, aging suddenly. "She's my only link with my late wife. I—" He looked away as if needing to compose himself a moment. "Do you have children, Campion?"

"He's Irish," the viscount said under his breath. "Of course he has children."

"No," Ian said, ignoring the nobleman. "But I do have a niece and nephews."

"Then you can understand my fears," Harrell said. "The thought that Lyssa has been gone this week and more, without a trace . . ." He looked at Ian. "I want her home."

"When did you last see her?"

"A week ago Thursday. She left with her maid and a footman to visit the lending library. Lyssa bid them sit in a chair in the front of the store to wait while she browsed the book aisles, and she never returned. She disappeared, vanished, with nothing but the clothes on her back."

Ian frowned. "Did the Runners find any information?"

"Nothing, not a trace. I put Parker on it and even he, the most resourceful of men, has come up empty-handed."

Ian hesitated in asking this next question because the idea had obviously not struck her father yet. "Could she have deliberately run away?"

Harrell raised his eyebrows as if shocked by the idea. "Why? Lyssa has always been the most obedient of children. She'd have no reason to run away."

Ian could not resist sliding a glance at the viscount. If he was a young woman, he wouldn't want to marry the man, and the woman in the miniature he still held appeared to be anything but docile. Especially if she had even one of her infamous father's traits.

The Viscount Grossett did not mistake his meaning. "What are you implying, Irishman?" he demanded.

"I imply nothing, my lord," Ian countered calmly.

"He is suggesting that perhaps our Lyssa has

reservations about the marriage and has taken matters in her own hand by running away," a feminine, musical voice said from the doorway. The men turned to find a blonde, beautiful woman standing there, one hand still on the door she'd quietly opened.

She blushed, the color becoming to her face. "Please pardon my interruption, gentlemen, but sometimes a woman must eavesdrop if she is ever to know what is going on." She had the most charming lisp. This was the former duchess of Lackland, who upon the ancient duke's death had married Harrell and provided him an entrée into Society.

She walked into the room, jewels sparkling in her hair and on her fingers, her movements smooth in spite of her advanced stage of pregnancy. Obviously, money was a significant inducement for a duchess to choose a commoner's life.

The men all rose to their feet, Harrell coming around the desk to meet her. "My dear, you should be in bed."

"You worry too much, Dunmore, and I wanted to meet the gentleman who is to find our Lyssa." She looked to Ian and offered her hand. "You will find her, won't you?"

Ian took her hand, flattered that she treated him with a modicum of respect. "I will endeavor to try—" He hesitated, uncertain of how to address her. Even though she was married to a commoner, he thought she still retained her title. He'd heard her referred to only as "Duchess," whether because of fact, or the speculation surrounding her marriage, he didn't know. It was apparent Harrell took pride in his wife's station, yet Ian decided to err on the side of caution. "—Mrs. Harrell," he finished, and she nodded, letting him know he was correct.

"Especially if I pay him well enough," Harrell answered, and Ian wondered if matters always came down to money with him.

Mrs. Harrell smiled. She was half her husband's age and a true catch. "You are not quite what we expected, Mr. Campion. Is he, Dunmore?" She did not wait for her husband's response but provided her own, "Find Lyssa, sir, find her so she can discover happiness, as I have, with a husband and a child." She removed her hand from Ian's and proudly rested it on her stomach, and he found himself wondering if it was money or love that had persuaded her to marry the "Pirate."

"He will, he will," Harrell said, clearly worried. "Now please, go lie down. I don't want anything to happen to my son."

Mrs. Harrell laughed, enjoying his concern. She slid her violet-blue gaze toward Ian. "My husband longs for a son, but he also loves his daughter. And Viscount Grossett—he, too, is most anxious. Are you not, sir?"

"Absolutely," the viscount echoed although Ian was certain his concern stemmed from the fear of losing Miss Harrell's fortune more than true worry for her well-being. The man lacked the anxiety of a lover. He met Ian's gaze with defiance. "My family is pleased with this match."

"Even your mother, my lord?" Mrs. Harrell asked archly.

"*Especially* my mother," Grossett returned evenly.

"Well . . . then it is settled." Mrs. Harrell walked to the door. She paused. "I believe, Mr. Campion, you will have your work cut out for you. Lyssa is as headstrong as her father."

"Do you believe her kidnapped?" he dared to ask.

A secret smile lingered on her lips. She shook her head and then shrugged. "I'm not certain, but knowing Lyssa, no one could take her by force without a fight on their hands. She is much like her father. And I do not feel here"—she pressed the tips of her fingers to her breastbone above her heart—"that she is in danger. After all, her books were missing."

"Books?" Ian looked to Harrell.

"My daughter is a bit of a bluestocking, except, of course, she prefers novels with, well, you know, with romance. She's also fond of poetry." He said the last word as if it left a bad taste in his mouth. "But to think she ran away just because some books are missing . . . ?" He shook his head. "She could have given them to the library or to friends."

"Not Lyssa. Her books were her companions," his wife answered. She looked to Ian. "My step-daughter packed her favorite books with her every time she traveled. She'd also much rather have a book in her hand than a possible husband by her side." And Ian knew by her answer that his suspicions were correct—the viscount was Harrell's choice for a husband, not his daughter's. And would a spoiled, petted young woman fond of romantic novels and poetry run away rather than face a betrothal distasteful to her?

Ian almost snorted his answer aloud.

He could feel Mrs. Harrell studying him and knew she shared his suspicions. "Good luck, Mr. Campion," she said and floated out of the room, Harrell watching her leave with the longing of the truly lovestruck.

Reluctantly, he brought his attention back to Ian after his wife had shut the door firmly behind her. "Find Lyssa, Campion, and see that whoever helped her pays."

"I'm no murderer," Ian said quietly.

Harrell's gaze hardened with undisguised irritation. He looked to Parker who kept his expression carefully neutral. A muscle worked in Harrell's jaw, and then he said to Ian, "I don't want a murder. Retribution, yes. But I've no desire to see a hangman's noose. Right, Parker?"

"As you say, sir."

"We've heard you are the man for such a job," Harrell said. "And I believe you are. You are no one's fool, and you handle yourself well. Lyssa's maid will travel with you. Proprieties must be observed."

Now Ian understood why Harrell clung to the notion his daughter had been taken against her will. He was a socially ambitious man, not only for himself but his children. Society could be harsh on runaway young women, especially heiresses with common backgrounds. Still a maid was an encumbrance. "A maid will slow down my hunt. And I have no idea where I will be forced to go to learn your daughter's whereabouts."

"Her reputation must be protected at all costs," Harrell answered. "She is to be a viscountess. I'm certain viscount Grossett will wish her reputation to be unsullied."

Ian was equally certain the viscount would have taken Harrell's daughter in marriage if she'd been a one-eyed hag with no teeth—but thought it best not to say such to her father.

His opinion was confirmed when Harrell added, "At Viscount Grossett's suggestion, we've put out the word that Lyssa is visiting my wife's uncle who is the ambassador to Rome. That buys us some time but not much. Bring her home quickly. I wish to see her married before her brother is born."

Looking down at the miniature in his hand, Ian decided finding one missing lass should not be difficult. Especially with hair like hers. He could see a hint of her father's tenacity in the determined set of her chin and the sparkle of intelligence in her eyes.

He prayed she was safe and had not been harmed.

This was one job he would like doing. "My price is two hundred pounds." The amount sounded astronomical to Ian. He was surprised he could dare to ask it.

Harrell didn't blink. "Done."

Immediately, Ian wished he'd asked for more—but the lawyer in him knew it was too late. "I need funds in advance."

"Fifty pounds and the balance on your return."

"One hundred."

"Seventy-five."

Ian thought it odd a father so anxious for the return of his daughter, a man who had all the money he could need would barter . . . but then, that seemed to be the way of the very rich.

Mentally figuring the expenses he would need to move his family temporarily out of the Holy Land's squalor, he agreed, "Seventy-five and two horses."

"What? And that is to include no murder?" Harrell said, and then quickly waved his hand. "I'm jesting. Seventy-five and cattle it is. Parker, pay him and make the arrangements for the horses and the maid. Start your search immediately, Campion. Too much time has passed already."

"If she has not met foul play, sir," Ian reminded him gently.

Her father shook his head, his expression fierce. "I am like my wife. I believe she is alive and well. If not, I would know it."

Ian prayed he was right. "I shall find her."

"I know you will," Harrell agreed bluntly. "Because you are a man who wants money."

He was right.

Not only that, but this would be easy money. After all, how hard could it be to track down one romantic-minded heiress lugging a load of books?

Not hard at all.

Chapter Two

Six days later

RUNNING away was the best, most adventuresome idea Lyssa Harrell had ever had, and she was enjoying herself immensely.

For the first time in her life she was free. Here, no patronizing lords or snobbish debutantes laughed that her hems smelled of Trade when they thought she wasn't listening or gave her the "cut" because they enjoyed feeling superior. Nor did anyone compare her to an elegant, beautiful stepmother who had completely supplanted Lyssa in her father's life.

However, most of all, she was happy there was no insufferable Robert, Viscount Grossett, to let her know what a favor he was performing to offer her marriage. And she was more than tickled at the prospect of never setting eyes on his gambling-crazed, high-and-mighty mother again.

Ah, yes, freedom was a fine and wonderful thing.

Lyssa wrapped her blue-and-green plaid, the

tartan of the Davidsons, around her and smiled into the campfire's flames. Traveling by Gypsy wagon was a wonderfully romantic way to reach her destination. All was exactly as she liked it. She had new friends in Abrams and his wife, Duci, a motherly mentor in the guise of Abrams' mother, Madame Linka, and a pleasant colorful mode of transportation where no one knew her or cared to ask questions, because Gypsies were rarely welcome anywhere. She rather liked playing the role of an outcast, since she'd been one in Society for years.

Better still, anyone her father sent to hunt her down would not think to look for her here.

Oh, yes, she had engineered her running away as carefully as her father plotted shipping schedules. In another day or two, they would arrive at Amleth Hall, the seat of her mother's clan, the Davidsons, in the Highlands. Her mother's people would take her in, and fortune-hunting Robert could kiss her money good-bye.

Of course, she did have a pang of conscience over her poor papa worrying about her . . . but she also had a healthy respect for his ire. The smartest course she could take was to place plenty of England between herself and him . . . or would he even notice her missing?

He was so besotted with his "duchess," especially now that she carried his "son," it seemed he had little care for Lyssa anymore. Yes, she was three and twenty, and the Duchess was right, she should think about marriage—but Lyssa wanted to pick her own husband. And she missed how close she and her father used to be.

His new wife had stepped in between them. She'd pushed Lyssa's father to force her out for a Season when Lyssa felt too old and too awkward. She'd orchestrated the courtship with Robert and had campaigned for Lyssa's father to accept the marriage offer over Lyssa's protests.

And all the while, she had expected Lyssa to befriend her. She'd even wanted Lyssa to call her Frances. Lyssa would never do that. To do so would be admitting that the Duchess had taken her mother's place—and Lyssa would not let her.

Now, as Lyssa listened to the night chirping of frogs and crickets, she felt she had finally had the last say—*no marriage*. At least, not to Viscount Grossett . . . or anyone else of her stepmother's choosing.

"It is time for sleep," Abrams announced, returning to the ring of light around the campfire. He'd gone off in the woods for a moment alone. He would sleep in front of the fire while the women climbed into the cramped quarters of the red and purple painted wagon.

Duci and Lyssa rose dutifully; Madame Linka, however, did not move. Instead, puffing her pipe, she said, "I need my cards."

Duci looked at Madame Linka in surprise. "Now?"

"Yes. I must read Viveka's future. The time is at

hand." "Viveka" was Madame's name for Lyssa. Duci had told her it meant "little woman." The name pleased Lyssa, and since she didn't want anyone to know her identity until she was safe in the arms of the Davidson clan, she continued to use it. Even Abrams and Duci called her by this name.

"It is late, Madame," Abrams protested wearily. "We have a long day ahead of us on the morrow. Certainly this can wait?"

"No. Now."

The tone in her voice brooked no argument. The hairs tingled at the back of Lyssa's neck and she knew she wasn't alone. Duci's eyes widened and even Abrams appeared surprised. From the beginning of the trip, Lyssa had been begging Madame Linka for a reading. She'd even offered to pay a goodly sum—and been refused.

So why did Madame wish to do one now?

Abrams did not question his mother a second time. "I will fetch your tray and your cards."

While her husband climbed into the wagon, Duci asked, "Do you wish a drink of gin, madame?"

Madame Linka shook her head. "Sit here, Viveka. I need you to watch my hands move over the cards."

Lyssa sat on the log stool across from Madame's chair. They were as close to the fire as they could be for the light. Abrams set up a folding table and then reverently handed Madame her tarot. He was very proud of this ability of hers. He'd told

Lyssa that Madame had predicted his meeting Duci and everything else of importance in his life. He said she'd once given a reading for the king of Spain, who'd been so taken with what her cards had revealed, he'd gifted her with the gold ring that hung on a chain around her neck.

Madame removed the deck from their velvet box. "Here, Viveka, shuffle the cards."

"For how long?"

"You will know," was the enigmatic reply.

Lyssa's fingers trembled in anticipation. The tarot were more than ordinary cards. Abrams had told her this set had been handed down from one fortune-teller to another amongst his tribe. No one knew how old the cards were, but they could only be given to one who had the "gift." The medieval characters on the faces were hand painted, and the gilded edges and bright colors of the cards, with their legends in French and Arabic, had been dulled by the passage of time.

The large size of the cards made shuffling difficult. Lyssa shuffled once, then started to shuffle again but stopped. A whisper of a voice in the recesses of her mind said *This is enough.*

Lyssa set the stack of cards facedown on the table.

Madame Linka smiled. "Good."

Duci and Abrams had pulled up a log for seats for themselves. Now, they held their breath just as Lyssa did as Madame lifted the top card from the deck and place it and two other cards face down.

"This is the Past," Madame said. "Here is the Present." She laid a row of three cards beneath the first. Then, she took the next card off the deck and pressed it into Lyssa's hands. "This is your Future. Hold it tightly and do not look until I am ready."

Lyssa nodded, conscious of the power of the card in her hand.

"Why do you not give her three cards for her Future like you have for the Past and Present, Mama?" Duci asked. "I have not seen you do this before."

"I do as the cards bid," Madame replied dismissively and turned over the first card in the row signifying Lyssa's past. Her eyebrows came up and she made a soft sound of acknowledgement. "The Seven of Cups." Her dark gaze met Lyssa's. "The Lord of Debauch."

Lyssa stared at the drawing of seven cups spilling their contents into what appeared to be a river of wine. "What does it mean?"

"That you have been surrounded by a multitude of many pleasures in your past. Pleasures that perhaps you don't trust and may even fear."

"This is true," Lyssa whispered under her breath. She did fear the *ton*, their many excesses, their different codes of conduct and double standards. In spite of her father's wealth and the grand home and beautiful clothes, she preferred a simpler life. Her books were her most valued possessions. Nor did she like the idea of being married to a husband who thought about nothing but spending money. She wanted a man like her father had been, one who had cherished the memory of his wife, until he became besotted of that woman.

Madame turned over the second card. Her smile turned grim as if she were not surprised. Ten silver staffs crisscrossed yellow-orange flames. "The Lord of Oppression. You have felt frustrated, angry. You want to be free."

"I want to find my roots," Lyssa acknowledged. "I want to meet my mother's clan." She leaned forward. "Will I?"

"We still have a card in your past," Madame replied and flipped over the last in the row with the tip of her nail. A huge wheel covered the face of the card. Tapping the card, Madame said, "The wheel of fortune turns and we poor mortals struggle." She shook her head. "I don't know why. There is abundance enough for all in the world. This card holds the secret of turning events to your advantage. And that is what you have done in leaving your past."

Reverend Billows might claim fortune-telling was nonsense and even heresy but Lyssa felt immense relief that the cards seemed to be saying she'd made the right decision when she ran away.

Smiling now, Madame flipped over the first card of Lyssa's Present and then frowned.

Duci gasped and said, "Death." Abrams crossed himself.

Lyssa did not like the picture of a grinning

skeleton that appeared to be dancing on a grave. "What does it mean?"

"Nothing like what you fear it does," Madame hurried to assure her. "When Death appears, it means there will be a change in your life, the kind of change that will alter you forever."

"Well, that's what I have right now," Lyssa responded, relieved.

Madame shook her head. "No. Death would be in your Past if that were its meaning. Here, it is telling us something completely different. The change is now. This moment . . . and something beyond our simple camp."

Lyssa glanced around at the darkness beyond the ring of firelight. Was it her imagination or did the shadow of the fir trees seem closer and more looming than before? She looked back to Madame. "My father—?"

"You will not be with us much longer." Madame did not wait but overturned the next card. What it revealed was even more alarming.

"The Hanged Man," Abrams said. The card was of the figure of a man hanging upside down from a tree branch. His hands appeared tied behind his back.

Madame Linka nodded. "You are vulnerable, Viveka," she said, her raspy voice menacing in the silence. "Whatever will be, you must accept. Your destiny is at hand and you must find strength within to meet it."

Lyssa did not like this fortune . . . especially

when deep in her bones she sensed an element of truth, of warning.

Madame turned over the third card of the Present. A naked woman sat astride a giant creature that was half lion, half man. The woman's head was tilted back as if in joy, one hand raised toward a shining star. The card made Lyssa uncomfortable, yet there was power in the strength of the girl's legs hugging the creature.

The card upset Madame Linka.

She started muttering to herself in Romany and pushed the cards on the tray before her, attempting to create a new alignment. Duci and Abrams understood what she was saying. They exchanged glances and Duci touched the cross hanging from the leather tie at her throat.

"What is it?" Lyssa asked. "What do you see? Why are you upset?"

Madame raised dark, concerned eyes to her. "The cards do not speak sense," she said, her voice full of foreboding.

Lyssa reached toward the card of the woman. "What is the meaning of this card?"

With a sharp gesture, Madame pushed Lyssa's hand away. Then, reverently, she placed the card in a row, flanked by Death and the Hanged Man. She held her palms over the cards as if they radiated some hidden power only she could divine.

An owl hooted in the night. A sudden wind picked up energy and swept through the small camp, giving the fire's flames new life. There was the snap and cracking sound of green wood being burned.

Lyssa leaned toward Madame. "What does it mean?"

"It is Lust," Madame answered.

The way the woman in the card sat on the man-lion's back took on a new significance. Lyssa's mouth went dry.

Madame tapped Death. "Change is now. Here. Soon. What was will be no more." Her pointed finger moved to the Hanged Man. "You are to meet your destiny. You must have courage, Viveka."

"And Lust?" What was its meaning? Lyssa had to know.

"You must use your powers," Madame said. "You must take hold of the moment and find strength. Joyously accept what is to come."

Lyssa tightened her grasp on the card in her hand—her future. "What is to come?"

"Show me," Madame said with a grave sincerity as if she accepted all possibilities.

She held out her hand but Lyssa did not want to surrender the card to her. Instead, she looked first. The picture was that of a galloping horse, its eyes wide. A runaway.

On its back rode a knight holding a sword high over his head as if ready to attack.

"What is it?" Madame demanded, her eyes angry.

Lyssa turned the card face around to show the others.

"The Knight of Swords," Madame whispered and then repeated the words as if she did not quite believe what she said. "This does not bode good. He is a dangerous man, one who is intelligent and yet clever and subtle. You will not know his true intentions until he reveals them to you."

"You are saying I will meet this man?" Lyssa questioned.

"Yes. The sword in his hand will enable him to cut to the heart of a thing and sometimes, Viveka, you will not be comfortable with what he reveals. Beware the darkest qualities of this card. This man can be ruthless. He is an angry man who, for his own reasons, searches for truth. Be careful . . . for he is a man who sees everything."

"How do I protect myself, Madame?"

The seer's gaze met hers. "You can't."

"Then what am I to do?"

"Accept." Madame's features softened in understanding. She lifted the card of the woman riding the man creature. "Lust will give you strength. You face danger. Do not shy away. Use the Knight, Viveka. Use your woman-power to make him your protector. But treat him with caution."

For a moment, Lyssa couldn't speak. There was a tightness in her chest, a sense of looming misfortune . . . and after she'd prided herself on everything going so smoothly. "Will I see Amleth Hall?"

"The cards do not say."

Smoke rose from the green wood in the fire. The wind blew it in Lyssa's direction. "I almost wish I had never asked for a reading," she confessed.

Madame leaned forward and lightly touched Lyssa's cheek. "You can't escape your fate, Viveka. Trust the Knight, but beware his sword."

Lyssa nodded, rubbing her thumb along the gilt edge of the card.

It was Abrams who broke the somberness of the moment. "Let us not be too grim, eh?" he said. He rose, offering his wife a hand up as he did so. "The future can wait until the morrow. Tonight, I need my sleep."

Madame nodded. "You are right, my son, and very wise. Come, Viveka. You will dream tonight and, in the morning, tell me every detail. Then perhaps we shall know more."

"I don't know if I'll be able to sleep," Lyssa answered.

"Keep the card close," Duci advised. "Your Knight will protect you."

She said the words in earnest and yet they sounded strange, because, for a moment, it had been the Knight that had frightened Lyssa. Her uncertainties dissipating, Lyssa laughed at her own gullibility. Neither Reverend Billows nor her father would be pleased.

Madame rose. Duci gathered the cards while her husband put away the folding chair and the reading table. No one seemed to notice that Lyssa still had the Knight of Swords. She stole a look at it and then turned to secretly tuck it into her bodice—

And that is when *he* appeared.

He stepped out of the darkness into the waning firelight, as if appearing out of nowhere.

For a second, Lyssa thought her eyes deceived her. No man could be so tall, so broad of shoulders. Smoke from the fire swirled around his hard-muscled legs. His dark hair was overlong and he wore a coat the color of cobalt with a scarf wrapped around his neck in a careless fashion that would have done any dandy proud. His leather breeches had seen better days and molded themselves to his thighs like gloves. A pistol was stuck in his belt and his eyes beneath the brim of his hat were those of a man who had seen too much.

Here was her Knight come to life.

He spoke. "Miss Harrell?" His voice rumbled from a source deep within. It was the voice of command.

Lyssa lifted her chin, all too aware that her knees were shaking. "What do you want?"

The stranger smiled, the expression one of grim satisfaction. "I'm from your father. He wants you home."

Chapter Three

IAN was well pleased with himself. His entrance had been perfect—especially his waiting until *after* the card-reading mumbo jumbo. At the sight of him, the self-named "Gypsies" turned tail and scattered off into the woods. They knew the game was over. But best of all, the headstrong Miss Harrell stared up at him as if he were the devil incarnate.

Good.

This task was turning out to be easier than he'd anticipated.

With a coin slipped here and there in the dark corners of London, he'd learned of a wealthy young woman who had hired some "Gypsies" to transport her to Scotland. Supposedly, the heiress was to stay hidden in the wagon, but after time, she had felt safe enough to show herself along the road and thus became very easy to track. More than one person, upon seeing the miniature, told

Ian that the young lady's red hair was a hard thing to forget—especially among dark-haired gypsies.

Now he understood why they had felt that way. Here in the glowing embers of the fire, the rich, vibrant dark red of Miss Harrell's hair with its hint of gold gleamed with a life of its own. She wore it pulled back and loose in a riotous tumble of curls that fell well past her shoulders. It was a wonder she could go anyplace in Britain without being recognized.

And her clothing would catch anyone's eye. It was as if she were an opera dancer dressed for the role of "Gypsy" . . . except the cut and cloth of her costume was of the finest stuff. The green superfine wool of her full gypsy skirt swayed with her every movement. Her fashionably low white muslin blouse was cinched at the waist with a black laced belt and served to emphasize the full swell of her breasts. She must have had some sense of modesty, because she demurely topped off the outfit with shawl of plaid that she wore proudly over one shoulder.

He was surprised she didn't have hoops in her ears.

Her awestruck silence was short-lived. She tossed back her curls, ignored his hand, and announced, "I'm not going with you."

"Yes, you are," Ian countered reasonably. "Your father is paying me a great deal of money to see you home safe, and see you home safe I will. Now come along. Your maid is waiting at an inn down the road with decent clothes for you to wear."

Her straight brows, so much like her father's, snapped together in angry suspicion. "You're Irish."

Ian's insides tightened. Bloody little snob. But he kept his patience. "Aye, I am," he said, letting the brogue he usually took pains to avoid grow heavier. "One of them and proud of it."

She straightened to her full height. She was taller than he had anticipated and regal in her bearing. Pride radiated from every pore. A fitting daughter to Pirate Harrell. "I don't believe you are from my father. *He* would *never* hire an Irishman."

"Well, he hired *me*," Ian replied flatly, dropping the exaggerated brogue. He rested a hand on the strap of the knapsack flung over one shoulder. "The others couldn't find you. I have. Now, are you going to cooperate with me, Miss Harrell, or shall we do this the hard way? In case you are wondering, your father wants you home by any means *I* deem necessary."

Her eyes flashed golden in the firelight like two jewels. "You wouldn't lay a finger on me."

"I said 'by any means I deem necessary.' If I must hog-tie and carry you out of here, I shall."

Obviously, no one had ever spoken this plainly to Miss Harrell before in her life. Her expression was the same one he imagined she'd use if he'd stomped on her toes. The color rose to her cheeks with her temper. "You will not. Abrams and my other Gypsy friends will come to my rescue. Won't you, Abrams?" she asked, lifting her voice so that it would carry in the night.

But there was no reply save for the crackling of green wood in the fire and the rustle of the wind in the trees.

"Abrams won't," Ian corrected kindly, "because, first, he knows he's not a match for me. I have a bit of a reputation for being handy with my fists, Miss Harrell, and that allows me to do as I please. And secondly, because he's no more a Gypsy than I am. Are you, Charley?" he called to "Abrams."

"Who is Charley?" Miss Harrell demanded.

"Charley Poet, a swindler if ever there was one. You probably think Duci is his wife?"

"She is."

Ian shook his head. "She's his sister. And your fortune-teller is his aunt, 'Mother' Betty, once the owner of a London bawdy house until gambling did her in."

"That's a lie!" a female voice called out to him. "The house was stolen from me!"

"Is that the truth, Betty?" Ian challenged. "Come out of hiding and we'll discuss the matter."

There was no answer.

The color had drained from Miss Harrell's face, but still she held on to her convictions. "I don't believe you. I've been traveling with these people and

they are exactly what they say they are—Gypsies.
They even speak Romany."

"Charley," Ian said. "Get out here."

A beat of silence and then sheepishly, Charley
appeared at the edge of the woods. He was slight
of frame, and with a scarf around his head Ian supposed he could pass for a Gypsy. "Tell Miss Harrell
the truth," Ian said with exaggerated patience.

"We didn't mean no harm," Charley said, his
"Gypsy" accent gone. "And we got her to Scotland. We were going to take her where she wanted
to go. She paid us—you can't be angry at us, Campion."

"It's her father you need to fear, not me," Ian answered. "And I'll warn you right now, Pirate Harrell wanted me to bring back your head on a pike.
Head west, Charley, don't show your face around
London for a year, and we'll call ourselves even."

Miss Harrell took a step forward. "You *lied* to
me?" she accused Charley in round tones, as if she
couldn't believe the truth.

Charley shrugged. "Not really. Mother Betty
has a drop of Gypsy blood in her. Her talent with
the cards is real."

But Miss Harrell was not placated. Her anger
was swift and sharp. "I should have known. Gypsies don't drink gin."

"Some do," Charley hedged and started backing away.

"Don't you dare leave!" Miss Harrell ordered.

"I've *paid* you to take me to Amleth Hall and so you shall—this, this"—she sputtered for words before deciding on one—"ox of an Irishman notwithstanding."

Ian had been called worse. "Well, it was money wasted, Miss Harrell," he replied philosophically, "because you are returning to London with me. And, by the by, my name is Campion, Ian Campion . . . but you may call me Mr. Ox if it makes you feel more comfortable."

The look she shot him could have fried bacon.

He couldn't give a care. "Go on, Charley. She's in my hands now."

"Well, I'd like the wagon, Campion," Charley answered, taking another timid step forward.

"You can have it—" Ian started but Miss Harrell contradicted him, moving to confront Charley.

"This is *my* wagon. I paid for it and it is full of *my* belongings. What did you think you were going to do? Steal everything I brought with me?"

"Ah, now, Miss Harrell, Duci, Betty and I were good to you," Charley reminded her.

"The three of you lied to me! I trusted you."

"We were only being what you wanted us to be," Charley said sympathetically. "And you had a good time. But now, Campion's right. You should go home and marry that viscount your papa wants you to marry. If you'd been in the hands of less honest folk, you could have been in real danger."

Her answer was to turn to Ian and, cool as you please, say, "I will pay you *twice* what my father offered to take me to Amleth Hall on the Firth of Lorne. In fact, we are not very far from there now."

"Twice?" Ian questioned with amusement. "You don't have the blunt."

"I assure you, sir, I do."

"And what of proprieties? What will your relatives say when you appear on their doorstep with an Irishman by your side?"

She made an impatient sound. "We can go to the inn and pick up the maid you brought along if you wish . . . although I would prefer not wasting the time."

Ian was taken aback by her boldness. She was no milk toast debutante, nor was she as smart as she thought she was. He was both intrigued and put off. If she'd been one of his sisters, he'd be tempted to lock her up.

"I'm taking you home," he said. "You've already been more than foolish, Miss Harrell, and you've been fortunate not to have had your throat slit, or worse."

Her chin came up. "There's something *worse* than having your throat slit?"

Ian suspected her of being impertinent and his temper flared, but Charley came to her rescue. "Here now, take it easy, Campion. She's more than a bit naïve. You know how the Quality are. You have to treat her with kid gloves a bit and talk to her like she's ten."

Miss Harrell whirled on him as if set on fire. "You don't need to coddle me!"

"Beg pardon, miss, but we did."

Here was the last bit of treachery and it hit Miss Harrell hard. "You didn't," she insisted.

"We did," Charley confessed. "And you'd best go with Campion. You really shouldn't be hanging with the likes of us." Duci and Betty had ventured to the edge of the woods and they sadly nodded agreement.

"It's been good fun," Duci added, "but you must return home."

Miss Harrell looked to Betty. "What of my tarot reading?"

"Ah, now, Viveka, that was real . . . and was I not right? Here is Campion and your course has changed."

"This man is no Knight," Miss Harrell pronounced. "And I am not going with him, even if I must *walk* the distance to Amleth Hall."

With that grand pronouncement, she turned and would have marched off into the woods—save for Ian's hooking his hand in her arm.

He swung her around. "It looks like I must carry you then."

"You wouldn't *dare.*"

"Oh, I'd dare, Miss Harrell. I'd dare." He slid his other arm through a strap of his knapsack, ready to pick her up. She stepped back, clenching her fists as if preparing to give him a punch if he came nearer.

"Come now, Campion," Charley pleaded. "Give her a moment to calm down." He came forward to mediate when a pistol crack sounded in the air. The heat of the shot whizzed past Ian and missed Miss Harrell's head by inches, burying itself in the side of the wagon.

The only thing that had saved her was her step back at his approach.

Ian pushed Miss Harrell behind him and turned on Charley, who immediately declared, "Wasn't me, Campion. I don't do guns."

"It must be Harrell. He wants your hide, Charley." And it would be completely in character for him to have had Ian followed to exact his revenge.

"Yes, but the shot was aimed at me," Miss Harrell argued.

"No, it was aimed at Charley," Ian replied, irritated beyond words with her countermanding everything he said. "Your father wants him dead."

The next shot almost struck Charley. "Run!" Ian ordered impatiently.

The Londoner didn't have to be told twice. His feet moved so fast they churned up dirt, while the women melted into the woods.

Ian held a hand up in the air and turned to confront the unknown assailants. "Wait! I have Harrell's daughter. She's safe."

The answer was another pistol shot, this one most definitely marked for Miss Harrell.

"See? He's shooting at me!" she insisted.

"Yes," he agreed, pushing her around the wagon.

"Why?"

"I don't know." A third shot splintered wood at the corner close to his head.

"Damn," Ian swore. "There's a party of them." He shielded her with his body while pulling his pistol from his belt. "Climb in the wagon. Take cover."

"Perhaps we should run for the trees?"

"Climb—in—the—wagon." He bit each word out, in no mood to argue any longer. Turning, he fired his pistol toward the shots, not expecting to hit anything, but he wanted their assailants to know he was no easy mark.

In answer two shots were fired back. And Miss Harrell had yet to move.

His temper short, Ian put his hand on Miss Harrell's rump and boosted her up into the wagon in a most ungentlemanly manner. He then dove in after her, feeling the shot as it breezed by his feet.

It was very dark in the wagon and he landed right on top of Miss Harrell who was attempting to roll over in a flurry of petticoats and skirt. He found himself between her legs, his hand on her breast.

"Pardon," he murmured quickly. With difficulty he moved off of her. There was little floor space, and the walls were covered with well-stocked shelves, so that every square inch was used to advantage. Ian banged his head on an iron kettle. Ducking, he reached for his knapsack, fumbling in the dark for his shot and powder flask to reload his gun.

"You honestly don't know who is shooting at us?" she questioned.

Ian spit out the cap to his gunpowder. "I thought perhaps your father had sent someone after Charley. I'm wrong."

She snorted her agreement . . . and Ian began to like her even less. He reloaded his pistol, his movements economical and efficient in the dark from years of practice.

"And you say they must have followed you to me?"

"Apparently," Ian said. He tucked his gunpowder back in his knapsack.

"I was safer with Charley," was her tart reply.

At that moment, the shadow of a head poked around the front opening of the wagon, directly behind Miss Harrell. Ian didn't hesitate. He fired the pistol and hit his mark. Miss Harrell screamed and scrambled to Ian's other side. The victim gave a soft grunt and fell to the ground.

"One down," Ian said with satisfaction.

Outside there were shouts of alarm. Whoever

thought he was easy pickings was wrong. However, now that he and Miss Harrell were in the wagon, their attackers had the upper hand. Ian didn't like feeling trapped, but he was certain he could stave them off until morning. In daylight, the game would be different. He reloaded the pistol.

Scrunched beside him, her arms around her knees, Miss Harrell read his mind. "Do you believe we can escape them?"

"I'm hoping Charley has gone for help."

"Do you really think he will?"

"No."

There was a space of silence. Ian listened, straining to hear any and all sounds. The night was deadly quiet. He sensed that their attackers were regrouping—but to what purpose?

His eyes were growing accustomed to the dark. He felt the walls with his hand, hoping there was another weapon of some sort he could use hidden there. Instead, all he found were books. Stacks and stacks of books. Miss Harrell's precious books. He couldn't stop a chuckle. Here they were, fighting for their lives, and if push came to shove, he supposed they could throw books at their assailants.

He'd start with the romantic novels, then all books of poetry.

"Who *are* you?" she said softly. "You aren't like any of the other men in my father's employ."

"He hired me special." He slung his knapsack on one arm.

"But he doesn't like the Irish."

"No one does."

His answer was not what she had expected. Even in the dark, he could feel her staring at him, as if taking new measure.

But she was nothing if not her father's daughter. "How do I know you've come from him?"

Ian wanted to ask who else would be willing to serve as her human shield, but bit his tongue. "You took these books from the house. They are the only possessions you left with, save for the clothes you were wearing when you left."

"You are correct." There was a beat of silence. Then she asked, "Who do you think is shooting at us?"

"I don't know. For all I know, they could be *with* your father."

"He doesn't want me dead," she said with certainty.

Ian wasn't so certain. A man with a beautiful young wife didn't need an obstinate daughter who runs away before her betrothal could be announced. "Then who does?"

"No one."

"You're obviously wrong."

She released a shuddering breath—a response more telling than words—and scooted a fraction of an inch closer to him. "I'm afraid."

He knew how much fear it took for her to make such an admission. "We're not done for yet," he promised.

She nodded and they sat still for a moment, listening and waiting. She started to speak again, but he silenced her by raising his hand to her lips.

Something was afoot outside. He was experiencing the tingling between his shoulder blades that usually warned him of trouble. Why his war-heightened senses hadn't picked up on the fact he was being followed, he didn't know . . . and it concerned him. Deeply concerned him. Too often his life had been saved by his gut instincts. He hated the idea he might be getting too old for these games.

Minutes passed like hours.

What the devil were the bastards up to out there?

He thought he heard a rustling. He stared at the black wall of the wagon in front of him, wishing he could see through it. He raised his pistol. With his other arm, he protectively pushed Miss Harrell back against her books, keeping her close to his side.

Let the bastards come. His temper was up now, and he knew he could have the strength of ten men when he was this angry. He'd make them think twice before they took on Ian Campion.

But when the attack came, it wasn't what he expected.

They set the wagon on fire.

There were three thumps on the roof and then quiet. Ian frowned, uncertain. It was Miss Harrell who understood. "The roof. They've taken wood from the fire and have thrown it on the roof."

As if to confirm her words, smoke suddenly billowed in through every unseen crack in the ceiling.

Ian pushed Miss Harrell down to the ground and threw his body over her, preparing for the possibility of the roof caving in. "We've got to get out of here."

"They'll be waiting for us."

He nodded grimly. "That's their plan." And how would he combat it?

"There's a door beneath me," she said.

"A what?" He wasn't certain he'd heard correctly.

"A trapdoor," she explained, a touch of impatience in her voice. "There is a trapdoor in the floor."

Ian ran his hand along the floor. He could feel the door's outlines. "Why didn't you say something earlier? Let's get out of here."

"I would if you weren't lying on top of me. You are a heavy man. I can't move."

Ian frowned down at her. "Has anyone told you there are moments when absolute truthfulness is not appreciated?"

"Often."

"You should listen to them." He rolled off of her, pulling her close so he had room to reach for the handle. The wagon was going up like a tinderbox. Already, flames lapped the roof.

She reached beyond him for a book.

"What are you doing?" he asked.

"I can't let my books burn. Especially this one."

"Yes, you can," he answered, and holding her close, clasped his fingers around the iron ring handle of the trapdoor and pulled up. Without a heartbeat's waste of time, he shifted his weight and sent them both tumbling to the ground.

Chapter Four

$\mathcal{L}$YSSA would have screamed, save she didn't have time.

They plunged through the trapdoor where, at the last moment, the Irishman flipped himself so he hit the ground first, cushioning her fall with his body.

His breath left him with a soft grunt. He lost no time in rolling them both from under the wagon, away from their attackers. When they came to a stop, Lyssa threw a dizzy glance backward. The wagon was engulfed in flames and she could see the silhouette of someone peering inside to see if they were burning to death.

The Irishman didn't give her time to think. He was on his feet in a blink. His pistol in one hand, he grabbed her with his other and half lifted, half dragged her to the protective darkness of the forest. Nor did he stop there. He ran her through the trees with enough speed to make her think he had a direction in mind.

In seconds, they burst into a small clearing. The Irishman skidded to a halt with a succinct, "Damn!" He released her arm and whirled with his fist clenched as if searching for something to hit in frustration.

Lyssa struggled to catch her breath. The pins had fallen from her hair and she clutched her plaid to her bosom. "What is the matter?" she managed to get out.

"The horses. They've taken the horses—"

A man's shouts interrupted him, "They're here! I've got the girl here!" From seemingly out of nowhere, a man attacked on foot, running straight for Lyssa, the moonlight gleaming off the wicked blade of a sword.

Without missing a beat, the Irishman stepped in front of her and punched out with his fist, hitting the man squarely in the nose. There was the sound of cracking bone and the man dropped.

Stunned, Lyssa asked, "Is he dead?"

"I hope so," came the unsympathetic reply. "Come along. We can't stay."

The truth of his words was proven by the sound of someone crashing through the woods. "Mason, do you have her?" a man called.

The Irishman took her wrist and started running. Lyssa followed blindly, anxious to put distance between herself and the scene of such quick violence.

They ran for what seemed like hours but was

really only moments. He lost his hat, but did not turn back for it. Behind them, Lyssa could hear the angry shouts of the downed man's friends when they found his body. Suddenly, the Irishman veered right and plunged them down a steep hillside and into a narrow stream. Water seeped into her fashionable new walking shoes, the leather still stiff. Her feet stumbled as they climbed up the ravine beyond the stream. The Irishman moved behind so he could help her keep her balance.

The plaid caught on a thorn bush. She stopped to untangle it, scratching her knuckles. "Leave it and keep going," he ordered.

But she couldn't leave it.

The plaid was now more than a symbol of her clan: It was all she owned.

Numbly, she realized her precious books, including the one she'd hollowed out and used to hide her money, had been burned in the wagon. She had nothing. Her fingers refused to move and the plaid seemed to become more tangled.

The Irishman solved the problem by pushing her hands out of the way and ripping the material. "Go!"

She dared not disobey.

Higher they climbed up the ravine. Once at the top, he kept her running, taking her by the arm and hurrying her faster than she'd ever moved in her life. They followed a rutted wagon road but it didn't make travel any easier. Her chest hurt from trying to breathe. She had a pain in her side and her feet stumbled over each other, her shoes not made for such strenuous exercise.

Abruptly he ordered, "Here, get down," and pushed her beneath some bushes. Before she could think, he followed her, covering her body with his own and edging them both closer to the shrubbery's roots. He even took the time to tuck her plaid close around her body. They lay so close together she could feel the racing beat of his heart against her own.

Lyssa was thankful for the rest. However as her heartbeat returned to normal, she became aware of how uncomfortable her position was. He held her against the muscled wall of his chest, their bodies spooned together. Her arm, trapped under her body, began to hurt. Rocks and small twigs on the ground pressed painfully into her. The earth was rich here with the smells of rotting leaves and moss.

She wiggled, needing to find a more comfortable position. His arm around her tightened. "Hold still."

"Do you think they are coming?" she whispered.

"If they do, I don't want the bush to be shaking."

He made sense. But Lyssa still had to pull her arm free, which he let her do. Lying on her stomach, she cradled her head on her arm and tried not to think about what sort of insects would be crawling around on the ground at night.

Her nose itched. She dared to scratch it.

All was still in the night. Not even the frogs croaked. She waited, expecting something to happen.

Nothing did.

Finally, she could be silent no longer. "What are we doing?"

"Hiding."

His curt, obvious answer brought out a healthy flash of temper, an emotion she seized to keep other fears at bay. She rolled over to face him, intent upon giving him a much-needed rebuke. He accommodated her by shifting his weight and she ended up on her back. However, once there, Lyssa knew she *didn't* want to be underneath him this way.

There was even less space here than in the Gypsy wagon and she found herself practically nose to nose with him . . . not to mention the fact they were fit together—intimately.

All anger vanished from her mind as the slow heat of embarrassment stole up her body. Her heart suddenly kicked up its beat. His lips were less than an inch from hers and his breath smelled like Cook's warm buns when fresh from the oven, a scent that could lure her to the kitchen at any time and was disconcerting when connected to him.

However, he was clearly annoyed with her maneuvering. His "Are you settled?" was like a slap in the face.

"I'm trying to be," she returned. "Are *you* enjoying yourself?"

He did not mistake her meaning. Tension tightened his body. He raised his upper torso to glare down at her, the movement joining their lower bodies even closer. Lyssa caught her breath at the bold intimacy, realizing it was one thing to tweak the pride of a dandified lord on a dance floor and something else completely to challenge this man, who knew no rules . . . or boundaries.

But then he slid over as if the contact had been of no consequence and wedged himself closer to the shrubbery roots . . . and she felt a disquieting stab of regret. Uncertainty was not a comfortable feeling. She didn't know if it came from the loss of his body heat and the safety his strong presence provided or the possibility that she had insulted him—not that Lyssa was afraid to stand up for herself.

However, as she and the Irishman lay side by side, quiet as hunted rabbits, she remembered that even a so-called gentleman would take advantage of a woman if he thought her beneath him. She'd learned to be wise to the nuances of male behavior and knew how to protect her reputation. She'd even administered a slap or two.

But the Irishman was a completely different species of the male sex than any who had crossed her path before.

This time, he broke the silence, his voice low and deep in the darkness. "If they discover us, I want you to run as fast as you can. Don't worry about where you are going, just keep moving."

"What about you? Where will you be?"

"I'll hold them off here."

Her pique of temper vanished. "You can't do that. There are at least two or three or more of them. And they are armed."

The flash of even white teeth gave his grin a wolfish expression. "*Now* you are worried about me? Miss Harrell, you could have saved us *all* the trouble by staying quietly in your bed back in London."

His criticism hit home—especially when she thought about how completely she'd been gulled by her Gypsy imposter friends. The feel of the tarot card tucked in her bosom only rankled her more. "I doubt if I'm much trouble to you. Not with the reward I'm certain my father is paying."

"You would be less trouble if you would be quiet."

Lyssa's temper flared red. Didn't he know who she was? Who her father was? *The man paying him?*

And she was going to tell him. She was going to rise up and give him a piece of her mind—

His hand clamped over her mouth. He lay one leg over hers, pushing her down to the ground while his right hand above her head raised the pistol. His thumb cocked the hammer.

Startled, she listened and heard what he'd heard: the sound of men beating through the bushes.

She edged closer to him. He removed his hand from her mouth and placed his arm protectively around her.

A moment later, their pursuers stood mere feet from when they hid. One man held a lantern, and Lyssa, too frightened to move, prayed she'd pulled in all of her plaid so it could not be seen from the road.

Go on by, go on by, she wanted to whisper to them, and for a moment she thought they would—until the beat of horses' hooves vibrated through the ground.

Two mounted men rode up and her mind frantically attempted to assimilate the horrid fact that a party of over five men had been sent to murder her. She leaned even closer against the Irishman.

"Have you seen anything?" one man asked the riders.

"Nothing. But hell couldn't be blacker than this night."

"A big man like Campion couldn't hide, no matter where," said a man with a muffled voice.

"Well, he has, damn him," the rider countered with no small amount of frustration. He had a deep bass voice that sounded as if it came up all the way from his toes. A voice that would be hard to forget. An English voice.

His companion on horseback added, "Not only

that, who would have thought he'd fight instead of turning tail and leaving the girl to us? What's she to him?"

"Money," the first rider answered. "Well, we're wasting our time at this point. How's your nose?"

"Broken. The bloody sod will pay for it when I get my hands on him," the muffled voice responded, and Lyssa knew this must be Mason. So, the Irishman hadn't killed him. Now Lyssa wished he had.

One of the others asked, "What do you want to do, Fielder? Your call." They all had London accents.

Mason growled out that he wasn't leaving until the deed was done. "She could have seen me. I've no desire to have my neck stretched for attempting murder. And beware, lads, if I go, you'll all go."

Even from her position on the ground, Lyssa could sense an instant negative response to his words from the others. No one liked to be threatened, especially murderers. Two of his comrades started to complain, but the man called Fielder, the one with the deep voice, cut them off.

"Are you certain they could recognize you, Mason?"

"How could they not?"

"How unfortunate," was the only warning Lyssa, or apparently even Mason had, before a pistol shot was fired.

Mason hit the ground with a thud, falling on his

back, his left hand outstretched toward where she and the Irishman hid. She could even see his fingers twitch one last time.

She wanted to cry out, to gasp, to react in some way to the horror. The Irishman caught her in time, raising his fingers up to her lips, his own mouth close to hers as if he would swallow any sound she made. They both waited, their bodies tense, the smell of gunpowder lingering in the air.

"Did you have to kill him, Fielder?" the other mounted man complained.

"Couldn't you see him shaking? He would have broke and turned us all in. Here, you two bury him."

"With what, Fielder?" one of them asked.

"There's a ravine down that way. Throw him in it and put some logs over him. He'll decay before he is discovered."

Mason's body was unceremoniously picked up by his arms and legs and carried off.

Once they were alone, the horseman with Fielder said, "We started off with six and now we are down by two, and we still haven't gotten the girl. Campion is better than we thought. What do you want to do? Keep searching the woods?"

"No," Fielder responded. "It's a waste of time. We'll head back to the inn. Campion needs to get the girl to London as quickly as possibly or else he won't get paid. After all is said and done, he's still nothing more than a mercenary. I'll wager he'll try and beat us to the inn where the maid and coach wait and then attempt to outrun us to London. He knows it will be harder for us to kill her on English soil."

"What if he gets by us?"

"He won't," Fielder answered with certainty. "We'll guard the roads."

"By ourselves?" his companion asked incredulously.

"We'll hire help," Fielder answered. "The girl's hair is a damn beacon. Anyone who sees it doesn't forget her. They can't go far on foot. We'll catch up with them and then we'll see if Campion feels like such a bloody hero." There was a clicking sound that she remembered from recently and she realized Fielder had been reloading his weapon.

The two other men tramped back to join the party. "Is it done?" Fielder asked.

"Aye," was the answer.

"Then get your horses and let's head to the inn."

"What about the maid?"

"We'll pay her off. She did a good job of leaving signs of the path they were taking and deserves her money. She is also smart enough to go running off and keep her mouth shut."

One man asked what they were going to do with Campion's horses.

"Sell them," Fielder said. "He won't be needing them." The others laughed with confidence, as if he'd made a great joke. They moved off down the road.

Lyssa's heart beat in her ears and she tasted fear. The Irishman didn't move and so she dared not.

They waited for what seemed hours but was in actuality fifteen minutes, maybe less. The Irishman removed his hand from her mouth and crawled over her. "Where are you going?" she asked.

"Seeing if it is all clear." He rose to his feet. A moment later, he offered her his hand. "Come. We're safe." He pulled her up as if she weighed nothing.

Lyssa ran a distracted hand through her hair. It hung loose, a hopeless mess, and she didn't have a pin to use to tidy it—such an odd thing to think about when one had murderers on her trail . . .

She reached for her precious plaid and held it out for inspection. There was a hole torn in the corner but it was not completely ruined. She wrapped it around her shoulders, needing something to help her combat the terrible coldness stealing through her.

The Irishman spoke. "Who wants you dead, Miss Harrell?"

She didn't know, didn't want to think on it. Instead, she said, "Which maid did you bring?"

"Harriet."

Harriet. The maid was newly arrived in London and had been so willing to please that Lyssa had championed her. The pain of betrayal ran deep. "You were a soldier?"

"Yes."

"You seem to know what you are doing." She had to make her mind work, to make sense of the violence, of what was happening. This was all to have been a lark. An adventure.

She forced herself to stop shaking by clasping her hands together. "I don't think anyone wants me dead."

"Obviously you're wrong. Someone has gone to a great deal of trouble and a good expense to achieve that objective, including using me." There was a beat silence and then he added, "That was their first mistake." She understood what he was saying. This was personal to him now.

"Do you think your father could be behind this?" he hazarded.

His suggestion staggered her. "No. I told you earlier, he'd never want to see me dead. He loves me! If anything it would be my stepmother."

"Your stepmother?" The Irishman shook his head. "Murder is a bold crime. I've met her. She hasn't it in her."

"Of course," Lyssa agreed sarcastically. "Every man thinks my stepmother is fragile. Trust me, she is far more resilient than most give her credit."

"But what does she stand to gain by seeing you dead?"

"A more substantial inheritance for her child?" Lyssa suggested.

"To what purpose? She has all the money she needs."

"Does anyone ever have all the money they

need? The moment my stepmother came out of mourning for her first husband, the duke, she threw herself at my father. No one can convince me it was love at first sight. Consider their age difference. She chose him for his money, and it's a pity my own father isn't wise enough to see it."

"But is she jealous enough of you to stoop to murder?" he asked.

Lyssa threw her hands in the air. "What more proof do you need? Who else would want me dead? I'm not a threat to anyone. Or perhaps you are right about my father. It seems I've ceased to matter with the advent of a baby. But then again, he is determined I marry for a title. A son can't give him that."

The Irishman put his pistol in his knapsack and adjusted it around his shoulders. "What about your betrothed?"

"We're not betrothed yet, not formally." She didn't like to think about Grossett. Conscious that the Irishman watched her closely, she said stiffly, "He only gains if he marries me. If he wants me dead, he'd be wiser to wait until after I am his wife."

"You don't like him much?"

She despised him . . . but she'd not admit that to the Irishman. "He is my father's choice, not mine."

Even in the night, she could see him frown. "You could be more forthcoming, Miss Harrell. This isn't some game, not anymore. These men want to kill you, and me if I stand in their way."

Was he criticizing her? "I understand the severity of my position. I've told you everything I know. I haven't any idea why someone would pay men to murder me."

He crossed his arms. Matching her clipped tone, he said, "Then let us start with what you know. Why did you run away?"

"I told you I want to go to Amleth Hall."

"Why?"

She hated how with one word he could make her feel she had no choice but to answer . . . and how vulnerable he made her feel when she did so. As Dunmore Harrell's daughter she'd rarely explained herself to anyone.

"Amleth Hall is my mother's family seat. She was the laird's daughter and a famed beauty. They called her 'the jewel of the Davidson clan,' and she was expected to marry well. Instead, when she was younger than I, she eloped with my father who then was nothing more than a shepherd. It was a terrible scandal and her father disinherited her. She never regretted her decision to marry Papa because she loved him with her whole heart. But I know that up until the day of her death, she always missed Amleth Hall and Scotland."

And Lyssa missed her mother.

"Why didn't you just ask your father to take you to Scotland? Why this running away nonsense?"

"I *did* ask him, years ago. Right after Mother died." Lyssa shook her head. "He's washed his hands of Scotland. He doesn't even like people to think he is Scottish—especially now that he has his 'duchess.' He refused to take me."

The Irishman paced a step to the right, then stopped. "Wait a moment. There is more here. Pirate Harrell is known to never refuse his daughter anything."

"How would you know that?" she demanded.

"Rumors on the street. When a chit is worth her weight in gold, people notice everything."

Lyssa had always been uncomfortable with the speculation her father's money brought her. Coldly, she said, "My father is no different than any other. He wants his daughter to do exactly as he says, and when she doesn't behave—"

"Such as marrying the man he has chosen for her?"

"Such as marrying the man he has chosen for her," she confirmed, "then like any other father, he can resort to harsh measures."

The Irishman actually laughed. "Measures like what? Bread and water for an hour? Confined to your bedroom with servants to wait on you hand and foot for the day?"

His mockery hit home—especially because his jests were true. And she saw herself through his eyes: a vain, pampered creature who had taken off for Scotland in a snit and was now deeply in trouble.

"You may laugh, Irishman," she returned tightly. "You know little of my life."

"Ah, but I can dream," he said.

Her temper broke. "Dream about what? About being just barely tolerated in Society because your father has wealth? About being forced on people who do not want to have anything to do with you? I smell of Trade, Irishman, and there are those amongst the *ton* who will never let me forget it. My father doesn't mind forcing his way through, but I do. And I *hate* the idea that I am to be married to a man I have not one thing in common with, just because of his title. I am being treated like little more than a broodmare. Once my husband has an heir from me, he won't want to talk to me again. He'll have my fortune and my child and I will be nothing."

"Such is the lot of most women," the Irishman observed. "I'm not saying it is right," he hurried to add, "but it is the way of the law."

"It was *not* my mother's lot. She married for love. She defied all convention and *chose* her life and her mate."

He frowned. "Don't tell me you are going to be looking for a mate in Scotland?"

"No," she said firmly, suspecting he was teasing her and almost hating him for it. "I'm going to Amleth Hall because even though I have everything I want—all that money can buy—what I desire most eludes me."

"And what is that, Miss Harrell?"

"Acceptance, Irishman. *Welcomed* acceptance. I'm tired of being the outsider. The one they poke little jibes at as if I have no intelligence or feelings and am certainly beneath notice. I hope to find a place amongst my mother's family and at her home. She's been gone so long and yet, inside me—" She tapped her breast right above her heart. "—I have a need to be there, close to where she was. A need I can't explain with reason."

She'd said too much. She knew it by the sudden silence between them and she wished she had been more circumspect. Her temper and her tongue had betrayed her again!

Of course, there was something about the Irishman that provoked her into speaking her mind. That is why she'd foolishly revealed more to him in the last five minutes than she'd ever had to anyone in her whole lifetime.

Now she stood in front of him completely defenseless.

And she hated the sudden silence between them.

Shifting her weight from one foot to the next, she crossed her arms protectively over her chest. "Well?" she challenged. "Don't you have anything to say? Some comment about how ridiculous I am?"

"Where did you say this Amleth Hall is located?"

Lyssa feared she hadn't heard him correctly. She pulled her plaid tighter around her shoulders.

"Close to Appin. Abrams—I mean, *Charley*—told me we were perhaps only two days from there."

"Heading north, right?"

Her heart skipped a beat. "Yes."

"Then let's go." He didn't wait for her response but turned and started in the opposite direction Fielder and his men had gone.

Lyssa stood rooted to the ground, stunned by his sudden change of mind.

The Irishman paused, looking over his shoulder. "Are you coming? I assure you, Miss Harrell, the walk won't be easy. We'd best get on with it and put as many miles between ourselves and Fielder as we can."

"Why?" she asked bluntly. "You were set against it when I offered money. And my father won't pay you until I'm delivered to him in London."

"Aye, but north is the direction Fielder and his men don't expect us to take. You are certain you still have family there?"

"Yes, I should."

"Then we can hope they will help us get you safely to London. There are many roads to the capital. We're merely taking one that is unexpected. Now, we'd best start marching."

Still Lyssa did not move. There was more here—her women's intuition told her so—and she wanted to know what it was. "Is that your only reason, Irishman, to avoid Fielder?"

The moonlight turned his eyes to quicksilver,

and she sensed he saw everything, knew all. His answer surprised her. "I understand wanting to be accepted, Miss Harrell. I understand all too well—and my name is *Campion*, not 'Irishman.' I'll thank you to use it. Now come."

He didn't wait for her response, but turned off the wagon path and started walking through the woods.

Chapter Five

DUMBFOUNDED, Lyssa stared after the Irishm—

Her mind stumbled over the appellation as she broke off the thought. *Campion.* He wanted her to call him *Campion.*

She frowned. The pride in his voice nagged at her conscience. The man had saved her life, but he was too high-handed by half. And at this moment, he was walking away as if he didn't care if she followed or not.

No. He *expected* her to obey.

Which she did, because she had no other choice.

She picked up her skirts and followed, but rebellion brewed in her mind. Think what he may, she was *not* returning to London.

She would *not* marry Robert or go through another humiliating Season of idle, patronizing chitchat from those who only pretended to like her to please her stepmother or even her father. She was too old for such nonsense.

She wanted purpose in her life, and she knew she would find it here, in Scotland, the birthplace of her parents.

In the meantime, she would contrive to be everything a proper, biddable young woman should be. After all, when they reached Amleth Hall and she refused to return to London with him, the Irishman would be cheated out of a great deal of money, and he wasn't going to take it very well.

So, Lyssa did her best to "march," but keeping up with him was a challenge. He had a long stride and moved as if he planned to cram the two days of travel inside this one night. She wasn't about to complain. Living with her father had taught her it was best not to pull on the watchdog's whiskers, and this man was definitely a watchdog.

Of course, it didn't help that her stockings were wet from their dash through the stream, and that water had seeped into her tight shoes, causing blisters to form on her feet.

She ignored the increasing pain each step caused her, and focused on placing one foot in front of the other.

She stumbled over a root growing over the path.

For a second, she was in midair, heading for the ground. But Campion turned, with that uncanny ability of his to know everything that was happening, and in the next instant, her cheek was against the solid wall of his chest. He set her on her feet. "Are you all right?"

"I'm fine." She took a step away from him. He wasn't the only one with pride. "I'll be better when we arrive someplace where we can hire horses."

"We won't be hiring horses."

Lyssa almost stumbled over her feet again in surprise. "You don't mean to *walk* all the way to Appin?"

"How else did you think we would travel?"

"With Charley and Duci, I had the wagon."

"There is no money for a wagon either, unless you have some."

She didn't. Her money had been hidden in the wagon that was burned to the ground. "You came after me without a shilling?" She'd never imagined herself without money.

"What little I have can be better spent than hiring horses."

"I doubt that."

Her flat reply startled a laugh out of him. "Oh, come now, people walk the distance across Scotland and back all the time, Miss Harrell. We shall manage."

"But not with my—" She stopped just in time. She'd been about to complain of her blisters, but she wouldn't give him the satisfaction. She'd heard the touch of satisfaction in his voice over having the power to make the rich man's daughter walk. Oh, no, like the noble Joan of Arc, she vowed to keep her personal sufferings private.

"Not with your what?" he prompted.

"Not with the present company," she improvised. "I'm certain walking is more pleasant with better company." He didn't like that response one wit, and she liked getting a bit of her own back—even though each step was agony.

And yet, she kept on, refusing to complain. She was her father's daughter for a reason.

The Irishman led the way, holding back low-hanging branches that would have swiped her in the face or helping her scramble up the often steep climbs in the forest path. She hid her suffering. Behind his back, she would hobble like a troll, but once he turned, she forced herself to walk upright.

In truth, the longer they traveled, the friendlier he became. As the first rays of the sun signaled the approaching dawn, he appeared ready to smile—until he caught sight of her limping.

"What's the matter?" he demanded.

"I've a blister. Nothing more, nothing less." They had come to a smooth road which she hoped would make the walking easier. She attempted to pass him, her head high . . . but parts of her feet felt like hot coals.

He held out his arm, blocking her path. "Sit down on that rock and take off your shoes."

"I have no intention of doing any such thing." And she would have ducked under his arm and continued on her way, except he hooked his hand in her elbow and swung her around to face him.

Lording his height over her, he asked, "What? You'd rather walk until you have nubs instead of feet?"

"That won't happen," she said.

"It will and it has," he shot back. "I've seen grown men lose *all* their toes because they didn't take care of a blister."

Lyssa frowned, slightly unnerved by his accurate diagnosis of her problem and yet not believing such a preposterous statement. "You're hoaxing me."

He shook his head. "Sit on that rock. We've been walking most of the night and the time's come to take a breather."

Her pride tempted her to nobly wobble on in spite of the pain. She wondered if he would be more contrite if she *did* end up with nubs instead of feet.

However, what won her over was the idea of sitting. He was right. They had been moving all night. Letting down her guard, she gratefully sank onto the round, flat stone half buried in the hillside beside the road.

Who would have thought "sitting" could be such heaven?

He dropped to his knees in front of her and reached for her shoe. She pulled her foot back. "What are you doing?"

"Easing your laces a bit," he said. "As I am your father's agent, your health and well-being are my responsibility."

"I can look after my own feet," she informed him primly. This didn't seem proper, his playing with her feet. It was too, too . . . intimate.

His gray gaze measured her a moment. His voice took on the coaxing gentleness one used with a skittish horse. "Aye, I'm certain you can. However, I've a bit of experience from my days in the army. So, if you'll allow me . . ." He didn't wait for permission but pulled her right foot to him, and she let him. Maybe because she was tired. Maybe because she was a bit susceptible to that fabled Irish charm.

Either way, she didn't argue. Instead, she watched as he deftly untied the laces of her shoes. The morning breeze ruffled his hair. It wasn't as dark as she'd first thought it was. It was sleekly straight and as feathered as a bird's wing with brushes of red on the tips as if he'd spent hours in the out-of-doors.

He needed a haircut. By a good barber. She wondered if there would be some curl . . .

He pulled off her right shoe and shook his head. "What kind of socks are these to wear for walking?"

"They're French," she protested as he drew off her other shoe. "Nor was I planning to walk."

"They should be wool or good cotton."

"I always wear silk—"

Before she realized what he was about, he reached up her skirt and untied her garter, his fingers tickling the tender skin behind her knee.

Lyssa slapped her skirt down before he could go for the other leg. "What do you think you are doing?" she demanded. No one had ever taken such liberties before.

"Don't worry, Miss Harrell," he cooed. " 'Tis only a garter."

"Located in a place where a gentleman shouldn't be placing his hands," she responded crisply. Even now her skin still tingled from the brush of his fingers.

He grinned, completely unrepentant, the slightly lopsided expression giving him a younger, more carefree appearance. "And what are you going to do now? Slap my face at the indignity?" He laughed. "Relax, Miss Harrell, I have sisters. Garters are no mystery to me, nor shall I go rabid and 'attack' you over the sight of one." He rolled the stocking down over her ankle with a journeyman's attitude.

Lyssa didn't know if she should be relieved by his words or insulted that he obviously didn't find her attractive. Of course, she was three and twenty and the duchess had been warning her she almost in her dotage . . . but surprisingly, this minute was the first time she'd ever cared about her age.

"I don't imagine most women, *including* your sisters, let you untie their garters?"

"Some have," he disagreed without looking up but his mind obviously wasn't on the conversation. Instead, he frowned at the angry blisters on her toe and heel.

His attitude changed, and he looked up at her. "These must be treated immediately," he said. "I can't believe you were walking on them. Take off your other stocking." He took his knapsack off his shoulders, dropped it to the ground, and began rummaging inside until he found a tin and a small sewing kit.

Holding the stocking she'd just pulled off her other foot, Lyssa frowned as he pulled a sharp needle from the kit. "What are you going to do?"

"The salve in this tin will cure anything." He unscrewed the lid and set it aside.

"And the needle?"

"If you are squeamish, close your eyes."

"Why—?" she started to ask and then gasped as without a moment's hesitation he lifted her foot and slid the needle into the base of one of her blisters.

Lyssa struggled to be brave but the truth was, she'd never been a good patient, especially after years of watching the doctors treat her mother. However, the Irishman moved quickly, doctoring one foot, then the other. It was all done before she realized it.

He covered the last blister he worked on with the warmth of his hand. "Didn't hurt, did it?"

She shook her head, mortified into silence, her

hands gripping the edge of her stone seat for courage.

If he noticed her distress, he gave no indication but went about his business applying salve.

Slowly, she began to relax—

"Do you mind?" was the only warning he gave before he reached for the edge of her petticoat and began tearing the hem.

Lyssa grabbed his hand. "Now what are you doing? Ripping my petticoats off my person?"

He didn't even look up. "We need to wrap your feet with bandages, or you'll have even worse problems. Silk stockings provide no protection, and we must make do with what we have."

"You're leaving me nothing to wear." Her words sounded as if she were being petulantly ungrateful or suggesting something not quite proper, neither exactly what she'd meant to say.

Her awkwardness was not helped by his curt, "Miss Harrell, your virtue is safe."

She grabbed his wrists. "It's not my virtue I'm worried about, but my clothing."

"Your father will buy you new clothes."

"But I like *these*," she returned through practically clenched teeth.

"Pardon me then, for it must be done," he replied and ruthlessly finished tearing her favorite petticoat hem into one long strip. Splitting it into two narrow ones, he bound her wounds, giving her no choice but to accept his ministrations.

Lyssa crossed her arms lest she give in to the temptation to pound him around the ears. Where had her father found such a man? He was high-handed, arrogant . . . and rather attractive, shaggy hair or not.

There had to be Nordic blood in his ancestry. It appeared in the lean line of his jaw and the planes of his cheeks. His nose was long and straight save for a bump on its bridge, as if it had been broken. The bump ruined the symmetry of his face and gave him a masculine, defiant air.

A glance at the size of his knuckles confirmed her suspicions that he was no stranger to fisticuffs. However his long, tapered fingers moved with grace and would seem to have been more those of a swordsman than a pugilist.

"I thought the Irish were more often blond or redheaded," she said. Her words were a peace of-fering of sorts. Did she really want to quarrel with him when they were being forced to spend so much time together?

He seemed to have reached the same conclu-sion. "Some are," he said not looking up from his task. He slipped her stocking on over her ban-daged foot. "But not all."

She was struck by his contradictions. He spoke with barely a trace of an accent, and yet he could be rude in his bluntness. She had no doubt he was used to rough living . . . but she also sensed he could be a gentleman if he so desired . . .

He raised his gaze, and for a moment, they seemed to take each other's measure without rancor. In the early morning light, she could see his eyes were not completely gray but had flecks of blue around the pupils. He still held her left foot, her arch against the warm palm of his hand.

"What is it?" he asked. "What are you thinking?"

Lyssa couldn't answer him. She had the strangest sensation that through those extraordinary eyes of his, she was truly seeing him for the first time. Honest, razor sharp . . . and yet there was passion in their depths, too, as well as a bright, burning flame of life. *Intelligent. Clever. Subtle.* She could even recall Madame's exact inflection as she'd described the Knight of Swords.

Breathing had become unexpectedly difficult. The tarot card was still tucked safe in her bodice and she was never more aware of it than at this moment. "Nothing." The word was little more than a whisper.

A heartbeat of silence passed between them, a silence she didn't quite understand. A frown formed between his brows.

Suddenly uncertain, she broke the silence. Wetting dry lips, she said, "Are you done with my foot or do you plan to hold it all day?" Her words came out sharper than she'd intended.

He abruptly released her, and she quickly tucked both her feet under her skirts and reached for one of her shoes.

The Irishman began putting the needle and salve back into his knapsack with great care, deliberately avoiding her gaze.

"You must have everything in there," she murmured, wanting to amend her brusque words.

"It's wise to be prepared." He still didn't look at her.

She ran a self-conscious hand through her disheveled hair. "You wouldn't have hairpins in there, too?" It was a small joke, but she owed him something. Already, her feet felt much better.

"No, but I've a leather cord if you'd like to tie your hair back." His glance touched her hair. "I imagine it is a heavy mane."

She nodded, again feeling that tightness in her chest. She was edgy and too aware of him for her own comfort.

He didn't seem to suffer the same malady. Instead, he searched in his knapsack and pulled out a foot-long leather cord which he offered to her.

Unhappily, her hair was too much of a tangled mess to tie neatly. She attempted to comb it with her fingers but using the thin cord to hold it in place was impossible.

"Let me help," he said.

"It's fine—" she started, but he took the cord out of her fingers.

Rising on his knees, he held her hair up with one hand and wrapped the cord around it several times with an expert's touch. He concentrated on the task at hand, oblivious to how close they were . . . whereas her senses seemed full of him.

The man was rock solid. With his looks he'd probably charmed more than stockings off of many women, and the idea that she might be just as susceptible to his charm was sobering. After all, he was completely unacceptable. Her father would rather see her dead than in this man's arms.

"Do you do this for your *sisters*, too?" She'd meant her tart words as a set down. Instead, they conveyed an alarming amount of feminine interest.

He ignored both sullenness and possible interest to answer honestly, "Occasionally." Then, as if she'd asked, he explained, "I have two sisters. One older, one younger. And a niece who enjoys being prettied up."

"Prettied up?"

"She's five." He let go of her hair, allowing it to cascade down around her shoulders but free of falling in her face.

"I also have two nephews," he volunteered. "My sisters and their children live with me."

"And your wife?" The question sizzled the air between them. She told herself that, again, she hadn't meant it the way it sounded, but held her breath for his answer.

His sudden grin turned cocksure.

She almost hated him and could blame no one but herself.

"I'm not married," he said.

"Oh." She infused in that single word complete disinterest. She knew how to do it with mastery. She'd learned that lesson protecting her own feelings in the drawing rooms of the *ton*.

And the impact on the Irishman was like a slap in the face.

The humor vanished from his eyes.

Rocking back on his heels, he stood with easy grace. "Here, you are probably hungry." He took several pieces of dried beef from the knapsack and dropped them in her lap. Taking a tin cup out next, he said, "Let me see if I can find water." He didn't wait for her answer but walked off into the forest bordering the opposite side of the road.

Lyssa watched his broad, straight back until he disappeared from view. She lowered her gaze to the three strips of beef and felt guilty. She told herself she'd done nothing wrong. Society had a pecking order and it would not be wise for her to become too familiar with Mr. Campion.

Mr. Campion.

For the first time, his surname came readily to her mind . . . and she was ashamed of herself for not using it earlier, because *she* of all people knew what it was like to be treated as if she didn't matter.

Still, he was only an Irishman . . .

She put her shoes on. The bandages he'd tied around her feet prevented the still wet leather from rubbing the blisters, and she found she could move reasonably well. After taking a moment to seeing to her needs, she returned to the rock and chewed on the salty beef while waiting for him to return with water, which he did presently.

He offered the cup to her.

"Thank you," she murmured, not meeting his eyes and yet knowing she could not avoid this unpleasant task forever. So, she took a sip, forced herself to look at him and said, "Thank you for your doctoring. And I'm sorry for my"—she paused for the right word—"my earlier churlishness, Mr. Campion."

The apology was not so hard to speak aloud as she had feared. However, instead of being gracious, he grunted a response.

Grunted.

Like some hack driver.

After she'd apologized!

Lyssa had rarely apologized to anyone in her life. Of course, she'd never had a need to until this moment, another crime she could lay at his arrogant Irish feet.

She stood abruptly. It was either do that or throw the cup of water in his face—which she was very tempted to do.

Chapter Six

IAN knew Miss Harrell had her temper up, and he didn't care. She was a job, nothing more, and he couldn't wait to wash his hands of her once they got to London.

No woman, *no person*, had ever held the ability to make him feel this small. But she could.

And he didn't know why.

One moment she could be warm and inviting and in the next, with a haughty lift of her chin or a cold stare, she could say clearer than words she thought him beneath her notice—even if she had finally condescended to calling him by his name.

Meanwhile, he'd been noticing her more than he should.

Of course, what man wouldn't? Those firm, round breasts of hers begged to be touched. He'd not been so busy saving both their hides from the fire he hadn't noticed them.

Her waist, in that ridiculous cinch belt, appeared so tiny he thought he could span it with his hands. And she was long-legged, too. He couldn't help but notice that fact when he'd boldly untied her garters. Nor was he immune to her tousled mop of hair, as red as a ripe apple and smelling just as sweet . . . or those green-flecked eyes that revealed a startling intelligence—and a wealth of naïvety.

God save him from bloody supercilious self-important virgins.

Of course, it was far wiser for him to carry a grudge against her, especially since they had to be practically joined at the hip until he saw her home safe *and* untouched. Pirate Harrell would not take kindly to having his precious daughter shagged by an Irish bounder. He'd probably draw and quarter *any* man for the offense, and Ian was not about to make such a powerful enemy.

"Ready to go?" he asked, deliberately brusque.

"Of course." She stood, regal as a queen in her tartan, and flipped her shining tangle of curls over her shoulder practically whacking him in the face as if he wasn't there.

Ah, yes, he could use the anger.

"Then let's go," he said. As they set off, he made sure to keep his eye on her first steps. He was pleased she moved better now that her shoes weren't rubbing her feet raw.

For the next few hours, they traveled without speaking. The overcast day offered them no encouragement. Ian knew she was tired, and yet, she didn't even complain once. He was exhausted himself. He knew they needed some good luck. They couldn't keep on this way.

His prayers were answered when, coming to a crossroads, they met a farmer with an oxcart loaded with grain bags heading in the direction they were walking.

Without hesitation, Ian asked for a ride for his "wife."

"An Irishman, are you?" the farmer asked in a heavy Scots' brogue. "I knew an Irishman once."

"Didya now?" Ian countered, drawing out his own accent.

"A good laddie he was and always one with a joke. What are you and the missus doing up here?"

Ian had his tale ready. "She's Scottish and I'm taking her home to see her family." Then, in a lower voice, he added, "She's in a delicate condition," as a bit of sport and was repaid with a horrified glare from Miss Harrell.

The Scotsman caught the look and had surprising sympathy for Ian. "A mother-to-be? Come up in my wagon and make yourself comfortable. I've got seven wee ones at home and know this isn't easy. Is this your first?"

He'd asked the question of Miss Harrell but Ian answered smoothly and with just the right touch of pride, "Yes, it is. Here, Sweetie, let me help you up." He offered his hand to help her up into the wagon.

She appeared ready to slap it away with more

vigor than she'd shown when he'd removed her garters. She leaned close and with a smile over clenched teeth said for his ears alone, "What sort of game are you playing? We are not married!"

"Would you rather I tell him the truth?" he mused. "I wonder what would happen if Fielder found out there was a man and a red-haired woman traveling singly around the countryside?"

"Fielder is watching the border. You heard him say so yourself."

"I don't take my enemy's movements for granted. Besides," he said soothingly, "what if someone were to find out you were in my company for days on end? It's a simple ruse but necessary. We pretend who we are not and no one's the wiser."

He'd caught her there. Reluctantly, she agreed. "But I can walk faster than that animal can pull this cart."

"True," he answered, "but you need to stay off your feet." He raised his voice on the last so the Scotsman would think she was having a bit of pregnancy pique. "You have the opportunity to ride, don't be foolish." He held out his hand again.

This time, she took it.

The farmer's name was William Rae and he was a good sort, solid and honest. "My wife calls me a laggard and I refer to her as an anvil. Ah, to be young again!" He shook his head as if remembering and then enjoyed offering Ian advice on rearing children and the handling of pregnant women. "Not to say they are easy to manage when they aren't in the family way," the farmer said. He dropped his voice. "And you've a red-head. I hear they are difficult."

"If only you knew the truth," Ian said fervently, and could almost feel the burn of Miss Harrell's temper.

In the back of his mind, he had assumed she would sleep. They both needed some.

She didn't. She wouldn't.

Of course.

She only lay on top of the grain, looking daggers at him, which only encouraged Ian to spin tales of his own about their imaginary happiness as man and wife. He particularly relished his new pet name for her, "Sweetie."

Rae also gave him good information on what to expect of the countryside on their journey to Appin. He'd visited the area more than once. "Tough going, if the weather is not with you. You'll most likely see rain, maybe some sun, and possibly snow—all in the same hour."

"We shall take our chances," Ian answered.

All too soon, they had to part ways. Ian thanked the man and gave him a coin for his trouble.

The farmer had barely taken the bend in the road and disappeared from sight when Miss Harrell turned on him. "I thought you didn't have any money, *Sweetie*."

Ian choked back a laugh. "I have enough to get us where we are going and pay for passage to London, if we are careful."

She hummed her disbelief, then changed her tack. "Well, at least I should be able to sleep in a bed tonight."

It was on the tip of Ian's tongue to contradict her. At first he thought they'd be wiser to sleep in the open or borrow a night on some farmer's hayloft. But then he changed his mind. He'd had his hands full resettling his sisters and their brood before charging off to Scotland. He needed sleep. It would be easier to guard Miss Harrell in a room at some local inn than to sit watch in the open. If he put himself across the doorway, he might even manage a few winks of sleep.

Mentally calculating how much money he had in the leather bag he wore on a cord around his neck and how much they might need for passage to London, he decided that a night in a modest inn would be a good investment.

"We'll see what we find," he answered and walked on.

She followed. They moved upward, through the forests with its rivers and small burnies and into the mountains and shaggy beauty of the Highlands.

He thought she did little more than concentrate on putting one foot in front of the other. However, an hour on their way she surprised him by asking, "Where is your family?"

Ian paused. "Where . . . ?"

"Yes. Are they are in London? Do you live there, or in Ireland?" she asked.

"London." Why the devil was she asking these questions? And then, for reasons he couldn't fathom he elaborated, "I put them up in a decent inn in Chelsea. A good place. A safe one." Or so he hoped they would be safe until he returned.

He could feel her glance at him, and he self-consciously regretted revealing so much. His story was not one he was proud of. Lengthening his stride, he pushed forward even harder, and she fell silent.

Three hours later, as evening approached, they came to a village with an inn nestled beside a small lake. Ian knew it was time to stop. Miss Harrell was exhausted. He led her inside and was surprised to see the taproom crowded with sportsmen of all shapes and sizes.

The moment they saw Miss Harrell, even as tired and bedraggled as she was, every male eye centered on her.

Ian guided her to a table in the corner and looked around for service. The innkeeper was nowhere to be seen, and the sole barmaid and lad working the ale keg were too busy to pay attention to them. He frowned at the staring company of men and they turned their attentions back to their drinks and conversation.

"Sit here while I find the innkeeper and speak

about a room," Ian ordered. "I'll also order supper. Do you have a preference?"

She shook her head, too tired to talk. He knew how she felt.

Then, as he started away, she said, "Tea. I'd like a pot of tea. Keemum, please."

"*Kee*-what?"

She made a soft, exasperated sound, as if this question was always so tiresome. "Keemum. It's a tea."

Of course, my lady, he wanted to drone like a footman, but bit his tongue. "I'll see what I can do."

She nodded and he felt dismissed.

Pulling his temper in hand, Ian sought the innkeeper. Catching the attention of the overworked barmaid, he ordered their dinners and a cup of tea for both himself and Miss Harrell. He didn't even bother mentioning a specific type of tea.

The innkeeper was in the hallway outside the taproom door. As Ian had feared, rooms were at a premium.

"There was a fight and a horse sale over in Douglas today," the landlord said. He was a portly fellow with a florid complexion and a head full of curly black hair. "However, you are in luck. We had some lads staying here—Daniel MacGregor and his brother, both bad news—" He took a moment to spit on the floor at the name. "I had to throw them out. I've their room left. It's in the front of the house, over the door. Top of the stairs, second one to the left."

"It's mine," Ian answered and paid for the night, the cost a bit more dear than he'd planned. He started back into the taproom, but when he caught sight of Miss Harrell, he paused for a moment.

In the dingy, smoky light, her hair was as bright as a torch and, with her delicate bone structure and innate grace, she could pass for a princess among thieves.

Even as Ian stood there, a tall, thin man in a well-cut coat—and booted heels that weren't round like Ian's—approached her. The man said something, and instead of sending him packing, Miss Harrell actually acted flattered by his attentions. She blushed and lowered her gaze in a manner she'd not practiced on Ian.

He was across the room in a snap. "Is there something I can do for you?" he asked the intruder, pleased to note he was several inches taller than the man.

"I was asking this young lady about her tea," the man fawned congenially. "The scent of it is unique."

"Aye, it is," Ian answered, not believing a word. "It's Keemum." He looked the man in the eye, daring him to carry the charade further.

The stranger's gaze slid from Ian to Miss Harrell, and although there was hint of regret, he said,

"Thank you." He had no choice but to turn and leave, not with Ian ready and willing to take his head off.

Ian sat down heavily on the bench against the wall next to Miss Harrell forcing her to move over.

"He only asked about the tea," she said quietly.

"If I hadn't walked up when I did, he would have had you upstairs with your skirts over your head."

He'd spoken recklessly, and immediately regretted how crude he'd sounded, especially when fire lit her eyes at the effrontery. He attempted an apology of sorts, "I'd have said the same thing to my sisters."

"And would they be as insulted as I am?" She practically snarled the words.

"Yes." He took a sip of the damned tea, finding it so bitter he wanted to spit it out.

Fortunately, the bar lad arrived with their meals—lamb shanks and peas—and Ian gave the food his attention. It wasn't fancy fare but it was tasty enough for a hungry man. He was finishing his plate when he realized Miss Harrell had barely taken a bite.

"What is it?" he asked.

She made one of those feminine shrugs that said louder than words that something did not please her even as her lips said, "Nothing."

Ian set down his fork, embarrassed at how quickly he'd eaten. But he'd been damn hungry. "You don't like the food."

"I'm not fond of lamb," she murmured. A heavy sigh and then she added, "Or this place. It's different . . . Do you think the sheets are clean?"

Once he'd left his mother's home, Ian had never worried about clean sheets again, but now, looking around the taproom, he began to feel dirty. Coarse. Clumsy. Because at one time, he would have noticed those things.

He hated the regrets. Regrets that he'd made rash decisions that had cost his family so much of their pride. Regrets that nothing had worked as he'd planned. Regrets that he was here and not on his way to London.

He took himself in hand. There was no crying about the past, because there was no changing it.

Brutally, he forced himself to say, "If you aren't going to eat yours, I'll have it."

With a shudder, she pushed her plate toward him and he pretended to enjoy the meal with great relish. And why shouldn't he? At three shillings five, the meal and the tea cost him more than whiskey.

But he didn't feel good when he was done. If anything, he was more disgruntled than ever, and dead tired. Why else would he be deliberately provoking her into a fight? Or thinking of matters best left untouched?

Fortunately, she had the good sense to keep her vaulted opinions to herself, although much of what she was thinking shone in her expressive green eyes.

Ian pushed the table away. "Come, we're both tired."

She didn't argue but rose and followed him out of the taproom. He led her up the stairs and opened the door to their room. The furnishings were simple—a bed beneath a window, a wash-stand, a chair—but it appeared a haven.

Miss Harrell glided past him into the room like it was her divine right. "Well, good night," she said briskly and attempted to shut the door before he'd even entered.

He stopped the door with his hand. "Wait, I sleep here too."

Her brows flew together. "Oh, no you don't. You can't. You must get your own room."

"Even if there was a room to be had, and there isn't, I've not the money for it. Don't worry, I'll sleep on the floor."

"I don't care," she said crossly. "It wouldn't be right for us to be in here together. What if the innkeeper found out?"

"The innkeeper doesn't care—"

"Did you tell him we were man and wife?" she accused, her eyes narrowing.

"No," he said, his temper breaking. "I told him you were my bloody mistress.

She slammed the door in his face so hard the wall shook.

Chapter Seven

🐎🐎 LYSSA received so much satisfaction out of slamming the door in Mr. Campion's face, she was tempted to open and slam it again.

As if testing her, he knocked on the door, a single, insistent rap.

She wanted to ignore him. She couldn't.

Opening the door no more than a crack, she demanded, "Yes?"

He shoved the tin of salve for her blisters on her feet. "Don't open this door again. Not for anyone." He then shut the door for her.

Steam could have come out of Lyssa's ears. Dear Lord, there was only so much she could take of that Irishman in one day and she'd had her fill. Leave it to her father to find the one man on earth who had the ability to irritate above and beyond all others.

Over supper, he'd been a bullying, ill-mannered bear and she'd had enough. He could go to the devil for all she cared.

As if in answer to her thoughts, he settled himself on the floor outside her door. He relaxed, releasing his breath with a groan that sounded much like the growl of a tired bear. She could almost picture him, his back against the heavy wood, prepared to spend the night in front of her door like the good bodyguard he was . . . and for a moment, she did feel a bit of guilt—but she quickly pushed it aside.

He was being paid very well for his trouble.

She was going to have a good night's sleep, something she knew she wouldn't have if he spent the night in the room with her. There was something about his presence that was too disturbing, too overwhelming. When he was around, she found her thoughts and her senses overpowered by him . . . and it was making the trip very difficult.

Frustrated, she removed the tarot card from her bodice. Why couldn't this card have had a picture of someone bland and inoffensive? Someone who didn't have the power to make her feel both nervous and excited? Or who was more amenable to her needs?

She unlaced and pulled off her shoes and slipped the card into one for safekeeping. Tossing the salve onto the bed, she crossed to the washstand and poured cold water from a heavy ironstone pitcher into the bowl. Undressing down to her ripped petticoat, she hung her clothes on a peg and washed the dirt from the road off her person. There was no soap, but the meager bath helped. Refreshed, she sat on the bed, removed the bandages from her feet, and used the salve. She had to admit the oily paste was doing its job.

At last, Lyssa climbed into bed, ready to relax—and got right back up again.

The sheets were not clean.

She'd suspected as much. After seeing the clientele in the taproom, she hated to think who might have been sleeping here before her. So she redressed in everything but her belt and shoes and lay on top of the bedclothes, using her plaid as a blanket.

At last, she attempted to sleep. Unfortunately, the noise from the taproom carried right up through the wood floor. Whenever someone climbed the stairs, she could hear every clumsy *clomp* of their feet on the treads. Too many of the guests seemed to bounce back and forth against the walls while walking down the hall, as if they'd had more than their share of drink.

She was now glad Mr. Campion was outside her door.

She wondered if he'd gone to sleep, or was he still awake, still alert? He was a hard man. The floor would suit him fine . . . still, she could have let him sleep inside the room . . .

At some point, Lyssa drifted off without realizing she slept, but hers was not a dreamless sleep. Instead, she saw herself running and running, pursued by nameless men wishing to kill her, and all she wanted was to find someplace safe.

And then the pounding started, shaking her dream world like a battering ram—

Lyssa sat up, startled awake by the realism of her dream. She felt as if she'd barely closed her eyes, and yet the hour must have been quite advanced, because all was quiet.

Unsettled, she started to lie down again, when there was a loud bang and the wall next to her bed shook as if something had been rammed into it.

With a cry, she rolled off the bed and onto the floor.

Mr. Campion didn't knock but burst into the room. He stepped on the mattress, threw open the shutter to the window over her bed, and looked outside.

Lyssa scrambled to her feet. "What is it?"

"Drunks," he said with disgust. Lyssa quickly climbed upon the mattress beside him so she could see too. Sure enough, there were six men gathered in the yard. One carried a torch and two carried a good-size log, which they heaved back and rammed into the front door again while the others cheered them on. She was surprised the door held.

She turned to Mr. Campion. "Why are they doing this?"

"Why do drunks do anything?" he returned. He sat on the bed and tested the mattress as if to sleep there.

Lyssa chose to ignore him as she grew caught

up in the drama outside her window. One of the men, a rawboned, greasy-haired fellow with a face that resembled that of a weasel's, stepped away from his companions and in a slurry, booming brogue yelled, "MacGregor, ye'd best come out 'ere! Do ye 'ear me?"

There was no answer, but there were plenty of people to hear him. To Lyssa's left and right, windows had been opened and necks craned to see what was going on.

"Veeerry well," the Weasel said, rolling his *r*'s, "we'll have to come in for ye."

His words were met with drunken grunts of agreement from his comrades. They heaved the log into the door again, and Lyssa fell back on the mattress, almost landing on top of Mr. Campion, who had stretched himself out, taking up most of the bed with his long body.

She scooted over. "Why doesn't this MacGregor come out and speak to them?"

"You can't be serious," Mr. Campion said, not even bothering to open his eyes.

"They won't stop pounding on the door until he answers."

"Yes, and they'll start pounding on him instead."

"How do you know?" she challenged.

"Drunks don't get together in the middle of the night to exchange recipes for face cream."

Lyssa frowned. He was right.

Suddenly, the innkeeper's sharp voice shouted, "Here now! What are you doing trying to break my door down and frighten good men out of their sleep?"

She clambered up on her knees to look out the window. The innkeeper, dressed in his nightshirt, nightcap, apron, and a pair of boots, had come out to confront the drunks. His bare legs looked white and scrawny in the torchlight.

"We want MacGregor!" one drunk said. "He owes us money, and no one will sleep this night until we get paid."

"Daniel MacGregor is not a guest here," the innkeeper answered. "I kicked him out. Now go on your way."

The Weasel took a menacing step forward. "Let us come in and see for ourselves."

The innkeeper blocked the front door. "Now see here, you'll do no such thing. I run a clean house and the likes of you will not cross my threshold. Now get on your way or I'll send for the magistrate."

His threat was a mistake. "You'll not be talkin' to anyone until we see MacGregor," Weasel returned and before Lyssa could blink, he picked up the innkeeper as if he weighed no more than a sack of grain and handed him off to his comrades, who dropped their log, pulled his nightshirt up over his head, and tossed him into the horse trough.

Lyssa was too shocked to speak.

"They tossed him into the water trough," Mr. Campion surmised.

She found her voice. "How did you know?" He hadn't even opened his eyes.

"I heard the splash. Come on, away from the window. Those lads will get tired of the play and drift off."

But the door to the inn opened again. The innkeeper's son, the bar lad minding the ale keg earlier, came out. He was young and thin and his voice cracked with his fear. "Leave my father alone!"

"Here now," the Weasel said. "Do you want us to stop doing this?" And to illustrate, as the innkeeper climbed out of the trough, the Weasel pushed the man back in. His friends cheered.

"Yes," the boy said, his voice quavering.

"You'll have to take his place," the Weasel answered and took a step toward the boy.

Suddenly, Mr. Campion rose from the bed. Nudging Lyssa aside from the window, he leaned out. "Touch that boy and I will break every finger in your hand."

The Weasel squinted up at their window. "And who are you to talk to us this way?"

"I'm the man who is going to teach you some manners."

"I'm ready for my first lesson," the Weasel countered.

"I'll be down to teach it." Mr. Campion pushed away from the window. He paused at the door.

"Don't you admire the Scottish?" he asked derogatorily. "They get a little whiskey in them and they become so charming. My rule still stands—don't open this door to anyone." He started down the hall.

Lyssa followed him. "Wait! What are you going to do?"

"Set matters right. It's the only way I'll get a good night's sleep."

"Alone?" She took a step after him. "You can't take all of them on alone."

"Watch me." He took a step, then stopped. "Get back in your room and keep the door closed." He disappeared down the stairs.

Lyssa hovered between charging after him to talk sense or running to the window to see the fight.

She ran to the window.

What she saw made her blood boil.

One of the other bullies had taken the boy and thrown him into the trough on top of his father. They all laughed uproariously at their own mean-spirited humor, and Lyssa doubled her fists in anger.

And then Mr. Campion walked out.

The pack didn't notice him until he spoke. "I told you to leave the boy alone."

They faced him. Lyssa could see they were impressed by what a big man Mr. Campion was. Still, the Weasel took a cocky step forward. "And who might you—?"

Mr. Campion's fist shot out so fast, Lyssa could have imagined the movement save for the sound of flesh hitting flesh and the way the Weasel practically flew back into the arms of his comrades.

A cheer went up from the other inn guests and Lyssa's chest swelled with pride. He'd done it!

But then, at a snarled, "Get him," from the Weasel, the gang of drunks fell onto Mr. Campion all at once. Fists flew and there were grunts of pain.

Alarmed, Lyssa called out to the other guests, "Please, someone, help him."

No one moved. Instead, they started making wagers on the winner—and the odds were not on Mr. Campion.

Lyssa could stand by no longer. Turning from the window, she reached for the ironstone pitcher and flew out the door, heading toward the steps.

Ian thought he was holding his own very well. He understood bully boys. They weren't that hard to beat once you got the first punch in.

One lad was down and out or faking it; it really didn't matter. Another joined him in short order. Still a third was backing away. Ian's final trick was to pick up the lightest of the remaining three and toss him like a caber into his fellows, which included their ill-tempered leader. The three of them tumbled down, and before Ian could pick up the little one to do it again, one man held up his hand, a sign that he'd had enough.

Ian stepped back. "I think you'd all best leave now."

"We're going, and too sober for our own good," the Weasel admitted. He turned to help pick one of his friends up off the ground. The others stumbled off toward the road to the jeers and calls of the inn's guests, who had witnessed their humiliation.

Ian turned to the innkeeper and his son. They'd both climbed out of the horse trough and were shivering wet in the night air. "Come, let us get you both a toddy and return to our beds."

"Thank ye, sir. They are a rowdy bunch and I tell ye I am glad to see them get a bit of their own back. Ye've been in the ring, haven't ye?"

"A bit," Ian answered. He was tired. He needed sleep. Unfortunately, the innkeeper was in even worse shape. The poor man lost his balance and fell against Ian, who held his elbow to steady him.

At the same time, a blur of flaming red hair rushed out the door. Both Ian and the innkeeper turned in surprise.

"Leave him alone!" Miss Harrell announced and before Ian realized her intent, she smashed a pottery pitcher over the innkeeper's head.

The man straightened in surprise, then his eyeballs rolled up and he fell backward, hitting the ground with a thump.

"My father!" the lad shouted, dropping to his side.

"His father?" Miss Harrell repeated.

"His father," Ian confirmed.

* * *

Two hours later, after doing everything in their power to repair the damage, Lyssa and Mr. Campion were unceremoniously thrown out into the night.

Mr. Campion was not happy.

They walked down the moonlit road in silence, his long legs eating up the ground so fast that Lyssa had to skip every fourth step to keep up. She knew he had good reason to be angry . . . He was tired . . . and every once in a while he'd flex his fingers, clenching and unclenching them as if they hurt.

Finally, she could take the silence no longer. "I have the tin of salve. Perhaps it would help your hand?"

He didn't answer.

"How was I to know the fight was over?" she argued. "I was running to your aid, which is more than anyone else back there was doing."

He shifted his knapsack from one shoulder to the other, not looking at her.

"Don't you believe the innkeeper may have overreacted?" she said. "After all, I didn't intend to hurt him."

Mr. Campion stopped so abruptly, she ran into him. In the darkness it was like running into a iron wall. She took a step back. His eyes glittered in the night.

"You cracked the man's pate open," he said, the Irish in his voice stronger than normal, a sign of how tired he was. "It took a good half hour for him to stop seeing double, and I've spent what little coin I had paying to have him stitched up. I know you don't have a concept of money, Miss Harrell, but I do, and being without means we live by our wits, which lately seems to be in short supply."

"I thought I was helping you."

"You weren't." He took another step forward, then stopped as he thought of another crime to lay at her door. "Furthermore, I told you to stay in the room. Do you remember?"

She pulled her plaid tighter around her. "Yes . . ."

"The next time I tell you to do something—do it."

She nodded, stung by the sharpness in his voice. And she felt like the outsider. Again. In fact, she didn't know when she'd ever felt so alone. "Yes, *Irishman*, you've made yourself very clear."

Tension lashed out between them. She had stepped over the line. Yet she would not call her proud words back.

His strong hands took each of her arms. He leaned down until his face was at her eye level.

"You are a job, Miss Harrell, nothing more and nothing less," he stated as if he'd been repeating the phrase over and over in his mind. "I am going to take you safely to London and collect my money. And then, I'm going to pack up my sisters and their children and escape this infernal land for someplace where we won't be having our heritage thrown in our face whenever someone wants to insult us. Where we can be who we are and what we choose to be. So be thankful I need the money your father is paying me. Otherwise, I'd turn on my heel and leave you right here."

"You wouldn't," she whispered, fearful that he would.

They stood so close they were practically nose to nose. He pressed his lips together, his jaw hardening, and for a moment she could see he struggled with himself before admitting, "Damn me for being a fool, I wouldn't."

His hands released her and he turned away. Running an exasperated hand through his hair, he said, "Damn, I wish I had my hat . . . If there truly is a patron saint of lost causes, I'd best light a candle to him."

"We aren't in *dire* straits, are we?" The idea hadn't even occurred to her. Frankly, with him at her side, she'd not worried about the details.

At that moment a fat drop of rain landed on Lyssa's shoulder, followed by another, and another. The moon was still out, but quick-moving clouds were taking its place.

Mr. Campion swore under his breath and didn't even bother to comment. Hooking his arm in hers, he said, "We'd better run for shelter." The truth of his words was proven as the rain started coming down harder.

They dashed off the road to what little protection the forest could offer. Within minutes, lightning also made an appearance. Lyssa pulled her plaid up over her head.

Coming out into a clearing, Mr. Campion had started to turn them back toward the woods again, when lightning lit the scene and he gave a shout. "Over there. A run-in shelter. Come on."

They made it to the shelter just before the skies opened and the rain fell like sheets. For a moment, they sat in the dark, thankful for dry ground and catching their breaths. From what Lyssa could tell, their safe haven was only a few feet deep and perhaps six feet wide.

Mr. Campion moved first. He took off his jacket. "Here, get out of your wet shawl or else you'll chill."

She dropped her plaid, setting it to the side, and crossed her arms. "Where do you think we are?"

"In a shepherd's shelter," he answered, leaning against the back wall, one leg stretched out, the other knee bent.

Lyssa's shoes were soaked—again. She took them off and placed them next to the shawl. Her toes were cold, so she drew her legs up and tucked them under the hem of her skirt.

"Do you think it will rain long?" she dared to ask.

"I don't know." After a beat, he said, "Lie down

and try to get some sleep. We have a long day on the morrow."

"What about you?"

"I'll keep watch."

"You must sleep, too."

With dogged stubbornness he said, "I earn my money keeping watch."

Lyssa sensed she'd best not press the issue. She stretched out on her side, resting her head on her arms, careful not to touch him.

However, sleep didn't come. She didn't like the tension between them. She wanted to make amends.

Mr. Campion rubbed his face and yawned. She could hear the scratch of his whiskers. He settled himself more comfortably against the back wall.

At last she dared to say, "I've always enjoyed the sound of rain. If I listen closely, I believe I can hear someone whispering as when it falls through the branches."

Lyssa didn't expect him to answer her, so she was doubly surprised when he said, "The whispers you hear are the fairies complaining they've had their sleep disturbed."

She laughed, delighted with the image. She relaxed, cradling her head in her arms, but her mind was even more awake now. The air smelled of rain and wet earth. She waited, debating with herself whether or not she should say anything . . . and in the end, as always, curiosity won out. "You said you have the keeping of your sisters and their children. Where are their husbands?"

"Dead."

He was not one to mince words, but the way he said this one sent a chill through her.

Lyssa sat up, brushing her hair back from her face. "I'm sorry."

He didn't answer but she could see the silhouette of his profile as he stared straight out into the steady rain. His arm rested on his bent knee and she noticed he rubbed his thumb against his index finger, a sign he wasn't completely as stoic as he seemed.

Before she questioned the wisdom of it, she reached out and touched his shoulder. Nothing more, nothing less. A quick, simple touch.

Slowly, he turned to face her, his features masked by the night. "I told them to stay where I'd left them, but they came after me. They worried about me and couldn't stay behind."

Exactly what she had done.

"Where were you?"

"Portugal. I knew the fighting would be brutal. I wanted them both to remain back. They didn't need to be in the first assault."

"But *you* were there," she said, instinctively understanding. "How could you expect them to stay behind?"

"I knew what I was doing," came his answer. "They didn't.

"Of course, it's my fault they were even there," he said "Their only reason for joining the army was because I was going."

"Were they not grown men and capable of making their own decisions?"

"They were followers. Whatever I did, they did. It'd been like that all our lives. I knew it . . . and in truth, I encouraged them. I had to go; they didn't . . . but I didn't want to go alone, you see?" He shook his head. "They should have stayed in Ireland."

There was guilt in his voice and a touch of shame, too. The raw emotions touched her deeply. "Sometimes we can't do what is prudent," she whispered. "Sometimes we must just leap into life."

He made a low hum of acknowledgement in the back of his throat. "Is that why you've run away, Miss Harrell? You are taking a 'leap' into life?"

Lyssa didn't know if she wanted the conversation shifted to herself, especially by this man who had more layers to him than one would first suspect. Layers her always active curiosity could not resist. "Why did you leave Ireland?"

"That's *my* tale, Miss Harrell, and not one I share."

The rebuke stung, especially since she felt she'd been open about her dreams and motives.

Nor was she one to give up. "So, if you have turned your back on Ireland and choose not to live in England, then where will you go?"

"The Americas. British America or a place called Maryland. I don't care. I'll go where the land is plentiful and cheap."

Land he would buy with the money from her father. In fact, she could see many similarities between Mr. Campion and her father. Both were men who went after what they wanted. Some thought such single-minded tenacity a disparaging trait, but not Lyssa. She'd cut her teeth on it.

The rain had let up a bit, its gentle sound calming. For a long moment she listened, wishing she could be like Mr. Campion and travel wherever her will took her. She turned to him—and with a start realized he'd fallen asleep.

He would not be pleased, and yet she did not wake him. Leaning closer until she could make out his features, she was struck by how much younger he looked when he wasn't scowling.

A low snore rattled in his throat and his head fell at an awkward angle. He'd be awake in a thrice in this position, and she didn't want him to wake.

No, he needed this sleep. She understood that now. Much of his frustration with her had been from the lack of it.

She would keep watch. Then he'd know how truly sorry she was for the trouble she'd caused him—and *would* cause him when she refused to return to London.

Lyssa knew what it meant to have a dream, and she regretted that in reaching hers, she would deny him his. "I can't go back to London with you," she said quietly. He slept on, peaceful . . . and this was the way she wanted him to stay.

She lightly pushed on his shoulder and his sleep-deprived body needed no more urging to lie down on the hard earth. She moved so his long legs could stretch out and he appeared more comfortable.

Of course, he was a big man and there wasn't much room in the shelter for her. She managed to wiggle a space for herself by the bend in his knees.

A lock of his hair fell forward over his eyes. For a second, she was tempted to push it back, but she didn't.

In fact, she'd already dared too much. He would not be pleased in the morning, still he needed sleep.

Squaring her shoulders, she was determined to keep watch. Then he'd know she wasn't as pampered and spoiled as he obviously thought her.

Ian woke slowly, not completely grasping his surroundings.

He hadn't meant to fall asleep, and yet he'd had the sweetest dream. He'd dreamed his body had been curled around a soft, beautiful woman and his sleep had been deep. It had been a long time since he'd been with a woman—too long, and his body was painfully aware of the fact.

Now, as he slowly came to his senses, he realized it had stopped raining. Dawn was just breaking. The birds were calling, and a squirrel sat not more than ten feet from where he lay and watched him with round, curious eyes.

Not only that, the woman hadn't been a dream. Miss Harrell was snuggled up against him as trusting as a child, while his hand possessively covered her breast. His dick, as hard as a poker, was pressed against her bum.

All intelligence left his head. He couldn't think, let alone move.

She was beautiful, with her red curls loose around her face and her cheeks rosy from sleep. She hummed a soft sigh and her lashes fluttered as she stretched and opened her eyes.

She smiled up at him, as lazy and supple as a cat . . . and then she turned toward his warmth, her breasts brushing against his chest.

Lust—strong, powerful, needy—shot through him.

In that moment, he had only one desire, and that was to plow into her, cock strong and sure.

Chapter Eight

![horses] IAN reacted quickly before baser instincts could take hold. He rolled away from her and rose to his feet, careful to keep his back to her.

He focused on the outside. The rain had stopped and the early morning smelled clean. Heavy fog floated across the ground, and there was a bit of a nip in the air.

He struggled for sanity. He counted to one hundred, thought of the names of *all* the members of his family alive and dead, and started in on the sixty-three initial clauses in the Magna Carta before realizing sanity wasn't coming.

Lust still reigned supreme.

"Mr. Campion?" She still wasn't quite awake, still didn't know his reaction to her. Was still sleepily sensual. Warm. Inviting—

"Stay here. I'll be back. In a moment."

He strode off through the wet grass. Thick fog meant there had to be water somewhere, and his prayers were answered as he stepped through a parting of the trees and found himself on the edge of a good-size lake. Ian walked straight for it, tossing off his coat, pulling off his shirt, unbuttoning his breeches, kicking off his boots, and shaking off his socks until he was naked as the day he was born, and dove in.

The water was freezing—and exactly what he needed.

He planted his feet on the soft, muddy bottom and lifted his head and upper body out, gasping for air. All thoughts of Miss Harrell's breasts, her warm, round buttocks, and his strong desire for both were shocked out of his system.

A shiver went through him and he lowered in the water as he watched tendrils of fog floating across the surface of the lake. His body adjusted to the icy temperature and he took off swimming, needing the exercise while he came to terms with what had happened.

He'd fallen asleep on watch.

He'd *never* fallen asleep on watch.

Pulling his arms through the water, he feared what it meant. He was losing the honed edge, the hardness, and he couldn't afford to, *not with so much at stake*.

But then, everything he touched, he seemed to destroy—starting with his own youthful ideals years ago. He'd had to flee college, his studies, and his father's plans for his future.

Then had come the army. He'd hidden from the English right under their own noses. What he hadn't anticipated was for his brothers-in-law to die. It had been a stupid waste and he was tired. Bloody tired.

But he couldn't give up yet. Not with Fiona, Janet, and their children needing him.

Ian lost himself in the rhythmic movement of his arms. He could have swam forever. Instead, he turned and headed back to shore, the angry voices in his head growing less powerful, until he could live with himself again.

And what of Miss Harrell?

The simple task of fetching her for her father was taking on Herculean proportions, and it wasn't just because there was a group of murderers after her.

No, it was because she reminded him of the man he could have been. A man who could have presented himself to her. Who could have wooed and won her, even as an Irishman.

Instead, now, he was the outlaw, the pariah, the outcast. It wasn't so bad for himself, except he'd taken his family's honor with him.

Ian quit swimming and, curling himself into a ball, floated a moment, letting the water carry him.

His father had always boasted that Ian was like a fish in water. Floating, Ian thought he could hear echoes of his father's voice in the murky silence of the lake . . . and his mother quietly answering him. They'd both been so proud of him, even when his youthful arrogance had cost them all they'd owned.

He shut his mind, not wanting the memories. The past was behind him. He'd learned long ago he could not dwell on it. If he did, he might go mad.

There was only one choice before him. He had to see Miss Harrell safe and collect his money. Money meant freedom and he desperately wanted to be free of his past. Somewhere in this world was a place where a man could be who and what he was. He'd find it—and not let them break him.

Nor would he allow an idealistic bluestocking with uncertainty in her eyes and a taste for adventure lure him into making another grave mistake.

Ian Campion knew who he was. He was far from perfect, but he'd promised himself long ago he'd live life according to his own dictates.

He straightened his legs and stood, throwing his head back and letting the water run in rivulets down his chest and the flat expanse of his abdomen. The sun was burning off the fog and gilding the tops of the trees surrounding the lake. The chill in the morning air hit his warm muscles and he felt clean and whole again. He had direction—

Someone was watching him.

A prickle of recognition danced over his skin. He took a step deeper in the water for the sake of decency before slowly turning toward the shore, the water barely covering his hips.

Miss Harrell stood there, her mouth wide open.

Their gazes met, and for a moment the air between them was charged—and then Ian's sense of humor got the best of him. She appeared so shocked and he didn't know why. There was a path of his clothing spread on the ground for anyone to see.

He broke the silence. "You seem to have a problem, Miss Harrell, with staying where I tell you to."

Deep color flooded her face. She shut her mouth and he knew in that moment that he was the first man she'd probably ever seen the way God had made him. He was tempted to give her a better show just to see if her blush could grow more heated.

"I heard a splash," she said, slightly indignant, as if the fault was his. "I ran to see if you were all right."

A hundred quips leapt to his mind. With a more experienced woman, he might have said one, and depending on how she reacted, could have found himself spending the morning in a very pleasurable fashion.

But this was Miss Harrell. Miss Harrell, the "job," one that could make his fortune, and he'd best remember that fact.

Still, he couldn't resist teasing her a bit. Spreading his arms, he said, "I am fine. But I want to come out now. The water is cold." He moved two steps forward.

Her reaction was everything he could have hoped for. Her eyes widened and she scrambled backward so quickly, her feet slipped on the damp grass and she landed on her bum.

She popped back up to her feet, her face afire. "You need a haircut," she tossed out and then, turning, went running back the way she'd come, her red curls bouncing.

Slowly, Ian sunk beneath the water, swallowing his laughter until he could release it in bubbles.

Lyssa did not stop until she reached the shelter. There, she snatched up her plaid and threw it around her shoulders before collapsing on a log someone had once set there for a stool.

"Stupid! What a stupid thing to say," she chastised herself under her breath. Mr. Campion was no doubt laughing at her expense.

And how could she have thought about his hair when the man had been standing naked in front of her? Worse, when his back had been turned to her, she had gotten an eyeful of his bare buttocks.

It wasn't as if she hadn't seen the male form before. After all, she was a sophisticated woman. She lived in the city. She'd seen nudes many times displayed in art and in certain pieces of sculpture. She'd even seen workers and seamen without their shirts on rare occasions. No, she wasn't a stranger to the human body—but there was a big difference between cold stone or a scrawny chest and seeing the well-muscled Mr. Campion rise out of the water like some pagan prince.

He'd been a work of art . . . and in truth, she had followed the trail of clothing because she was curious.

Of course, *then* what had she done? She'd gaped like the village fool. She hadn't been able to take her eyes off of him.

Lyssa dropped her head to her hands. How was she going to face him again?

As if on cue, she heard him whistling. A second later, he came out of the woods. He was dressed, to a degree. He wore breeches and boots; his shirttail, however, was untucked and he carried his jacket and neck cloth. His hair was still wet and combed back with his fingers. He apparently had used his shirt for a towel. Damp, it molded itself to his chest.

She was struck anew by his casual elegance and athletic grace. He could have easily passed for a member of the Court with the right clothes.

Lyssa shifted around, uncomfortable.

He strolled into their small camp as if nothing was amiss and picked up his knapsack. From the corner of her eye, she watched him pull out a clean shirt. "Would you care to bathe, Miss Harrell? I do have a bit of soap." He tossed the clean shirt over his shoulder and smelled the sliver of soap he'd carried. "No scent, but it is of good quality. My sister makes it and Janet has a talent for soap. I also have"—he held up a tin— "tooth powder."

The minute he made the offer, she felt gritty. Still, she wasn't prepared to face him.

There was an awkward silence, and then he took two steps closer and prodded her with the bit of soap. "Come along and take it. You don't need to be embarrassed, the sea serpent has his clothes on."

The Irish lilt in his voice lent teeth to his teasing. She jerked her head around to glare at him while she took the soap and tooth powder. "Thank you," she forced herself to say, and stood, her back rigid.

"Here," he said and pulled off his shirt. "You can use this for a towel."

She didn't take the shirt from his hand or give him the benefit of comment but marched away, head high.

"I'll keep watch," he called, tossing the shirt aside.

Lyssa stopped. "You keep your eyes to yourself."

"Yes, Miss Harrell," he responded dutifully, and she knew he was implying that she hadn't. She hurried down to the lake before he could see the heated glow on her cheeks.

However, close to an hour later, after a leisurely washing, she did feel better. Her breath was freshened and the soap had been a luxury after the past two days. She was a bit embarrassed she had little to return to him. Of course, she'd not jumped in the lake naked the way he had. No, she'd maintained some decorum . . . although as a child, she used to swim with her father. Even cold, the water had been inviting.

The space of time by the lake gave her back her poise. After all, other than a glimpse of bare buttocks and his naked chest, she'd seen nothing, well, *damaging*.

No, what held in her memory was waking up beside him, of having her body cradled in his warmth . . . and of feeling his obvious arousal.

She had been confused when she woke. She hadn't realized what had happened. But after having tracked him to the lake, she instinctively understood exactly what had been poking into her backside—and she was not displeased.

Mr. Campion was the most handsome man she'd ever met. If he were in Society he'd be handsome enough to turn more than a few feminine heads amongst the *ton*, but nothing must happen between them. He was what she'd overheard one matron describe as a "guilty pleasure," a man one could dally with after she'd given her husband an heir.

Of course, Lyssa had no doubt her father would murder her himself if she were to lie with, of all things, a penniless Irishman. Whether she was married or not.

In the way of those who hungered for social status, he'd become more of a stickler than the sticklers.

However, such closeness as she and Mr. Campion had shared waking this morning was to be expected, she rationalized, and she was too honest to think he'd been taking liberties with her person. After all, she'd been the one determined to keep watch and he'd been right where she'd placed him the night before. If anything, she had been the one to move in her sleep toward him.

Mr. Campion had taken time in her absence to continue his toilet, and his clean-shaven jaw only served to make him more striking. He'd built a small fire to boil water for tea. Pulling a pouch with tea leaves from his magic knapsack, he brewed the tea in a tin cup.

"Would you like a cup?" he asked.

"It would be nice. What is for breakfast? Dried beef?"

"Funny you should be hungry for some," he teased back, offering her a strip of it.

They shared the tin cup of tea, an act more intimate than waking in his arms. Lyssa watched the way his fingers curved around the cup handle. A man's hands said a lot about him. His moved with grace and efficiency, whether he was putting out the fire or cleaning the tin cup. And his nails were clean.

They started walking. Her feet felt fine. The salve had done its trick and her shoes were breaking in.

The road did not make for easy walking. After last night's rain, there was deep mud in many places but they managed to find ground high enough to travel.

She noticed he had slowed his pace a bit, a kindness she was truly thankful for. However, he didn't seem in the mood for conversation. His earlier lightheartedness had vanished, replaced by his relentless determination to travel fast.

All right. She didn't have to talk either.

However, after about a half hour of silence, she could bite her tongue no longer, and talking would make the time pass faster.

"Do you think we'll make Amleth Hall by tomorrow?"

"It's doubtful."

More silence.

She fished her mind for something to draw him out. "I'm sorry I fell asleep last night. I meant to stand watch."

A muscle hardened in his jaw. "I was the one keeping guard."

"You can't go days on end without sleep and expect your body not to rebel."

"Making excuses for me, Miss Harrell?"

His cynical tone could have been a warning, but she sensed the anger wasn't directed toward her. "No, I'm being factual, Mr. Campion. And no harm came of our lapse."

"Do you always rationalize, Miss Harrell?"

Lyssa stumbled. "I beg your pardon?"

"Rationalize," he said. "I haven't known you long but—and please beg my pardon—I'm beginning to see a pattern. In mine, I see things as they are. It's the only way I can survive. The world isn't always safe or pleasant, but I know how to live with it. You, on the other hand, are like a character in one of your novels searching for adventure, the circumstances contrived of your own imagination. You believe you can change your lot. That you have control over your universe and that good triumphs over evil." He finally looked at her. "It doesn't.

Both his verbosity and his assessment caught her off guard. She didn't know whether to be offended or flattered. "I believe I'm more grounded than you give me credit for."

"Are you? Then why did you run away? Such a dramatic notion, that. And of course in the novels, all ends well, doesn't it?" He stepped up to higher ground and took her elbow to help her up. "Let's see, if you are the heroine, Viscount Grossett must be the villain who is keeping you from"—he paused for dramatic emphasis—"true Love."

"What is your point, Mr. Campion?" she asked crisply.

"That the reality is, Miss Harrell, most arranged marriages are more satisfying than those based upon whims. You are a wealthy young woman. If you were my daughter, I wouldn't leave anything to chance, either."

"Is my father paying you to say this, too?" she demanded crossly. "Or are you expecting an extra bonus. And you know nothing of the literature I read."

He jumped down from a rock and reached up to help her down. "Most men see eye to eye."

She slapped his hand away and jumped down

herself. "It's a new day, Mr. Campion. Women have minds as well as bodies."

"Yes, and it's their bodies I most admire. Their minds, especially when they are attempting to be logical, are a pain in the arse." He started walking down the road without waiting for her.

In three hurried steps, Lyssa caught his arm and pulled him to a halt. The muscles beneath the material were like tempered steel. They surprised her but she held her ground. Looking him in the eye, she said, "I am not chattel to be sold for a title. I want a man I can love *and* respect, and that man is *not* Robert."

"Unfortunately, under the law you *are* chattel," he replied blankly. "You can petition to change the law, Miss Harrell, but you might be wise to stay home to do it."

Lyssa could have stomped her foot she was so angry. She almost preferred his silence! "Why are you being so provocative?"

He started walking again and she followed. "I was merely making an observation."

"Yes, that you are sensible and I am not. That is what this conversation is about. How I should stay home, keep recipes, and do needlework."

"You aren't sensible," he agreed. "Sensible women do not take up with the likes of Charley and 'Bawd House' Betty—"

"I thought they were a family of Gypsies."

He didn't miss a beat. "—or want to be adopted by a family of Gypsies."

She followed him in frustrated silence. He argued with the efficiency of a barrister.

They had traveled maybe a quarter of a mile farther before she said, "Why shouldn't I have some adventure in my life? Why should I be expected to be happy attending a few routs, having a husband chosen for me, and then being carted off to some musty old estate to raise my children, count linens, and think of what to serve for dinner? Isn't there more to life than that? After all, you are a man who has lived fully. Would you be happy with my lot in life?"

"Idealism is a waste of time, Miss Harrell. A *dangerous* waste of time."

"And how would you know?" she challenged.

"I used to be idealistic."

Lyssa lengthened her stride to keep shoulder to shoulder with him. "So what are you now?"

"Pragmatic." He shifted the knapsack to his other shoulder, and taking her arm at the elbow, helped her jump a deep, water-filled rut in the road. A rushing stream curved close to this section of the way and it must have overfilled its banks during the night. The hem of her dress got wet. She ignored it.

"I can be pragmatic," she refuted. "But if one can change one's fate, why not try?"

"Because it is easier to flow with the current and not against."

With a jolt, she sensed there was a wealth of the unspoken in his words. She studied him from beneath her lashes, attempting to picture a younger and idealistic Ian Campion. The task was impossible.

He must have felt her staring. He turned, meeting her eyes as if daring her to say more.

She accepted the challenge. "Do you speak out of experience or because you lack the imagination to try?"

Her insult forced a reluctant smile from him. "What do you think?"

Considering a moment, she said, "I've never imagined you for a dreamer, Mr. Campion."

"All men are dreamers."

"Not pragmatic men."

"*Touché*," he said softly—and all she could do was smile back, inordinately pleased with his approval.

They started walking again. In some corner of her mind, she cautioned herself that she was too aware of him for her own good, but that didn't stop her from asking, "So what do you want?"

"Money," he replied, shattering her romanticism.

"And nothing else?" She couldn't keep the disgust from her voice.

"Plain and simple."

"For your land," she concluded.

"Exactly."

"And what exactly will you do with this money?" she wondered, wanting him to have a higher motive.

"Buy a farm."

Lyssa made an impatient sound. "That's it? A farm?" Her father owned several. Everyone she knew owned several.

"Yes, a farm," he said, mimicking her, and then elaborated, "A horse farm, like the one my grandfather owned."

"What kind of horses did he raise?"

"Race horses. The finest in Ireland."

"What happened to his farm?"

"It was taken for English taxes."

Taxes, she understood. Her father complained about taxes. "I see," she murmured.

"Do you?" he wondered aloud. "Do you really?" He stopped, turning to her, his gaze hard. "I doubt if you have the first inkling of what I'm talking about. You've lived a privileged existence, Miss Harrell, a life lived *as it should be*, with servants to bow and scrape for you. However, for the rest of us, life is damn hard. It's like climbing a slope covered in ice. Some make it—some don't. I'm trying to make sure I'm one of the ones who make it."

"Don't be so certain I don't know what you're talking about, Mr. Campion. My father cut his teeth the same way—and I *am* my father's daughter. Why else would I have struck out on my own?"

"Foolishness," he hazarded and before she could think, Lyssa slapped him across the face.

She didn't know who was more surprised—

herself or him. Her hand stung from the force of her blow, although she doubted if she'd hurt him.

For a second, she struggled with the urge to cry. Instead, her voice shaking slightly, she said, "I *can* take care of myself. I was there when my parents lived modest lives. I'm not what everyone thinks of me."

His gaze unreadable, he shrugged. "Perhaps."

Was there ever a more annoying man? "Perhaps *what*?" she demanded.

"Perhaps I deserved that." He opened his arms, holding his palms out as if to show he had no tricks. "Satisfied?"

No, she wasn't. If anything, she felt a little sick. "I wish you wouldn't keep talking to me as if I were a child or have had no experience in the world. I'm trying, Mr. Campion. I *am* trying."

He lowered his arms. "Well, there is something about the two of us that seems to bring out the worst in each other."

"Do I make you angry?" she asked, surprised.

"No," he hedged, then looked as if he was about to say something and changed his mind. He started walking. She fell into step beside him.

"What?" she prodded.

"Leave it."

For a second, Lyssa couldn't believe he'd spoken to her that way. Again, she wanted to lash out . . . and where would that get her?

Instead, she lifted her chin and, swinging her arms, charged forward, determined to leave him behind . . . and to prove to both him and herself that she could take on the world.

Ian watched her squared shoulders and tight back and knew she was fuming. That was just all right with him. Making her angry was the only way he knew to stave off the growing attraction between them. He didn't know if he actually *liked* Miss Harrell, but he was certainly *captivated* by her. He found himself deliberately annoying her for no other reason than to see sparks spring to life in her green eyes.

Whether she realized it or not, they were on perilous ground. Necessity forced them to be together. However, he would not let himself take advantage of it, especially since, in spite of her age, Miss Harrell wasn't truly knowledgeable in the ways of men. She thought she was, but she was no practiced flirt.

Still, she was curious. He'd caught a glimpse of the way she looked at him when she thought he wasn't watching, and he couldn't afford a misstep. More dangerous, he'd always been a easy dupe for idealism. The combination of idealism and red hair could prove fatal.

Fortunately, their class differences kept a wall between them. Her passion and her willingness to live life fully were qualities he admired. She was also the first woman to charge to his rescue. When he recalled the sight of her wielding the ironstone pitcher, he had to chuckle.

She was still a snob and too much her father's little girl for any man's comfort. But he had to agree with her on one point—marriage to Viscount Grossett would be deadly dull, especially for someone as vibrant as herself.

The going grew tough. Miss Harrell was forced to slow her pace and he allowed himself to catch up with her. This time, she didn't bother to initiate conversation, and kept her out-of-joint nose in the air.

The road wound up over a high hill. Beyond the trees, Ian could see the purple tops of mountains in the distance. That was the direction they were heading in and he hoped Amleth Hall was on this side of them.

They'd not met any other travelers. However, as they reached the crest of the hill, they heard a man shouting and the offended, exhausted snorts of horses.

Ian extended his arm in front of Miss Harrell, silently ordering her to stay put while he investigated.

Of course, she didn't.

Fortunately there was no danger. At the bottom of the hill, a farmer's wagon, heavily loaded with milled lumber, was mired in deep mud. The back wheels were buried to the axle.

Ian offered assistance. "Can I be of help?"

The farmer, who'd been too busy rebuking his horses to notice their approach, looked up. "These animals are mules. They weren't watching where they were going and we went off the road. Before I knew it, I was done up . . ."

His voice trailed off as he caught sight of Miss Harrell. He pulled off his low brimmed hat and smiled as if she were Venus personified.

To her credit, Miss Harrell appeared embarrassed by the sudden attention. Ian was merely annoyed.

"I've experience with this kind of situation," he said, drawing the farmer's attention back to him. "In the army, sometimes the cannon would get stuck. Here, let me push two boards under the wheels and I'll lift while you push the horses on. It should work."

"I hope it does," the farmer said fervently. "I promised my wife I'd be home well before nightfall. My uncle died and they are waking him tonight. It's going to be a fine *ceilidh* if ever there was one, because there wasn't a person in the village that could stand him. And I don't want to miss it."

At the mention of the word "wife," Ian didn't know whether to be relieved or alarmed. The farmer was a handsome man with sandy blond hair, a short nose, and strong shoulders and his gaze kept straying to Miss Harrell.

However, she didn't seem to hear what he wanted her to hear. Instead, she looked to Ian. "*Ceilidh*?"

"Dance," he translated.

"For a wake?" she asked, surprised.

"Aye, and it will be a bonnie good time, too," the farmer added, giving Miss Harrell a wink.

Ian stepped in his line of sight. "Are you ready to move the wagon?"

The farmer grinned, unrepentant. He knew Ian considered him a threat. "Aye."

Following Ian's instructions, they had the wheels out of the mud in a thrice. The farmer held out his hand. "I'm Angus Anderson. I thank you for your help. Are you traveling this road for long?"

He had a melodic brogue, the sort that could probably set Miss Harrell's romantic fantasies of Highlanders afire.

Ian wanted to get her away from him as soon as possible.

He was about to grunt a response, but Miss Harrell chirped happily, "We are on the way to Appin. My clan lives there."

"Ah, so you are Scottish," Anderson said with interest.

"My family is—" Miss Harrell answered and would have continued on, but Ian stepped in her way.

"We'll be seeing you," he said firmly.

"But you haven't told me your names," Anderson protested.

Ian frowned. Whatever happened to dour Scots who enjoyed their wall of reserve? This man was gregarious to a fault. He decided to cool the farmer's ardor a bit and introduce himself and Miss Harrell as man and wife. It was safest. "Ian Campion," he said ungraciously. "And this is my wi—"

"His *sister* Lyssa. Lyssa Campion," she interrupted.

Ian could have turned her over his knee.

Anderson was delighted. "What a pretty sister you have, Campion."

"Thank you," Ian said testily, refusing to look at Miss Harrell. "We must be going."

"I'm going Appin way," Anderson said, stepping into his path. "I can't take you all the way there, but I can put you up for a night. You can even come to the ceilidh. We always need another pretty girl to dance with."

"You *dance* at a wake?" she asked.

"Aye, and a lot more too," he added.

Ian didn't know if he'd ever seen anyone actually leer before in his life, but Anderson did. He almost licked his chops like a wolf eyeing a mouth-watering morsel.

Now Miss Harrell understood. She took a step back toward Ian. "Well, I don't know—" she started, but Ian wasn't going to let her get away with it.

"Absolutely," he said cheerfully. "Sounds fun, and there isn't anything like a bit of adventure, is there, *sister*?" He hopped up on the rear of the wagon. "You ride up front, Lyssa dear, with kind Mr. Anderson," he said, taking great relish from using her name.

"But I think I'd rather be in the wagon with you, *brother*," she said pointedly.

"No, you don't," Anderson said. His hand snaked around her waist. He hugged her close. "It's more comfortable up here with me." Before she could make another protest, he commandeered her up to the narrow wagon seat beside him.

Snapping the reins, he had the horses on the go, and Miss Harrell had no choice but to grab hold of the side of the seat or go tumbling off the wagon.

Ian stretched out, enjoying the scent of freshly milled timber and the hole Miss Harrell had obstinately dug for herself.

Chapter Nine

LYSSA knew she'd made a grave error in judgment.

Mr. Anderson obviously thought he was God's gift to women. She'd heard of men like him but she'd never met one. In the past, her father and her chaperones had kept her safe from this type of scoundrel.

However, it was very unhandsome of Mr. Campion to not come to her rescue. True, she had been a bit bold in insisting on the brother/sister relationship . . . but wouldn't any decent brother come to his sister's defense around the likes of Mr. Anderson?

As if answering her silent question, a snore came from the back of the wagon.

The bounder! She'd wager all her father's money he wasn't asleep but merely pretending, to egg Mr. Anderson on.

It worked. Mr. Anderson's hand came down on her thigh.

Lyssa went still, hoping he'd made a mistake about where he'd placed it and would remove it momentarily.

He didn't.

Now what should she do? "I'm sorry, was I crowding you on the seat?" she asked. "Here let me move." Of course there was no place to move to, but she made a pretense of doing so.

His hand stayed where it was. He didn't look at her, but kept his eyes on the horses. Lyssa debated whether she should pretend his hand wasn't on her person. She tried. They rode in silence, her hands in her lap—and then she could take it no longer. Although she was not anxious to make a scene.

"Your *wife* must be a nice person," she reminded him.

"Oh, she is," he agreed. "The very best."

Then what is your hand doing on my knee? Lyssa edged over, thought about crossing her legs and rejected the idea.

Instead, she picked up his hand and put it on his leg. "I can't wait to meet her."

"The two of you will like each other." He put his hand back on her leg.

Lyssa dodged, swinging her knees over to the far side of the wagon. Instead of being rebuffed, Mr. Anderson chuckled. "You are a tasty handful," he replied, and eyed her breasts so she knew exactly what he meant.

Wrapping herself tighter in her plaid, she an-

swered, "You'd best watch the road and not me."
A glance over her shoulder told her Mr. Campion
blissfully slept on . . . but there was a hint of a
smile around his lips.

Mr. Anderson leaned over to whisper in her ear,
"I'd prefer to watch you. The horses can watch the
road."

Lyssa swiped him away as she would a gnat.
Instead of being insulted, he laughed.

"Neither you nor your brother sound Scottish."

"Both of our parents are," she said coldly.
"Davidsons."

He shrugged. "If you say so. It's a shame they
never taught you the Gaelic."

"I speak English, French, and Latin," she answered haughtily, hoping to put him in his place
by the disparity in their education.

"I can help you with the Gaelic," Mr. Anderson
said, completely unimpressed, "but it takes a nimble tongue. Tell me, Miss Campion, do you have a
nimble tongue?"

It took a moment for the double entendre of his
words to sink in, and when it did her temper sizzled. No one spoke to her that way. No one. She
swerved in her seat to face him. "You, sir, are a
boor!"

Instead of being offended, Mr. Anderson
crooned, "When you get your temper up, you
make a man believe you'd be worth the ride." He
punctuated his words with a low growl in the
back of his throat.

Shocked, Lyssa doubled her fist but before she could punch, Mr. Anderson gave her a kiss—a wet, smoochy one right on the mouth. She wanted to gag. Instead, she struck out. Mr. Anderson laughed as if she played a game, reaching to catch her wrist—

"I had such a good nap," Mr. Campion said, coming forward. Without an invitation, he started to sit down between them on the wagon seat, putting his arm around Lyssa's waist so that she didn't fall off the side.

She'd never been so glad to see anyone in her life—although she did want to bop Mr. Campion for not rescuing her sooner. However, now was not the time to quibble.

"Hey," Mr. Anderson complained, "there's not enough space for the three of us on the seat."

"Of course there is," Mr. Campion answered, putting his muscular arm around Mr. Anderson's back in a gesture of bonhomie that had just a hint of threat to it.

Mr. Anderson understood the unspoken message, and Lyssa smugly enjoyed his dissatisfaction. Of course, that meant that she had to ride practically sitting on Mr. Campion's leg . . . something that didn't bother her at all. In fact, she felt very comfortable this close to him, and her shoulder fit beneath his very well.

Unlike Mr. Anderson, who reeked of unwashed male and sawdust, Mr. Campion smelled of the fresh wind and his sister's homemade soap.

For the next several hours, they made better time than they would have on foot. Mr. Anderson was forced to stop his advances with Mr. Campion between them, although the two seemed to get along well while engaging in "man talk" about crops and horses and what sports were to be had in the area. Mr. Anderson liked cock fighting, and once on the subject he carried on his own conversation.

The one thing she had to grow accustomed to was calling Mr. Campion by his Christian name. *Ian*. There was strength in the name. It suited him. Yet she preferred to refer to him as "brother." It kept distance between them, a barrier. "Ian" was warm, inviting . . . intimate.

On the other hand, *he* seemed to delight in calling her "Lyssa." He slurred the last syllable in a way no one else ever had, and she liked the sound of it.

Mr. Anderson attempted to call her "Lyssa" as well, but her name on his lips irritated her, and Mr. Campion quickly corrected him into a proper and respectful "Miss Campion." She was learning that when a man of Mr. Campion's size and presence said something, other men listened.

On the latter side of mid-afternoon, Mr. Anderson turned off the road and headed toward a village nestled against the mountain. "This is Meadhon," he said proudly. "The mill along the stream there is the one my uncle owned. He's the one we shall be waking this night."

"What will become of the mill?" Ian asked.

"He leaves behind a young widow who will not be a widow long," Mr. Anderson predicted. "Not that she's ever let marriage stop her from eyeing the lads, if you know what I mean." He said the last to Mr. Campion in a low confiding tone, one seemingly understood only by gentlemen.

Lyssa did not like him at all.

Several people out and about called a greeting to Mr. Anderson. They were all rushing through their chores so as to ready for the wake. The mood in the air was one of anticipation. They were all good-looking, hardworking people. Many spoke to Mr. Anderson in the Gaelic and they were all curious about Lyssa and Mr. Campion.

Mr. Anderson told everyone they had been invited to the wake, and several echoed his sentiments that visitors were always welcome— especially to a wake like the one the miller was about to have. No one expressed sorrow over the old miller's death. In fact, his wake seemed to be quite an event.

About a half a mile on the other side of the village, Mr. Anderson pulled into the yard of his own small farm. It was a handsome place with chickens running across the yard, several dogs, a good-size barn, and a solid manor house made out of the local stone.

As he pulled the horses to a halt, the front door opened and four towheaded boys came running out yelling, "Papa!" The youngest's fat legs had trouble keeping up with his brothers.

They were followed by a frazzled woman of ample proportions who was all too obviously pregnant with Mr. Anderson's fifth child. Stray wisps had escaped from her braided and pinned blonde hair and her cheeks were red from exertion. She appeared ready to have her baby at any moment.

He jumped to the ground and gave his wife a husbandly kiss on the cheek, apparently without any pang of conscience for having kissed Lyssa earlier.

"Angus, I'm glad you are home," the woman said without acknowledging the kiss. "The house is full. All of your relatives and their friends have come from far and wide to stay under our roof this night."

"It is to be expected," he answered. "Here now, this is Mr. Campion and his sister Miss Campion. They are bound for Appin. I had a wheel stuck in the mud and Mr. Campion helped me out. I offered them a bed for the night."

"But we haven't any," his wife said, worried. She glanced over her shoulder where several of the relatives had already come out on the step.

"We have the room in the barn." Mr. Anderson looked at Mr. Campion. "That should be fine enough for you and your sister? There's a cot there and we've plenty of blankets."

"It will be fine," Mr. Campion said.

"There, it's settled," he said to his wife, who looked to Lyssa.

"I am so sorry we can't offer you better hospitality," she said in her lovely lilting speech. "But my husband's uncle was not a beloved man."

"Do you mind my asking, why is everyone attending his wake?" Lyssa asked.

"Because we are all glad he is dead," Mrs. Anderson responded frankly. "There wasn't a one of us that James Potter didn't cheat, even his own nephew's family. There will be much to celebrate this night. But I go on and you look worn through from travel. Let me show you to your room."

Mr. Campion and some of Mr. Anderson's other guests offered to help unload the wood. Lyssa followed Mrs. Anderson into the barn, which was a large stone-and-timber structure almost a century old with a draftiness to prove its age. Stalls for livestock lined the aisle. Most were empty.

"We don't keep the horses in here during the summer, or the cattle or sheep either," Mrs. Anderson explained. "The room I'm letting you use was for a stable manager, if we were to ever have such a thing. My husband's family had been quite well off before they fought against the English at Culloden. Of course, then they lost all save for this piece of land."

There was a trace of bitterness her voice.

She opened the door to a dark room used for

storing tack. The overpowering smell of molder-
ing leather and a variety of liniments made Lyssa
take a step back to allow her nose to adjust.

Mrs. Anderson walked inside. The only light
was from the door. Lyssa had no choice but to follow.

"This isn't much," her hostess said, pointing
out a canvas-covered cot on a less-than-sturdy
wood frame. "But you should be fine for one
night."

Lyssa nodded, not ready to draw a full breath.

"Your brother can sleep in one of the stalls.
There is hay in some of them and he should be
comfortable. On the other hand, *you* will appreciate a door." She placed her palm on the worn
wood. "There's a hook to lock it closed." Her fingers lightly brushed the metal, before she added
thoughtfully, "Angus has a habit of, um, moving
around at night. You will want to lock the door."

"I will," Lyssa assured her.

"Good," Mrs. Anderson said, and gave Lyssa a
smile that said clearer than words that she was
glad they understood each other. Lyssa's heart
went out to her.

"By the by, I'm Maggie."

"And I'm Lyssa." How would it be, to have a
husband you couldn't trust? Then again, would
she have trusted Robert?

No.

"I'm sorry we can't offer you better. But we will
have a good time this night."

"I've never been to a wake that was fun," Lyssa said.

Maggie laughed. "Whenever there is whiskey and friends there will be a good time, no matter what the occasion. We'll be ready to leave in the hour. Meet us outside the barn."

"Yes, thank you."

"And don't forget to lock the door," Maggie whispered before leaving Lyssa alone.

Lyssa stood in the middle of the messy tack room and pulled her plaid close around her shoulders. Even the lowest servant in her father's employ had a better bed to sleep on than the mildewed canvas cot. Maggie had not even given her a blanket. Perhaps she thought Lyssa's plaid would be enough . . . still, Lyssa could feel her spirits dip.

What was she doing here?

The romance of her great adventure was quickly disappearing in the face of being without money and means. What had Mr. Campion said? They must live by their wits?

As if she had conjured him, Mr. Campion appeared at the door and gave a low whistle. "Our friend Anderson doesn't take care of his tack, does he?"

Relieved to have her dejected thoughts interrupted, Lyssa heartily agreed. "Worse, his wife wants me here because there is a lock on the door."

Mr. Campion eyed the hook. "It should work well enough."

There was a beat of silence and then Lyssa confessed, "I don't want to stay here."

Her words seemed to hang in the air . . . but instead of agreeing with her, he crossed his arms and leaned against the door frame. "You don't like your quarters?"

"I'd rather sleep on the ground."

"We were lucky to find shelter last night. We may not be so fortunate tonight if we leave."

Her nose was growing accustomed to the air in the room, but she wrinkled it all the same. "I don't feel comfortable with these people."

"Ah, now we are discussing the truth," Mr. Campion said with great understanding.

"What do you mean?" Lyssa demanded.

He leaned forward to whisper, "My lady does not like the lower classes."

No words could have been more damning, especially because there was an element of truth. A truth Lyssa would deny. "I don't even know what you are talking about. And why shouldn't I feel uncomfortable around Angus Anderson? The man is as crass as they come."

"You are a snob."

"Absolutely not!" Frowning, she took a step back from him. "I am anything but. Don't forget, Mr. Campion, my father made his fortune in Trade. I know what it is like to be looked down upon and I'd *never* do it to anyone else."

"You do it to me all the time."

His words brought her up short. He was right.

"Of course, I don't let my guard down," he continued, knowing his words had hit their mark. "Your vanity rolls right off me. But these people, they don't know your father's name or your past history. They've opened their home to you because that is what one does for strangers. Their only sin is they are treating you as if you are one of them. And, yes, Angus Anderson flirts with every female he meets, and I daresay does more if the woman is willing, but even his wife wouldn't turn you out."

Lyssa reeled from the accusation of *vanity*. "You must have a low opinion of me."

He shook his head. "I don't think you know any better."

"I do." The air in the room felt warm now with the Irishman so close. And she no longer noticed the odors of leather and liniment. "As a Tradesman's daughter—"

He interrupted her impatiently. "Being a Tradesman's daughter is your convenient excuse not to put yourself out for anyone."

The accusation was outrageous. "I don't know what you mean."

"Yes, you do." His eyes were silvery sharp as they met hers. "Look at yourself, Miss Harrell. You have the looks to set the Town on fire and your father's fortune to make you a worthy prize, but you whine that you were snubbed and are therefore unhappy. Poor little rich girl," he said without sympathy. "She doesn't like her stepmama—like a hundred other women don't—and has no friends. All right now, let's be honest. The only people who snubbed you were those who were jealous. But you use their small-mindedness to keep a wall between yourself and the rest of the world. You didn't even choose your own husband—"

"Wait a minute!" Lyssa leaped to her own defense. "Is this the same man who was lecturing me on the advantages of arranged marriages?"

"I did," he admitted, "but that was before you started turning up your nose at everything—"

"I have not turned up my nose—"

"You can't even say my Christian name!"

"I can too!"

"But you don't."

He was right.

And the reason she didn't was, as he'd said, to keep a wall between them. But not for the reasons he suggested. No, she needed the wall because he was too vital, too overpowering . . . too masculine for her comfort.

Nor was he done. "You expect me to jump at your every whim while you tap your little blistered foot with impatience. Meanwhile, you have yet to listen to sound advice and reason."

That accusation was doing it a bit too brown. She'd been following him around like a lap dog. "When have I not listened?"

He began ticking off the instances on his fingers. "You wouldn't go to London—"

"There were killers blocking the road. Killers who followed *you*, I might add."

He ignored her jibe. "I told you to stay in your room in the inn last night."

"We've already discussed this," she countered, since here was a legitimate case when she should have listened to him.

"And you introduced us as brother and sister." He poked his index finger in the air at her. "You got exactly what you asked for from Anderson. I've been trying to protect you from his kind and worse, and I'm tired of fighting with you—"

"We're not fighting. We're merely expressing our opinions."

"Well, I'm *tired* of your opinions. And I'm tired of being treated as if I were less than a man. Whether you'll excuse me or not, Miss Harrell, I need a bit of distance from you. I plan on going to the wake this evening and enjoying myself with good, honest people who don't have the money to buy everything they wish. You can stay here and pout, or you can walk to Appin. At this point, I'm heartily tired of your whole foolish adventure."

With that, he turned on his heel and walked out the door.

Lyssa stood stunned.

No one had ever talked to her that way before. In fact, Mr. Campion had not *yet* treated her in the way in which she was accustomed. This nonsense about his being tired of her—?

If anything, *she* was tired of *him*! He was

grumpy, incorrigible, bullish—and she would tell him. She hurried to the door. "Mr. Campion!"

He didn't stop.

She took three steps out the door. "Mr. Campion!"

He kept walking.

"Ian!"

He stopped.

Slowly, he turned. "Yes, Lyssa?"

All the things she wanted to rant at him flew from her head.

Instead, they stood facing each other in the near empty barn with shafts of light and dust motes streaming from the doorway and windows—and she knew he was right. She had put up walls between herself and the world. And she'd clung to her prejudices against him because otherwise she had nothing else to protect her against the fact that she was deeply attracted to him.

His attraction came from more than his being a handsome man. Here was a man she admired. A man she was growing to respect.

A man unafraid to speak plainly to her.

This sudden, new awareness of him and his impact on her senses was both startling and unnerving. She felt as fragile and disoriented as a baby bird coming out of its shell and not quite understanding what it wanted yet.

And she feared what she wanted might be something she shouldn't have.

Ian seemed to sense not only her change of temper, but her confusion. But did he understand why?

God help her if he did!

"Lyssa?" He raised an eyebrow in uncertainty.

She blinked, coming to her senses as she realized she'd been staring. It took her a moment to find her voice. "Maggie says we are to be ready in the hour. We're to meet everyone outside to go to the wake."

He shifted his weight, his ever-present knapsack over one shoulder. "So you *are* coming?" Her capitulation seemed to surprise him . . . and he was not a man to trust what he did not understand.

Consequently she took great pleasure in saying, "Of course."

His brows came together. He appeared baffled. So, she couldn't resist whispering in her sweetest voice, "I'm sorry for being so headstrong, Ian."

His puzzlement turned to suspicion. "I actually prefer your obstinacy. It's something I can count on." Then, as if he'd said too much, he murmured, "I need to go shave." He ducked out the barn door and walked away.

Lyssa watched him a moment and couldn't help but add to his list of admirable qualities the straight set of his shoulders. "It's too bad you aren't Robert," she said quietly and then turned to go into her depressing little room and prepare as best she could.

*   *   *

Ian walked out to the rain barrel, dropped his knapsack, threw off his jacket, neck cloth, and shirt, and stuck his head in the water.

He blew his breath out in bubbles and lifted his head out of the water to let it drip off his hair over the barrel.

What the devil was the matter with him? All she had to do was soften her green eyes and give him a hesitant smile and he had the oddest desire to melt at her feet. Especially when she called him "Ian." If he wasn't careful, Lyssa Harrell, the job, could start to become something more.

The thought was so radical, he dunked his head in the rain barrel again until he came to his bloody senses. She couldn't be more. Not ever. They were of two very different worlds. Not to mention Lyssa's father would see Ian a eunuch before he let him have his daughter—something Pirate Harrell could easily accomplish.

Straightening at the waist, he came up again, water dripping down his face—only to discover he had an audience. Three of Anderson's sons and their friends watched him with wide eyes as if they'd never seen anything more funny than a man with his head in a rain barrel.

Ian capped off the show by squirting a mouthful of water out his cheeks at the lot of them, and they ran away with shrieks of laughter.

He leaned over the barrel, bracing himself on the rim with his arms, and watched the boys run.

He was left to prepare hiself to escort his "sister" to a wake. While the truth of the matter was he was beginning to fall for the one woman he couldn't have.

God must be laughing.

Chapter Ten

![horses] WHEN Lyssa came outside at the appointed hour, the Andersons, along with a host of others were waiting for her. Always self-conscious about meeting new people in social circumstances, she found herself feeling a bit shy as she was being offhandedly introduced to the Andersons' relatives and neighbors, who had joined them for the walk to the village.

There were so many people that Lyssa couldn't catch everyone's name, not that anyone seemed to care. The women were busy talking amongst themselves about children and the men groused about farming. And when it became clear to them that she was Ian's "sister," their acceptance of her became warmer.

Ian had already made himself at home. He was trying to beat the Anderson boys in a chase after a barrel hoop. The adults laughed, enjoying the sight of such a big man getting his legs run off of him by their children.

And Lyssa was happy to blend in.

In the tack room while she'd been getting ready, she'd worried about the increasing shabbiness of her dress. The wool of the skirt was good, but both her skirt and blouse were showing signs of hard travel. She didn't have anything else to change into or even a bonnet to wear. However, when she saw how the other women were dressed, she relaxed.

There wasn't a bonnet to be seen. True, the married women all wore very high white caps, but the unmarried girls, her age and younger, either neatly braided their hair or plaited it in front and let it flow down their backs in the Grecian fashion. Since her curls were impossible to tame into braids, Lyssa had to be satisfied with her simple style of tying it back with Ian's leather cord, although she wouldn't have minded a snood or bit of ribbon like some of the girls had.

She was pleased to see that everyone, save for Ian, wore plaid, and her tartan was well received. The matrons wore plaid shawls with white kerchiefs beneath them. Several men wore kilts, including Mr. Anderson, who topped his off with a blue jacket, no doubt a sign of his former position and prosperity. Some wore their tartan as a wrap as Lyssa did, others as a drapery. Even the children had plaid, either tied around their waists or as garters.

What really raised Lyssa's eyebrows over Highland fashion was that most of the women were barefoot and seemed completely at ease with the fact. Thank goodness she had shoes, because she did not think she could do without.

Ian jogged up to her. "Put my knapsack in your room if you please," he said.

"Of course." Lyssa turned back toward the barn and was surprised when two young women offered to go with her. She found out why, when the first, a pretty blonde who was an Anderson neighbor and had the sort of lush figure any man would admire said in her melodic brogue, "Is your brother married?"

They had reached the door to her room. "No."

"Any sweethearts?"

"Not that I know," Lyssa hedged.

That was all the girls wanted to know. They left her like a shot, and by the time Lyssa came out of the barn after hiding the knapsack under her cot, she could see Ian was surrounded by lovely young lasses.

He didn't seem to mind.

"It's a nice night for a walk, isn't it, Lyssa, my dear?" Mr. Anderson said, coming up and attempting to put his hand around her waist.

"Yes, it is," she answered, skillfully avoiding his arm. "And I must help Maggie carry the basket she is holding." Staying by his wife should cool his ardor, although he didn't seem to be the least put off by her snub.

"Save a dance for me," he called softly, and she wanted to punch him. If Maggie overheard, she gave no indication.

Most of the women were bringing food for the wake. Maggie had a ham and a dozen hard-boiled eggs in her basket. She also had a pudding that David, her youngest son, had helped himself to. "Just like his father, he is."

Lyssa hoped not.

James Potter had lived in a good-size house built beside the mill, and it was there that the wake was held. The house was made of the same gray stone as the mill and outbuildings and there was a large yard of dirt beaten down into a hard floor from years of carts delivering grain to the miller.

The Anderson party was not the first to arrive. The house was so crowded, people stood outside. An ale keg had been tapped and a row of whiskey bottles set up. Lyssa was surprised to see that everyone had brought their own glass. Maggie had thought to bring one each for her and Ian.

All in all, the air was festive and a far cry from any wake Lyssa had ever attended. She was relieved to learn that no one could have a drink until they'd gone in and paid their respects to the dead, which seemed the least that people could do in sympathy to the family.

Lyssa had assumed she would not be expected to perform such a serious chore, because she'd never even laid eyes on the man. However, one of

Maggie Anderson's aunts, Jean, cheerfully said she'd hardly known the old miller either and now was as good a time as any to say hello *and* good-bye. She was all of sixty and as tiny as a bird with bright brown eyes to match. She took Lyssa by the arm and led her into the house.

The halls and rooms were packed with neighbors and friends greeting each other. Here, the atmosphere was a touch more somber, but not much. Food was being set out in the kitchen and children darted amongst the grown-ups, anxious to play until someone shooed them out.

"There's the widow." Jean nodded to a surprisingly young, sandy-haired woman with the plumpest breasts Lyssa had ever seen. "I do know *her*. She worked at her father's tavern a few miles south of Meadhon and was always a handful. Little better than a whore and would take anyone to her bed, until that goat James took a liking to her and offered his name. Now, look—she's wealthy," Jean confided. Approaching the woman, she immediately changed her tone of voice. "Mary, what sad news."

"He was my life," the widow murmured. Black was a good color for her complexion, something Lyssa sensed the woman knew.

"Yes, he was, yes, he was," Jean agreed. She patted Mary's hand twice and moved on without taking the time to introduce Lyssa, who hesitated.

"Shouldn't I let her know I'm here?"

"She doesn't care about you," Jean said. "Now,

when she meets your brother it will be a different matter. You'd best watch him close. Just because she's a widow doesn't mean Mary will want to sleep by herself tonight. She's carried on with Angus for years."

Lyssa was shocked at Jean's candor. "You're not serious? Why, he's her husband's nephew?"

"Aye, and I and the rest of the family don't have any use for him. We all worry about poor Maggie, but she seems blind to her husband's bad habits."

Lyssa also observed they were receiving more than their share of attention. Coming up to them, Mr. Anderson noticed, too. "Visitors, especially beautiful ones, are always welcome in the kirk." He laughed as if he'd made some small joke and steered Lyssa and a now frowning Jean into the low-ceilinged bedroom. Lyssa hoped Jean didn't think she encouraged Mr. Anderson's nonsense.

Nor was she ready to pay her respects to the dead. The viewing was in the bedroom and Lyssa wanted to hang back, but the movement of the other guests prevented her. People stepped forward and then to the side in what seemed a relentless tide and before she was ready, she found herself standing in front of the body of Mr. Potter, sitting straight up in bed.

The position startled Lyssa into a hiccup of surprise and a step back. Everyone else acted as if he appeared completely natural for a dead man.

He'd been shaved and dressed in a blue jacket with a drape of a red and green plaid over his shoulder. The few gray hairs on his bald pate had been combed to the side and he appeared to Lyssa simply to be a rather reluctant member of the party. His was not the expression of one "resting in peace." If anything, he appeared ready to bite someone's head off.

"That is him," Mr. Anderson crooned. "That's my uncle, looking as real as life."

Lyssa could see why no one liked him. Feeling remarkably awkward, she shifted the empty glass Maggie had given her from one hand to the other.

Mr. Anderson patted his uncle's leg, covered by the bed clothes. "James, we won't miss arguing with you at all."

"Amen," another gent said, a sentiment echoed by several other mourners.

Jean turned toward Lyssa. "*Och*, you look like you could use a wee dram. Come, let's go outside."

Lyssa thankfully followed her, slipping away from Mr. Anderson, who was waylaid by another guest. As she and Jean walked out the front door, a group of local musicians started tuning their instruments.

Because the night promised to be a nice one, they were set up outside by the house. This was no string quartet like the ones Lyssa often listened to at London soirees. There was a drum, a pipe, and a fiddle, and in a matter of minutes they set up a tune that filled the air.

"That is more like it," Jean said approvingly,

moving toward the bottles of whiskey. She poured a healthy measure into her glass and offered some to Lyssa.

"No, thank you," Lyssa demurred.

"No whiskey?" Jean acted as if she'd never heard of such a thing. "You have to have whiskey at a wake. It's the water of life. Why even the babies drink it." She proved her words by pointing Lyssa toward a group of children sipping on their whiskey.

"I don't think so," Lyssa said uncertainly. She'd never had strong spirits before and usually drank no more than a glass of wine at dinner.

"Come on," Jean pushed, filling Lyssa's glass whether she wanted it or not. "We are guests. We have to drink to the miller's health. How else is he to go off to heaven or hell without us?"

To her relief, Ian joined them. "Is there a problem?"

"No problem," Jean assured him. "We're just having a wee dram. Would you like some?"

He held out his glass, placing his arm on Lyssa's shoulder. "Take just a sip," he murmured in her ear. "Otherwise it is an insult."

Lyssa held out her glass and discovered her idea of a "wee dram" and Jean's were decidedly different. The older woman didn't hesitate to fill a glass half full.

There was nothing to be done. Jean held her glass in the air. "To James!" she chirped and Lyssa had no choice but to drink with the others surrounding them, who quickly seconded the toast.

She took a sip—and was caught off guard by the whiskey's burn. She choked as the fire of the liquor went down her throat and hit her stomach. Tears sprang to her eyes though she'd barely drunk more than a few drops.

"Is something the matter?" Jean asked.

Ian rubbed Lyssa's back. "My sister's never had whiskey before."

"But I thought she was Scottish?" Jean wondered.

"She is now," Ian said and silently toasted Lyssa before downing his own glass.

Lyssa watched the amber liquid go down his throat and wondered how he did it. Then Jean, laughing, did the same—and although she had close to forty years on Lyssa, she suffered no ill effects. In fact, she poured more for herself and Ian. Lyssa had no choice. She had to take a second timid sip.

This time, there was no burn, just a smooth, mellowy, not-too-sweet taste. She wasn't certain if she liked it or not, but let Jean pour some more in her glass and the third swallow was even better.

The sun was setting. The evening air was turning velvety, and a full, yellow moon, the kind Lyssa liked best, made its appearance in the sky.

The band finished its first selection and now started the dancing in earnest with a merry reel.

Couples quickly took their places while others flowed into the house for food.

"So you paid your respects to the miller?" Ian asked, his voice close to her ear. Jean had moved on to greet other friends.

Lyssa looked up at him. "I was shocked to discover him sitting straight up in bed. I've never seen such a thing. Nor have I seen such a crowded wake for a person no one liked, or at least, I haven't attended one. Did you pay your respects?"

"I managed to avoid it so far."

"Oh," Lyssa said, "so you haven't met the widow yet?" She made a great pretense of looking around him for the blonde neighbor and other Anderson female relatives. "And where is your entourage? I can't believe they are leaving you alone."

He held a finger up to his lips for silence. "I've steered them toward lads more their own age."

"That was thoughtful of you."

"That was smart of me. Did you see the jealous look on the lads' faces when I arrived? A wise man doesn't bait the pack. Let's go get something to eat." He placed his hand on the small of her back, directing her toward the house. The gesture felt good and—perhaps it was the whiskey—she liked being beside him.

However, before they could get far, Mr. Anderson came charging up with the Widow Mary Potter. "Campion," he said good-naturedly. "The widow says she has not had the opportunity to meet you yet."

Lyssa murmured, "Uh-oh," under her breath. Apparently, Jean's prediction was about to come true.

Mary Potter stepped in front of Lyssa as if she didn't exist and pushed her fantastical breasts at Ian. "I am so glad you could come. It is always a pleasure to welcome strangers."

Especially handsome ones, Lyssa wanted to add. She caught Ian's eye and waggled her eyebrows but then, suddenly, she had her own problem. "Let's dance," Mr. Anderson said. He didn't wait for an answer but pulled her toward the dancing.

Lyssa attempted to beg off. "I don't know the steps."

"You don't need to know the steps, lass," Mr. Anderson told her. "You just move." And he was right.

She danced once with Mr. Anderson, conscious that he attempted to swing her close to him every chance he could, but quickly escaped him. However, to her surprise, another young man asked her to dance, and when he finished there was another—although, as always, there were more women than men who wanted to dance. In fact, for the first time, she was having a grand time at a dance.

Some of the reels she recognized, but most of the dances were regional or seemed to be created right there on the spot. There was stomping and whooping and clapping and all sorts of behavior that would never have been allowed on a London dance floor—and she reveled in it.

Even the whiskey tasted good, and was it her imagination, or was she dancing better than she ever had before?

The one person she didn't dance with was Ian. He was being monopolized by the "Merry Widow" Potter. And when she didn't have him, the girls of the shire clamored for the next dance with him. Lyssa could understand why. Ian was the best dancer there, and unlike the majority of men who danced when they were forced to and drank when they weren't, he seemed to be enjoying the music.

But then, what man wouldn't like so much feminine attention? Other than when they'd had their earlier conversation, he'd barely glanced at Lyssa. He'd been too occupied with other women—not that she cared. After all, she was pretending to be his sister, and what brother asked his sister to dance?

Still . . . it would have been nice if he looked over to her once in a while, as if concerned about what she was doing. Especially when she found herself without a dance partner a time or two . . . as she did at this moment. Of course, she could have found herself a partner if she'd been willing to *throw* herself at men the way the other women threw themselves at Ian.

Jean and Maggie wandered over to her side.

"Your brother is making quite a stir," Jean observed.

"It's disgraceful the way Mary Potter is behaving," Maggie added. "You'd think she'd never been married, the way she is rubbing that bosom of hers against Ian, and every other man, every chance she gets."

"Did you expect her to change just because her husband is in the house waiting for his burial?" Jean wondered. "Here, Lyssa, you look thirsty."

Lyssa covered her glass with her hand. "No more whiskey or I won't make it home." Already far too many people had imbibed too much and the wake was growing raucous. Only a short while ago, she'd seen a young man cover his mouth and lurch off into the surrounding woods beyond the torchlights set up in a circle around the yard. A few minutes later, the man marched back to the wake to drink some more. Another two lads were proudly wrestling over in a dark corner while other men took bets. Here and there a few couples slipped off into the night.

If Maggie and Jean noticed these things, they didn't say, and Lyssa didn't doubt they weren't as pleasantly dulled by the whiskey as everyone else. In fact, she and Ian appeared to be the two most sober people in the crowd, and she wasn't certain he was all that clear-headed.

Just then, one of the musicians, an open-faced redhead named James, grabbed Lyssa's arm and pulled her toward where the dancers were forming two circles—an inner circle of women and an outer circle of men. "We need more for the circle dance."

"I don't know any circle dance," Lyssa protested.

"You don't need to," James answered and drew her forward.

"What do I do?"

He stopped. "You women take your place and the men take theirs. The circles move in opposite directions until the music stops and then you dance with whoever you are standing in front of. The game is only fun if everyone is a part of it."

Before Lyssa could ask another question or offer protest, he was off, heading toward the wrestling boys, who'd finished their match.

"Beg pardon," a portly girl with pink cheeks said, squeezing in between Lyssa and the woman next to her in the circle. As Lyssa stepped aside to make room, she discovered what the girl was after. Ian was several people down from her in the men's circle. All the women had their eye on him for the dance and were maneuvering for a position close to him, even to the point of poking elbows in ribs to gain their chosen place.

Meanwhile, the men noticed the attention Ian was receiving. Nor were they as good-natured about it as she had assumed. Out of the corner of her eye, Lyssa caught James talking to the wrestlers. They glanced at Ian with undisguised resentment and she knew none of the gentlemen at the wake appreciated how easily the Irishman had swept their women off their feet.

And the fact that James had little problem at all persuading the other men to dance made Lyssa suspect something was up.

Everyone took their places and the music started. Lyssa's suspicions were confirmed. The women all tried to place themselves in front of Ian and the men seemed to have another purpose in mind. Ian noticed them jostling him but he took it all in stride. His gaze met Lyssa's and he shrugged as if to say he didn't know what was going on.

Round and round the two circles went, the women lingering in front of Ian, the men pushing him on.

Lyssa tried not to pay attention to any of the games. After all, what did she care who danced with whom?

The music stopped. She found herself in front of a thin man with legs like walking sticks that made him appear comical in his kilt.

Then, suddenly, one man bumped another, and Ian was shoved to stand in front of her.

The men looked at each other in triumph. "Sad news," one of them said to Ian. "Looks like you'll be dancing with your sister."

His announcement met exultant shouts from the men and miffed mews from the women. The plump girl next to Lyssa walked off in a pique of temper rather than dance with the man in front of her.

But the music didn't wait for anyone. Immediately the music of a Scottish reel filled the air and everyone's feet started moving ... save for Lyssa's and Ian's.

She looked up to him. Not for the first time was she struck at how tall he was, except this time was different. There was music and laughter in the night air and somehow, being with him seemed more intimate.

He made a wry face. "Shall we?"

Lyssa had no choice. Everyone was dancing, and they were watching. Reluctantly, she placed her hand on the tips of his long fingers. His hand came down at her waist and she knew he felt as awkward as she did, because he barely rested it there.

They started dancing, joining the skipping line, and were surprisingly very compatible as partners. They moved together well and within heartbeats, Lyssa forgot the charade of being brother and sister, and even class distinctions. Instead, she enjoyed dancing with a man who did it well. A man who was attractive enough to command everyone's attention. A man who, when he laughed as they missed a step like he just did, made her stomach go fluttery.

Her stomach had never fluttered before. For anyone.

And she sensed she was not the only one affected. His hold at her waist had grown more possessive. He pressed her closer to him and did not shift when her breast brushed against the side of his chest. At one point, when the dance called for her to lean in to him, was it her imagination or did he hold her close for a moment? Very close.

She didn't question these intoxicating new feelings. She didn't put up barriers or walls. She accepted . . . and lost herself in the music, the night, and the presence of this man.

And when the music stopped, neither one of them moved away from the other.

Except that all of the men had come up to clap Ian on the back and laugh at him for the joke they had played. The women crowded in, too, wanting to win his attention . . . and Lyssa, still caught in a haze of bewilderment at her uncertain sense of longing, found herself pushed back and out of the way.

That was fine with her. She needed a moment to sort things out.

She wandered over to Maggie, who was busy comparing notes with friends on the births of her children. Jean giggled with some other women. Lyssa would have crossed over to her except that an older gentleman took that time to ask Jean to dance, much to the amusement of her friends.

The next set started and Lyssa drifted over to the whiskey table feeling very much alone. For a second, she was tempted to have another nip, but decided what she really needed was to take a bit of a walk to clear her head. Whiskey fumes were obviously putting her in a self-pitying mood. After all, what did she care who Ian danced with?

She checked to make sure Mr. Anderson was occupied dancing. She had no desire to run into him in the dark. He was . . . but she didn't see Ian. She decided to search him out and moved toward the edge of the torchlight.

Groups of people stood around, their laughter adding to the music. One or two men called to her, a sign the drink was getting to them, too. She ignored them.

Away from the house, the village was quiet. In the full moonlight, she easily found a path that led down to the millstream. She'd not followed it far when she heard the sound of whispering and recognized the low timbre of Ian's voice.

Lyssa started to call his name, but then some inner sense warned her to hesitate. In the silence, a woman giggled and there followed the rustle of clothing.

She should have stopped there. It would have been polite and prudent. But there was whiskey in her veins and a woman's curiosity to be satisfied.

Quietly, she moved closer until she could look around a bend in the path. There in the dark shade of a tree, Ian had his arms around the Widow Potter—or, to be more correct, she had her arms around him. She'd already removed his jacket and was laughingly trying to pull his shirt from his breeches, which he seemed to be trying to avoid even while they were both very involved with a kiss.

Lyssa didn't know what to do. To think that only moments earlier she'd been attracted to him to the point of confusion. Now, a part of her wanted to march over and pull the brazen widow off of him. Another part wanted to turn tail and run as far away from him as possible, especially when his hand came up to cover the widow's right breast. Lyssa could see where it was as plain as day in the moonlight!

The widow moaned like a cat in heat, her leg coming up to wrap around his thigh—

"Ian?"

The girl's voice on the path above Lyssa not only startled her, but also caught the lovers. Ian pulled away to put on his jacket while the widow hurriedly rearranged her clothing. "I can't be seen like this. Not tonight!" she said with belated worry.

Ian merely grunted a response and pushed a hand through his disheveled hair. Lyssa wondered if she'd been wrong about his sobriety. He didn't quite seem himself and there was a frown between his brows as if something bothered him.

As for herself, she slipped back into the shadows, bending down and hiding in the bushes beside the path.

"Ian?" the girl called again and came into Lyssa's view. She was dark-haired and had nubile features—why did everyone have breasts bigger than Lyssa's—and had been chasing Ian shamelessly all night.

A second later, the girl stumbled on Ian and the Widow Potter. "What are you two doing down here?" she asked, amazed. Obviously they'd righted their clothing or she would have known what was going on!

"I was showing Mr. Campion the millstream," the widow said.

"At night?"

Lyssa was so proud of the girl she almost stood up and rooted aloud.

"Of course, at night," Ian answered with smooth Irish charm. "Especially in the moonlight. How better to see two beautiful women?"

Lyssa had to cover her mouth to keep from making her opinion of such blarney known.

But the women giggled and the next thing she knew, it sounded as if he was kissing them both.

She couldn't stay in hiding but had to stand up to see for herself. Her ears were not lying. Ian had his arm around the waist of each and nuzzled first one, and then the other.

And they let him!

To think she'd begun to admire him. Had even started to grace him with all sorts of splendid heroic qualities. And now he was making love to two women!

Lyssa jumped out of her hiding spot and charged up the path toward the millhouse, crashing through the bushes without a care to any sound she might make.

Behind her, she could hear one of the women ask, "Who was that?" but she didn't wait for the answer to tell if she'd been seen or not.

Rushing back into the party, she quickly found Maggie, who had two sleepy heads resting in her lap. "Are you ready to go?"

"Past time," her hostess admitted tiredly.

"Come, I'll help you with the children." Lyssa lifted one in her arms. She didn't know how Maggie would carry the youngest, as far along in pregnancy as she was, but she did.

Jean had started to doze in a chair. Maggie shook her shoulder. "Come, Auntie, it's time to go home."

"What about the others? Is Angus coming?" Jean asked.

"You know Angus is always the last to leave," Maggie said. "And some of the others have already left. Come."

They'd gone no more than a few steps when Ian appeared back in the ring of light, alone. The moment he saw Maggie and Lyssa, he crossed over to them.

"Here, Maggie, let me hold the boy."

Maggie happily relinquished her son to his arms. "Thank you. He's getting too heavy for his mother to carry."

"I'll walk you home," Ian said.

"You can stay as long as you like," Lyssa said coolly.

"I'm ready to go home," Ian answered. She could feel him stare at her although she refused to even glance at him.

No one wanted them to leave. The women all called for Ian to stay and the men begged Lyssa to stay. Mr. Anderson shouted that another dance was forming and no one should leave now, but the time had come. Lyssa was exhausted and needed her rest for the next day.

They took off in the dark, she and Ian holding the children and Maggie and Jean supporting each other.

Ian fell into step beside her. "You're angry."

"Over what?" Lyssa asked breezily while inside she seethed.

"You *know* what."

"That you were kissing *two* women?" Lyssa managed a tolerably good shrug even with the boy's head on her shoulder. "What you do is none of my concern, Mr. Campion."

"Liar."

Lyssa whipped her head around to confront him. "I beg your pardon?" she demanded in a voice that could have frozen water.

"Oh, stop that upper-class cold shoulder. You're in a great pout and for what? Because I was kissing someone?" He snorted. "We have a full moon, a bit of whiskey, good music, and a willing lass. There is nothing wrong with kissing. At least not where I come from."

"Willing *lasses*," she corrected. "Don't you believe you were being a bit greedy?" She didn't wait for an answer but informed him, "This is really none of my concern. You are paid to protect me and if you think grabbing women in the bushes is giving my father his money's worth—"

"You weren't in any danger. And you were having as good a time as I was."

That was true, but Lyssa didn't want to admit it. In fact, for some perverse reason, she relished picking this argument with him. It was good to keep him at a distance, even comforting. "Mr. Campion, this conversation between us is finished. Believe me when I say I don't care what you were doing with those women. You could have been *fornicating*," she said dramatically, using the boldest, worst word she could think of in her vocabulary, a word she'd never been brave enough to use before, "and I would not care."

His reaction was swift. "You are being damned silly."

That was *not* the response she had anticipated. Her temper was ready to go up in flames except he moved away, the set of his mouth grim, placing Jean and Maggie between them, both women too tired to care about an argument between "brother and sister."

Fifteen minutes later, they reached the Andersons' farm. They helped Maggie put the boys to bed. Her two older sons were going to stay with friends in the village.

Lyssa didn't wait to say good night to Ian but marched off to her little room, shut the door, and hooked the latch. Moonlight lit the barn but her room was darker than pitch. She had to feel her way to the shabby cot. Removing her shoes and her belt, she wrapped herself in her plaid, expecting to fall asleep instantly. She didn't . . . or perhaps she dozed. She wasn't certain.

All she knew is that she heard a scratching on the closed door. "Ian! Ian, let me in," a woman's whispered voice said.

Lyssa lay still, immediately recognizing the Widow Potter.

"Ian?"

Then there was silence. Lyssa strained her hearing. Had the widow found him? She heard voices whispering beyond the door.

She sat up, pushing aside her plaid.

This was not her business.

Ian was his own man. As he'd said earlier, he didn't answer to her.

However, he was being paid to protect her, not flirt with women, and Lyssa came face to face with a hard truth.

She was jealous.

For a second, she sat quiet, uncomfortable with this new emotion.

Or was it an old one?

For the first time, she recognized how jealous she was of the Duchess, the wife her father had chosen to replace her mother, a jealousy she'd denied. Nor did she like confronting how childishly she'd behaved to her stepmother over the past three years.

She pushed unwelcome thoughts aside, but having these feelings now over Ian . . . ?

Knowing she shouldn't, Lyssa rose and tiptoed to the door. She leaned her ear against it. There was no more whispering, but there were sounds— soft sighs and a feminine laugh that was quickly squelched and turned into a gasp of surprise.

Lyssa stared at the door, wishing she could see right though it.

She couldn't. And she could not stand here any longer pretending nothing was happening. She had to see for herself. Maybe then she'd rid herself of this silly infatuation over Ian. She pulled on her shoes, lacing them quickly, flicked up the latch and threw open the door.

The moonlight gave the barn a silvery glow, but she didn't see anyone.

Listening, she heard a strange, rhythmic noise in the stall nearest the tack room. Curiosity propelled her forward. Quietly, she took one step after another until the stall came into view and Lyssa caught sight of a naked Widow Potter bouncing up and down on a man lying in the hay whose breeches were around his ankles.

Chapter Eleven

For a moment, Lyssa could only gape like some village fool until she realized what they were doing—and then, she was shocked to the core of her soul.

The man's naked thighs were pasty white and his hands gripped the Widow's breasts as if they were plow handles. They were both so occupied in their moans and groans and mutual sweaty activity, they didn't notice her.

Finally, Lyssa found her voice. "When I said fornicating, I didn't expect you to do it!"

Nor did she expect his voice to come from behind where she stood. "I'm not. But I do think you should mind your own business, Lyssa."

Turning, she saw Ian standing—fully clothed in shirt sleeves, breeches, and stockings—at the entrance of another stall.

"Then who—?" she started before turning in horror to see both the Widow and Mr. Anderson looking up at her.

Lyssa thought she would die from the embarrassment. Instead, she turned and ran out of the barn.

Outside in the yard, she stopped. What should she do now? Knock on the door and inform Mrs. Anderson of her husband's activities? Or sit out here until they'd finished and left?

She certainly couldn't pretend *nothing* had happened.

Ian came up behind her. Taking her arm in a grip as tight as a vise, he said, "Not one word, not until we are beyond the house." He'd pulled on his boots and practically carried her away from the house and the barn.

"But Maggie . . . she needs to know," Lyssa protested, trying to turn back.

"No, she doesn't," came his terse reply and he half carried her forward.

As Ian had anticipated, Anderson came out of the barn buttoning his breeches. He could almost hear the farmer's sigh of relief that his guests were heading off toward his pastures instead of knocking on the door to inform his wife.

He led Lyssa toward a pond on the far side of the field. Beneath the overhanging branches of a willow tree, he let her sit on the cool ground. She buried her face in her hands. He sat beside her, not saying a word, preferring instead to study the way the moonlight shone off the smooth surface of the pond.

"I didn't think it was done like that," she said at last, her voice completely serious. "That didn't appear pleasurable at all."

Her reaction startled a laugh out of him.

She turned to him. "This is not funny," she said. "Catching them was so humiliating." And yet, in spite of the stain of embarrassment on her cheeks, even she started to laugh, and covered her mouth as if to stifle the sound.

"Think how I felt with them going at it in the stall next to mine," Ian confessed. "I was hoping they wouldn't wake you up."

"How could they not? They were making so much noise."

Suddenly, the two of them were laughing so hard, Ian feared the sound would carry and Anderson would hear them. He put his arm around Lyssa's shoulder and shushed her. "We'll wake up everyone."

"I'd like to wake up Maggie," she said, sobering. She turned to him, sitting so close that her bouncing red curls spilled over his shoulder. "She should know."

"She *does* know. Anderson certainly doesn't hide his tomcatting."

Lyssa looked out over the pond. "What a life she must live."

"It may be the one she chooses," he observed quietly. "You can't convince me he is any different now than he was before he married."

"But why would she look the other way? If he

was my husband, I'd take a whip to him. I certainly wouldn't let him into my bed."

Ian had no doubt she wouldn't. But then Lyssa had a strong sense of self and more pride than was prudent—two things he admired about her. Two things they had in common.

"Look at the house she now lives in," he told her. "Back when he courted her, he was probably a jovial fellow with a wandering eye and a good piece of property."

"She told me his family had once been quite grand."

"So now you know why she married him and with four children and another on the way, no, she wouldn't appreciate your telling her about her husband and Mary Potter."

Lyssa leaned forward, hugging her knees. His arm was still around her shoulder and she did not seem to mind. "Love shouldn't be like that," she said half to herself.

"Too often it is."

He didn't remind her of Lord Grossett waiting for her and his share of her father's fortune.

Instead, he focused on Lyssa, on *wanting* her. Yes, earlier in the evening he'd been kissing any willing woman . . . but the one he wanted, the one he'd tried not to think about was right here beside him.

And what would she taste like if he kissed her?

"You don't believe in love?" she challenged, looking over her shoulder.

"When the moon is this full, I believe in everything," he answered recklessly. "Besides, I'm Irish. We're poets and fools."

"I thought you were pragmatic?" she returned, a sign there were no more whiskey fumes in her brain.

"Reality has hardened my idealism," he admitted.

"Not mine," she said proudly. "I believe love, *true* love, can overcome *anything*. And it is worth the price. Even if you have to live in a hovel. My parents had that kind of love."

Dear God, had he ever been so naïve? It seemed ages ago. "Why do you say so?"

"Because my mother gave up everything for my father. He was a shepherd who had come looking for work. He hadn't home or hearth. The Davidsons hired him and he lived in the meanest conditions. However, he said the moment he laid eyes on my mother, he knew he was in love, a love he couldn't deny even if he was poor. My mother felt the same. She believed they were destined for each other."

To a man who had nothing, her words were like water for a thirsty soul. Still, Ian knew the world too well. "Her family did not approve."

"Of course not. He had nothing. Her father tried to lock her in her room but she escaped and she and my father ran away to London to seek their fortune." She was silent a moment before adding softly, "Ironic, isn't it, that now he wants me to marry a man with money and a title?"

"Or that your mother ran away from Scotland to escape her fate, while you are running toward it."

She sat up and turned to him. "Yes, you're right," she agreed thoughtfully. "And instead of allowing me to choose my own husband, he's insisting on Robert."

Here was dangerous ground. Ian dropped his hand from her back, warning himself to be cautious. Lyssa was romantic and what she claimed to want was not always what she wanted . . . except a part of him, his pride, most likely, sought to be accepted for himself, in spite of his mistakes. In spite of his failures.

And pigs might fly someday, too.

"There is no wrong in a father wanting what is best for his daughter," he said.

"No," she agreed quietly, and then her expression hardened. "Of course, he destroyed my mother's memory and what they had together by marrying the duchess."

Ian knew he shouldn't touch it. After all, what was it to him if Lyssa insisted on portraying her stepmother as the villain? Still . . . "Your stepmother came down in rank to marry your father. Perhaps, there is deep love there, too?"

Her brows snapped together and her back straightened with indignation. She moved away from him. "How can you say such a thing? The duchess only married my father for his money. Her love has never been tested. And, have you forgotten she is behind the murder attempt on my life?"

"We don't know that," he answered—and in truth, in his gut, he didn't believe she was. "I have no doubt that the love your father and mother had was rare and special. That's the way it was with my parents and my sisters would have followed their husbands to hell and back."

"But—?" she prompted.

He smiled. How well she was beginning to know him. "But I believe there may be many different kinds of love. And while one may not be as intense as another, each is important."

"For example?"

Of course, she would expect him to build his case. Ian picked a blade of grass and rested his arms on his bent knees before saying, "Well, there is the love of parent and the love of a child. Both are important, but not the least bit similar. Then, there is the love in a friendship. I've had friends I would lay down my life for and although the feeling is different, it is as strong as the love between man and wife." He tossed the grass aside. "Each love is valid. In a remarriage who is to say which love was stronger, the love for the first or second wife? I can see your father loving your mother for being by his side. For believing in him when no one else did. Could he not love your stepmother for the same? Certainly she gave up some status in society for him. Of course, what he felt for your mother must have burned brighter. They were younger and there was much more at stake."

She studied him a second, considering his words. Her response surprised him. "You argue your point like a barrister, stating your case while appeasing mine."

The insightful accuracy caught Ian off guard. Unsettled, he pulled back, suddenly uncertain as to what he had revealed.

If Lyssa noticed his slight alarm, she gave no indication. Instead, she rested back on her palms and looked up at the stars. "I wish I'd known my mother when she was as young as I. My first memories of her were when she was ill. The doctors could never tell us what was wrong with her save she didn't have the strength to leave her room. I used to believe having me had made her ill but Papa said that wasn't true. I spent every moment I could with her. She was sick for so long . . ." Her voice trailed off wistfully and Ian thought he understood.

And now her father had a wife who was young and healthy, something her mother had never been in Lyssa's memory. No wonder she was jealous of her stepmother.

"Would you kiss me?"

Ian shook his head, thinking he'd imagined her words.

She sat up and faced him. "Would you?" she prodded.

"Are you serious?"

Her expressive widened. "Yes." There was a pause and she added, "I think I am."

"Why?" The word flew from his mouth before he could stop it.

Her cheeks darkened with color. She dropped her gaze and then said, "Because the only kiss I've ever had was that terrible one from Mr. Anderson."

Ian frowned. "I find that hard to believe."

"Well, you shouldn't." She pulled out a handful of grass, her fingers twisting the blades into rope. "I mean, I've received a peck or two. When Robert asked for my hand and my father gave it to him, he kissed my cheek."

"And what did you do?" Ian asked, curious.

"Initially? Nothing." She dropped her grass and dusted her fingers lightly before adding, "Later, I washed my cheek."

That was the answer he'd wanted to hear. And still, like a doubting fool, he hedged. "So why would you want a kiss from me?"

"Because you must know how to kiss. You seemed to be doing a good job of it earlier. Or so one would believe from the response you received." She placed her hand on his thigh, a bold move that was counterbalanced by the timidity in her wide eyes.

Suddenly uncertain, he said, "Miss Harrell—"

"Lyssa."

"Lyssa," he repeated, drawing out the syllables.

Her fingers were inches from his groin and he was having trouble thinking, since all the blood seemed to have left his brain and was now centered in his very strong erection.

If she noticed, she gave no sign.

Instead, she leaned close. "I'm three and twenty," she whispered, "and on the shelf, or so my stepmother tells me. After mother died, father and I spent three years wrapped in grief. But he recovered. I was twenty, Ian. My mother had been ill most of my life and I was already old in more ways than age. Then Papa met his duchess and married and I was forced to go out into Society. Do you know how awkward I felt? There were so many rules I had to learn and everything I did seemed to be wrong. Whereas my stepmother knew everything and everyone. She was graceful and poised, and I felt old."

"You are not old."

"There were girls younger than myself who were already matrons with babies—"

"Not many," he corrected.

"More than enough," she said. "And here I was, not even knowing how to flirt."

"You know more than you realize," he answered carefully, his heart pounding in his ears.

"I don't know how to kiss like you were kissing the widow. I don't know how to kiss at all, and I do want to learn." She punctuated her words by moistening her lips with the tip of her tongue, and Ian almost groaned aloud.

Here was the first sign that she saw him as a man . . . and the opportunity to taste her was very tempting.

"Please?" she asked prettily and closed her eyes, offering herself to him.

All Ian had to do was press his lips to hers and nature would take its course. What he'd give to have her body against his. Her nipples had tightened and he yearned to feel the weight of her breasts in his hands. Mary Potter had been a poor substitute for what he really wanted, what he ached for. What he could have right now if he would only take advantage—

Gently, he moved her hand from his thigh, placing it on the ground between them and holding it in place with his palm. *Dear God in Heaven*, he was going to regret this.

Her eyes fluttered open. Her brows came together in a question.

"I believe the whiskey is talking to you, Miss Harrell." He deliberately put a lot of Irish in his voice, needing to remind her—and himself—of their differences.

She gave her head a small shake as if in disbelief. "You won't kiss me?"

He didn't answer, knowing whatever he said, he was a doomed man.

His prediction was right. Lyssa rose to her feet, her fists clenched at her side. "You would kiss every woman at the dance tonight and *refuse* to kiss me?"

This was not going to be good.

Slowly, he came up to stand in front of her, needing his height in the face of her building temper. There were so many things he could say. He could tell the truth and possibly find himself entangled even further with her—or say something that would put her off him for good. Then he wouldn't have to worry about any messy complications like his own heart.

"Your father is not paying me to kiss bluestocking virgins who want to experiment."

He braced himself, fully expecting her temper to explode and for her to deliver another slap in the face for his impertinence.

She fooled him. Instead of anger, there was sadness. "Yes. Yes," she repeated. "You are quite right. Silly of me. I'm sorry—"

She turned and ran toward the barn.

Ian took a step, wanting to go after her—and then stopped. If he caught her, then what? More words? More arguments?

Or would he give her the kiss she craved? Kiss her until she bent to his will? Until he could swallow her whole and claim all?

And would that be enough?

No, it was better this way. Now, she would hate him and the job would be easier. They needed to keep a wedge between each other.

Still, she had finally seen him as a man.

He looked at the cold pond, thought about jumping in, and then decided he'd had enough of the "water cure" for what ailed him. Instead, he set off walking. It was a long time before he finally had himself in hand and could sleep.

Lyssa ran to her small room and slammed the door. The widow and Mr. Anderson were both long gone. She was alone.

She raised her hand up to her lips, tracing the line of them. She'd asked him for a kiss and he'd refused.

Sinking down on the cot, she unlaced her belt and threw it on the floor, struggling with an overwhelming urge to cry.

Instead, she fell asleep.

A few hours later, Lyssa woke, fully dressed, with a fuzzy mouth and a rapping sound in her ears. Someone was knocking on the door. She didn't want to wake and huddled into the warmth of her plaid. In the vague, dreamy recesses of her mind, she had her arms around Ian, her thigh wrapped around his—

She sat up, shocked into wakefulness. She had no idea where such vivid, erotic images sprang from, and remembered his refusing her kiss last night.

What a fool she'd made of herself. Bending over at her waist, she hugged her plaid to her chest and wished she could hide.

But she couldn't and she knew who was at the door.

Rising, she straightened her clothing as best she

could, crossed over to the door, and opened it. Ian stood there holding a steaming mug of tea and looking completely refreshed and more handsome than any one man had the right to. "I thought you could use this. Maggie made it for us."

With her dream still fresh in her mind, she could do nothing but blush hotly. Taking the mug, she shut the door in his face. She knew she had to look terrible. Her face was probably all smooshed from sleeping so hard and her hair was a complete tangle. "No wonder he didn't want to kiss me," she muttered to herself.

He knocked on the door again. She opened it. "We need to leave. We don't want to be here when Anderson wakes."

Oh, yes. She wouldn't be able to face him, not without losing her temper. "Absolutely. Give me a few minutes." She shut the door again.

And she truly meant to get ready. In fact, she gulped down the tea and put on her belt. However, as she was lacing it up, her gaze fell on the knapsack stored under the cot.

She knew she should leave it alone. There was no time to dally . . . but her breath needed freshening . . . and Ian kept tooth powder in his knapsack.

If she had any qualms about helping herself to his knapsack without asking, her curiosity squelched them. After all, she knew what some of the contents were—the gun, the dried beef, his tin cup.

But what else would she find? What secrets did he hold?

Her curiosity was overwhelming. With trembling hands, she pulled out the knapsack and opened the leather flap. She found the tooth powder immediately, with his shaving kit. The contents smelled of the strong soap he used.

She should have stopped then.

She didn't.

Instead, she pushed aside his pistol and the gunpowder flask. There was another cloth-covered packet that contained the dried beef, and the tin cup was in the bottom. She told herself she would need the cup for water and used the need as an excuse to probe to the very depths of the bag.

That is where she found the packet of letters and the crucifix.

For a second, Lyssa couldn't move. She stared at the amber prayer beads. She'd heard of them before. Every English child was taught about papist idolatry. She knew that even in London there were Catholics, although she didn't *know* any. A piece of ribbon tied the crucifix to the letters.

Without untying the ribbon, Lyssa scanned the letters. The handwriting was definitely feminine. *My dearest son* was the salutation on one. Leafing through, she could see they were all written by the same hand. Lifting an edge, she saw the closing, *Mother*. Holding the letters, she sensed an overwhelming air of sadness and she could not have stopped herself from reading the first if she'd tried.

Lyssa sat on the floor and glanced over a paragraph she could see without untying the ribbon: . . . *Matters are much better. Please do not fear for your father and I. None of this was your—*

The door opened without a knock.

Slowly, Lyssa turned fearing the worst. She was right. Ian stood there, his gaze dark.

She pushed the letters and holy beads back into the recesses of the knapsack. "I . . . um, wanted to borrow some tooth powder."

"Did you find it?" His voice was flat, his expression guarded. She could not judge his mood.

"Yes. Thank you."

He walked over and picked up his knapsack. He could tell she had rifled through his belongings and she was ashamed.

His gaze did not meet hers. "I'll wait for you outside. I need to shave."

"Of course."

He left, and Lyssa wanted to collapse. She knew he was upset. She shouldn't have pried . . . and she wished she'd not seen the crucifix.

Quickly seeing to her morning ablutions, she was putting on her shoes when she discovered the tarot card where she had hidden it a day ago. The Knight was looking the worse for wear. The gilt was coming off the edges and she interpreted this as a sign she should not have snooped.

Ian was a Catholic. She wished she didn't know, and yet now she did. Perhaps in the back of her mind she had suspected but confirmation had taken her back a bit.

She tucked the card in her belt, combed her hair with her fingers the best she could, picked up her plaid, and went out to face Ian.

The hour was very early after a night of partying. No one stirred at the house. Maggie didn't come out to wish them well. Even the village was quiet. Without a word, he filled his tin cup at the pump and offered her some dried beef. Her guilt had robbed her of appetite, but she took what he offered.

They started down the road that would lead them to Appin and Amleth Hall.

Neither of them spoke for a good hour. She kept her eye on the angry muscle working in his jaw. She knew she'd been wrong to go through his personal things.

Still . . . had her father known he was hiring a Catholic?

And even though she was silent, she was very aware of him. Since following in his footsteps was easiest, she couldn't help but notice the strength in his back or the way the muscles of his legs worked when he walked. The day before, she'd thought she was getting to know him better than she did any other person of her acquaintance.

Now, she didn't know if she knew him at all.

Ian's silence was reserved for her alone. They

met several travelers on the road and he always said the first word of greeting. A tinker walked with them a way, and his presence helped to ease the tension.

Around luncheon, they came upon a farmer's wife attempting to catch a runaway piglet. Ian charmed the pig into trotting right up to him and the woman was so grateful, she offered them meat pies she'd just made that day.

Ian and Lyssa sat by the road to enjoy their bounty . . . and she finally gathered the courage to say, "Even though we've been living by our wits, we've managed to eat well."

He shrugged.

This was going to be harder than she imagined. He gave her no choice but to confront the issue directly. "I didn't mean to pry." She took a bit of pie.

He didn't even look at her. "Yes, you did."

Her mouth full, she nodded, conceding without words that he was right. She took her time chewing. He was almost done. If she wasn't more forthcoming, she knew matters would not be settled between them.

And she did not like this distance between them.

"I'm sorry."

He didn't speak.

"Are your parents still alive?" she dared to ask.

"No."

One word. No more.

She studied the crust of the pie in her hand. She

broke a piece off. "I suppose I knew that. Otherwise, your sisters would not be with you."

She knew she should leave the subject there. She couldn't.

"The beads are lovely." She didn't look at him as she said the words. However, she could feel the heat of his silver gaze as, at last, he swung around to look at her. "Do you practice?" she dared to ask.

He didn't pretend to misunderstand her. "No."

"Then why do you have the beads?"

"They were my grandfather's. He gave them to my father, who passed them down to me."

Lyssa nodded. She ran her thumb along the top of the pastry in her hand. "I'm not very religious."

She was afraid to look up and see what he was thinking. She feared he'd be even more angry.

His hand tilted her chin up to look at him. The hardness about him had softened.

Tears of relief stung her eyes and she struggled to hold them back, not wanting to embarrass herself.

Still intent and serious, he ran his thumb along the line of her lower lip.

Her heart pounded in her chest so hard, she knew he must hear it. She waited for him to speak, wanting him to open to her, to trust her.

Instead, he made a soft, self-deprecating sound before saying, "Come, *Cailín*, we need to move on."

"Cailín? What does that mean?"

" 'Girl.' It's the Irish for 'girl.' " There was a melancholy about him. He removed his hand and stood. "Come, we must keep going." He helped her rise.

The wall had been breached between them, but it was not the same.

For the next few hours, they talked in generalities much as they had the previous days, except that she was painfully aware of the change. Lyssa had opened a Pandora's box, and now it wasn't the secrets that kept them apart, but the truth.

By dusk, they were both tired. Ian called a halt. "We'll arrive at Amleth Hall toward midday," he predicted. "Let's get a good night's rest, since we didn't have one last night."

His plan was fine with Lyssa. She was exhausted. He found a place for them to camp in a small clearing protected by a thicket a fair distance from the road. After building a small fire, he made a bed for her of pine needles over which he placed her plaid.

For their dinner they ate the last of the meat pies. Again, Lyssa didn't have much of an appetite. She discovered that instead of being excited at reaching their destination, she was sorry to let the journey go.

Ian stretched out on the ground three feet from where she lay with the scent of pine around her. Clouds blocked the moon and the fire was welcome, although sleep did not come. No matter how tired she was, she was too aware of him. And she shouldn't have been.

"So do you think you will marry Grossett?"

His unexpected question caught her off guard. "No, I will not."

"Good." She heard a smile in his voice and rolled over onto her stomach so she could see him. She would not tell him she had no intention of returning to London once she reached Amleth Hall. Honesty could only go so far, or so she reminded herself, and matters were still tenuous between them.

"What of you?" she asked.

He rolled over on his own stomach and rested his chin on his hands. "I'll go on with my plans."

"To leave England."

"Yes."

She didn't like the idea of him being far away. "You don't have to leave. My father is always looking for good men." She studied her thumbnail, worried by her own audacity. "He owns numerous farms and could put you in charge of one. You could raise your race horses and your sisters and their children would be happy." Of course, if she didn't return with Ian, her father would be angry with them both. But she wanted to believe all could work out. There had to be a way for her to have everything she wanted.

"I can't stay, Lyssa." His voice had gone flat again. "There's a price on my head."

For a moment, she thought she hadn't heard him correctly. She sat up. "A what?"

"A price." He was watching her closely and she didn't know how to react.

"For what?" she dared to ask.

"Treason."

Chapter Twelve

IAN had never told another soul what he'd just said to Lyssa. His family knew, of course. He'd destroyed their lives with his foolishness.

But he had to tell Lyssa. She had to lose the starry look in her eyes. Even when he'd captured the runaway pig, she'd looked at him as if he were a hero.

And he wasn't any damn hero.

But when she spoke, she surprised him. "Is it a very *large* price they are asking for you?"

"Why? Are you planning on collecting it?"

Tossing her magnificent mane of hair over her shoulder, she said, "I don't know. I'm assuming that men who do housewives a favor by chasing their pigs can't be that dangerous."

"Lyssa, that is a silly thing to say. Any man can be dangerous given the right provocation."

"Not you," she said seriously. "You'd not hurt anyone without cause."

Her faith in him conquered his reticence. "All I

wanted was what was right. I wanted justice."

She folded her hands in her lap. "Then tell me the story and I'll be the judge."

Ian ran his hand through his hair, not certain where to start.

"It's about your being Catholic?" she guessed.

"Hardly. It's more about Ireland being free to rule herself." The moment he said those words, the old passion rose strong inside him.

Lyssa doused it. "The Irish can't do that," she said logically. "The country is part of Britain."

"No, it isn't."

She shook her head. "I'm afraid there are many people who would disagree."

"I've learned that lesson. The hard way," he admitted. He sat up, resting his arm on a bent knee. "Lyssa, we are an independent country. We have the right to our own Parliament and our own religion—whatever that religion may be."

"I thought you said you weren't religious—"

"I'm not," he said, cutting her off. "I was the bane of the priest and my mother. However, I should be able to choose."

She didn't answer right away. He knew what he'd said was so radical to the thinking of the English mind, he didn't know if she'd be able to digest it. And that was the crux of the matter. He wanted her to understand. He wanted to believe she could grasp the depth of his passion that had led to such folly.

Tracing the red line in her plaid, she asked quietly, "So are those beliefs the reason you have a price on your head?"

"A price!" He waved the thought away dismissively. "Ten quid. Hardly enough for anyone to trouble themselves over . . . but enough to get me transported to Botany Bay if I should be turned in."

She took a moment to digest this piece of information. Releasing her breath on a sigh, she asked, "So, why are you telling me?"

Because I'm falling in love with you.

But that would be a foolish thing to say. He couldn't have her. Could never have her. "You should know."

"So that you can warn me off?"

Her precise assessment surprised him. "Yes."

She hummed a response as if words failed her. He wished he knew what she was thinking. He wanted her to care—even knowing it was wrong, even knowing nothing could ever happen between them, he wanted her to care.

However, for once, he could not read her thoughts.

"All right," she said at last, as if coming to a decision she feared she might regret. "Tell me your tale." She drew her knees up to her chest, tucking her toes under the hem of her skirt, like a child ready to hear a bedtime story.

"I don't know," he hedged. "Everything was so long ago."

"Oh, no." She shook her head. "You have played

me hot and cold and the time's come, Ian Campion. You've trusted me this far, tell the rest. I have to know."

And he sensed she did. Besides, why not clear the air between them? Then, when they parted, as they must, she would understand he was the worst possible man for her—and be thankful he hadn't given her the kiss she'd requested.

He began, "It all started after I returned from London. I'd been reading the law at Lincoln's Inn," he said, referring to one of the Four Inns of Court where he'd started his apprenticeship to be a barrister.

"You read the law?"

"Yes."

"I'm surprised."

He lifted a skeptical eyebrow. "Because I'm not as illiterate as you had assumed? I speak Latin and Greek along with your much-vaulted French and Spanish. Then of course, I'm conversant in Irish."

"I never thought you were—" she started, and then broke off. Indeed, she had insulted his intelligence on numerous occasions when they'd first met and well she knew it. The stain of embarrassment crept up her cheeks, yet Lyssa was one to hold her own. "What I meant is that I'm surprised . . . I mean, I didn't know Catholics had access to, um . . ." Her voice trailed off.

"Education?" Ian supplied. This was going to be a long conversation. "Catholics are educated," he said quellingly. "Granted, no university in England would accept us and we'd not attend a Protestant School in Ireland, but there are ways. Some of my friends were sent abroad for their education. My father tutored me. He was a learned man, and I had no trouble with my studies. I was even preparing to be called to the Irish Bar."

"A Catholic?"

"Lyssa! I don't practice the religion. But even if I did, there are places for Catholics in the law." Granted, it was a small place with numerous restrictions, but a place nonetheless. After all, they had to take a stand for their rights somewhere.

But Lyssa's active mind had moved on. "I surmised there was something more to you than met the eye," she said victoriously.

"You caught me off guard when you accused me of sounding like a barrister," he admitted and she grinned, pleased with herself. "At one time, my family had been a great and wealthy one. But our fortunes fell with the passage of each oppressive law over the years. We still had our property and raised the finest race horses in Ireland, but make no mistake about the matter, Lyssa, we knew we lived on borrowed time.

"Then I heard Daniel O'Connell speak. That man can speak. I can recall his words even now. He was a lawyer and a Catholic and he knew how to stand up to the English. I wanted to be exactly like him. So, with my parents' blessing, I left for London, where I did very well until I returned to Ireland."

"What happened?"

"I became too full of myself. I involved myself with a students' group. We were radical. We were angry."

"Wasn't that dangerous?"

"Yes," he said baldly. "In the beginning all we did was write a few pamphlets and hold a rally. However, the English have always been nervous."

"There have been uprisings in Ireland, Ian. The government has a reason to be nervous."

"They'd have no reason at all if they let the people who pay the taxes have a voice in the making of the laws that govern them."

He leaned back. There was no sense in being frustrated with Lyssa. She was merely parroting what she'd been taught and her attitude made him realize the differences between them.

"Anyway," he continued, "one night one of my friends was beaten by English troops on his way to a meeting. I wasn't there that night. My father had heard about my goings-on and had come to Dublin to see me. He lectured me for hours, but it was already too late. The others had one too many ales and decided to retaliate by beating an English guard. The next morning, my name was included with theirs as one of the culprits, and the hunt began."

"They actually hunted for you? Couldn't your father tell them you were not involved?"

"I suppose in an honest government." He didn't hide the bitterness from his voice. "There is no open voice in Ireland. All troublemakers are either hanged or transported, which is what happened to many of my friends. I wasn't at my rooms when the English came for me, so a price was put on my head."

A soft, distressed sound escaped her but she did not flinch. Instead, she asked, "What happened next?" as if dreading the answer.

"I would not turn myself in. I'm the only son and I felt my parents needed me. When one of my friends was found hanged in his prison cell, my father agreed."

"He hanged himself?"

"Not Dónall. Someone had to have helped him."

"I don't see why you had to run from any of it," she argued, her own strong sense of justice rising. "You had nothing to do with the beating of the guard."

"Oh, but I would have, Lyssa, if I'd been there. I was young, rash, and arrogant. I was as angry as the others. But my father knew better. He was a wise old bird who'd spent most of his life out-thinking the government. My future as a lawyer was gone. Even the Catholic lawyers in Ireland wouldn't have been able to help me. And I knew if I was transported, I'd never see my family again."

"So what did you do?"

"I join the British army. Father said the English would never find me there and he was right. Six years I served and the irony is I had a talent for it. I knew how to get things done and I know how to fight."

For a moment he sat silent, remembering. "They took the land away from my parents as a way of punishing them for my sins. They claimed it was for taxes, but in truth we had Protestant neighbors with government friends who had coveted our pastures."

"What became of your parents?"

"They moved to Dublin where my uncle lived. About two years later, they both came down with the pox and died within weeks of each other. Father always said he wasn't meant to live in a city."

"And all of this touched the lives of your sisters and their husbands, too, didn't it? What of them?"

Ian nodded. "They had all lived off my family's land, but it was no longer there. Cedric, Fiona's husband, was always a daredevil, and he didn't like to work. He thought the life of a soldier would be more interesting, and I was selfish enough to not want to go alone. Janet's husband, Jamie, had no choice. He got caught lying to protect my whereabouts and my father's solution was to ship him off to the army, too."

"It's not your fault they died," she said softly.

"Yes, it is. I volunteered to be in the first attack at Talvera. There was a bounty paid to those who went in first and survived. I really didn't care what happened to me back then. I told both of them to stay behind and we'd split the money. They didn't listen. Each took a bullet."

"And your view of life changed."

He smiled at her. Wise Lyssa. "Yes, I suddenly had responsibilities beyond my imagination. But I survived."

She tilted her head and asked, "Did you earn the extra money you risked your life for?"

"Umm-hmm," he said. "I sent it to Janet. She used it to move herself and Fiona to London to wait for me. There was nothing for them in Ireland. Once we lost our parents, we lost everything, and the children were starving in Dublin. We thought there would be a better chance in London, or at least until I returned."

"Has there been?"

"No." Ian hated to admit it. "All we did was separate ourselves even more from our birthright. The children don't even know their heritage." He leaned forward. "That's why someday, I'm going to re-create what I've lost and I don't care where, provided we are free to speak out minds and never have to live in fear again."

Lyssa shifted her weight, crossing her arms as if she were cold.

Something was wrong. He had told her the brutal truth to put her off him. Still . . .

"What is it?" he asked.

She gave him a little smile. "My father is paying you well to bring me home."

"Very well."

Her gaze dropped to her lap and he would have given his soul to know what she was thinking. He'd wager it wasn't good. Lyssa Harrell was far too direct and honest to not feel guilt.

For one wild moment, he toyed with the idea of asking her to go with him.

He didn't—because he had nothing to offer her . . . and because now that his story was done, she'd not said anything.

Ian had too much pride to be refused. It had been the risk he'd run by telling her all.

"Well, good night," he said, surprised at how empty he felt inside. He'd given her all he had. Tomorrow he'd sort everything out.

Tonight, well, tonight was lost.

Lyssa murmured a "good night," immediately sensing his withdrawal and not knowing how to react. She pretended to lie down and go to sleep; she was too troubled, however, to relax.

She knew why Ian had told her his story. He wasn't just sharing his secrets. He was offering, in his own tight-lipped, cautious way, the possibility of something more between them.

More. The word haunted her.

And she was uncertain. Especially now. Because the truth be known—she was a coward.

It wasn't just that he was completely unsuitable—without a doubt, her father would disown her—but because she didn't know if she had the courage to love an Irishman, let alone a Catholic traitor.

Did she have the strength to go against all she'd known? To be an outcast?

And she did love her father.

Staring into the dying embers of the campfire, she knew she'd not intended to be gone from him forever. With newfound maturity she realized that, in the back of her mind, she'd chosen a course that would not set him off from her forever. He would understand her wanting to return to her mother's home. He would think her foolish, but he would forgive her.

She could also admit now that her secret desire to have him realize how important she was to him—even more important than his duchess— was not going to happen.

He had a new family now. As Ian had said, there were many kinds of love. She had one form, her stepmother another.

Her father could not choose her over his second wife and soon-to-be-born child. Such an act would not be honorable, and she was embarrassed that she'd harbored such a hope in the back of her mind.

Funny, how at three and twenty a woman could still grow up.

She did not know what would happen when she finally had to tell her father of her stepmother's attempt to murder her. To lose two women he loved . . . ?

But then, she was discovering love was about loss, too.

Lyssa raised her head and looked over to where Ian slept. He faced the fire, the shadowy light highlighting the strong, masculine lines of his face. If she stretched out her hand, she could have touched the top of his head and stroked his hair to see if it really was as silky to the touch as it appeared.

"You need a haircut," she whispered.

He slept on, his conscience free of burden, dreaming of a place for his family where they were free to be who they were. She didn't know if she was strong enough to be a part of that dream—and Ian had known it.

Now she understood why he'd refused to kiss her, why he'd not taken advantage of her . . . and she grew all the sadder.

It was a long time before she fell asleep.

Ian lifted his head and studied the woman close to him who had finally fallen asleep. Something was bothering her. He'd been aware of the tension . . . and he would have given his right arm to know the cause.

Lyssa was headstrong and her silence was not a common occurrence.

Tonight, he'd opened his soul and she'd not said a word. No, instead, her redheaded brain had been busy working and he sensed it did not bode well for him.

He was glad he'd not been stupid enough to make some sort of romantic declaration.

Or to have kissed her.

Ian rose, uncertainties making him unable to sleep. Perhaps in a different place and a different time, he could have declared himself to Lyssa. But in this place and time, he had nothing to offer.

The fact did not set well. Not well at all.

Lyssa woke the next morning to the smell of cooking meat. Ian had poached a rabbit and was roasting it on a spit for their breakfast.

"Good morning, sleepyhead," he said jovially, an emotion that didn't quite reach his eyes.

He was so handsome, she couldn't help but smile—until she remembered the decision she'd made the night before. It took all her courage to keep her smile pasted on her face.

And Ian seemed to react to her inner thoughts as if he knew she was forcing herself.

"We reach Amleth Hall today," he reminded her.

Lyssa nodded dumbly.

"Is something the matter? I thought you would be happier."

"I'm still not awake," she murmured, and excused herself for a few moments alone. When she returned to their small camp, she had herself firmly in hand.

Watching him put out the fire and scatter the ashes, she told herself it was for the best. They were from different worlds. Her father would agree.

She recalled the start she'd had at finding the crucifix amongst his things, and it helped give her distance.

Not that Ian's demeanor to her was overly friendly. There was a detached air about him, a distance bordering on coldness. She was happy when they started traveling.

They hadn't walked far when their path crossed that of a Vicar George, from Appin. He was a pleasant companion and relieved some of the tension between her and Ian. Although the vicar did not know the Davidsons nor had he visited Amleth Hall, he knew something of its whereabouts.

"On the coast," he said. "The north shore about a mile from Port Appin. I've seen it by boat. It has a westerly aspect with a magnificent view over Loch Linnhe. I imagine you can see Lismore and Moren, too."

"Do the Davidsons so rarely come to town?" Lyssa wondered.

"I never see them," was the reply. Then, as if feeling sorry for her, the vicar added, "I have laid eyes on the Davidson Stallion. He's a beauty and he bears out his breeding. He's going to be a fast one."

Ian spoke up. "The Davidson Stallion?"

"Aye, he's just turned three. They say Ramsey

Davidson, the young laird, refused to let him run as a two-year-old. Knows his horses, he does. He doesn't like to push them, and I agree." The vicar nodded before adding, "When I saw him, he was the most docile I've ever seen. A temperament only a king could afford—and perhaps that is what Davidson has in mind. They boast he's the finest in Scotland. Mayhap in England or anywhere else."

"I didn't know the Davidsons bred horses," Ian said.

"For generations," Vicar George assured him. "This stallion is out of—"

"*Gealach*." The word had sprung into Lyssa's mind unbidden and in her mother's voice. She stopped, savoring the small memory.

"Yes, *Gaelach*, 'the Moon,'" the vicar said approvingly. "They say she was silver white and could run as if kelpies were chasing her." He laughed at his own description. "I heard that from John Islay, a local farmer who drinks more than he farms. I always fancied the image of kelpies chasing a horse." Again, he had a chuckle.

"And is the stallion also white?"

"More a gray with black legs. Good-looking, solid racer," the vicar answered.

Lyssa was elated. She leaned close to Ian, completely forgetting their earlier reserve. "My mother used to brag about *Gaelach*. She claimed the mare was the beginning of a dynasty—and now to learn she is."

"Your mother?" the vicar prompted.

"She was Isobel Davidson, the old laird's daughter."

The clergyman frowned. "I'd not heard of her."

"She left long ago, before I was born."

"Still, you would think her name would have been mentioned." The vicar shrugged. "Ah, well, the Davidsons are an odd lot. Ramsey Davidson doesn't mix much with the locals. No offense, please."

"None taken," Lyssa answered and then she changed the subject to ask about the vicar's wife and children. But she did not forget his verdict, especially when she and Ian finally reached the drive to Amleth Hall.

The drive was almost completely overgrown by hawthorn bushes, of all things. The woods were dense here when compared to the rest of the landscape. If they hadn't been carefully looking for the drive, they would have passed right by it.

Ian glanced at her. "Are you ready?"

She nodded. "I believe so."

He took her arm. The drive was really no more than wagon ruts with stone paving here and there. Lyssa grew uncertain. Something was in the air here, something she hadn't anticipated. It was like a humming in her ears. And was it her imagination or did the air smell different?

She realized it must be the mist coming in off Loch Linnhe. Or was it?

Even the colors of the plants and trees seemed darker and more foreboding.

"Are you feeling well?" Ian's voice startled her and she realized she was giving into some outlandish fancies.

"I'm fine. Just excited. I have waited a long time to meet these people."

"Well, let us hope they make us welcome," he said.

The drive was a good mile long. Just as she started to wonder if the house even existed, they came around a bend and there it was, Amleth Hall, its stone walls blackened with age.

Lyssa halted, stunned to be here at last. As if in blessing, the sun came out from behind a cloud and reflected off the glass window panes, giving the house an unworldly glow. The chimneys, almost too numerous to count, were of all shapes and size. Beyond the house stretched Loch Linnhe, the water so deep and cold it shimmered in the light.

Lyssa took in every nuance of this moment.

"Is it how you imagined it?" Ian asked.

"It's better," she whispered. "The house is exactly as my mother described it. Do you see the first-floor window on the far right?"

He nodded.

"That was her room. When she told her father she wanted to marry my father, she was confined to her room with a guard placed at the door. My father scaled those walls to reach her and then the two of them climbed the same way down to run away."

"He climbed the wall for her?"

"Yes."

"I'm not overly fond of heights, or crashing down to the ground."

"She always said she was never more frightened in her life than she was that night climbing down the dark walls of Amleth Hall, but she loved my father and refused to live without him. They both made it down safely and escaped in a boat smaller than a dinghy my father had hidden by the loch."

"And did they sail all the way to London?"

"Yes," she told him proudly.

"Well, I hope we make good time, too," he answered. "I have little more than a week to see you home safe. A boat may be quickest."

Lyssa kept her own counsel, the romance of the moment destroyed, and she saw the house as it really was. The grounds were completely overgrown and scraggly. The windows were filthy and there was an unkempt air about the place, almost a sense of desertion.

Lyssa took a step forward, anxious. She could not have come all this way only to find no one here. For a horrible moment, she feared she would swoon. To have traveled this distance, to have defied her father and to have held fast to a belief in a place that might not exist—

Ian took her arm by the elbow. "Steady," he said. "Don't give up."

At that moment, the narrow, paneled front door opened.

Chapter Thirteen

A young girl of perhaps sixteen came out the door. She did not wear a bonnet and her hair was unbound down around her shoulders in the Scottish way. The girl's hair was straight instead of curly and blonde rather than red, but she and Lyssa could otherwise have passed for sisters.

Here was family, the fragile connection Lyssa had longed for since her mother's death.

Her feet moved of their own will. In two steps, she wasn't walking but running. Behind her, Ian followed at his own pace.

The girl noticed them and hesitated, watching them approach.

Lyssa was suddenly aware of her appearance and forced herself to slow down. Her clothes were certainly the worse for wear, her curls were absolutely unruly from going for days without a brush to tame them, and she knew her complexion must be a sight from being out in the sun without a bonnet.

She stopped, embarrassed. This was not the way she had pictured meeting her Davidson relatives for the first time.

Ian came up beside her. Sensing her reticence, he took the lead, approaching the young woman.

"I'm Ian Campion and we're here to pay our respects to Laird Davidson."

The girl's gaze honed in on Ian with feminine appraisal, and she liked what she saw. Lyssa realized the girl was actually older than she'd first thought. Indeed she was a woman, and several years older than Lyssa herself.

"The Laird is my cousin," she said in a voice made all the more musical by its soft lilt.

"Will you tell him Miss Lyssa Harrell of London, a relative of his, wishes to pay her respects?"

"I didn't know we were expecting company," the woman countered.

"We were unable to announce our travel plans," Ian answered.

The woman's gaze swung back to Lyssa. The color of their eyes were different. Lyssa's were green like her father's. Her cousin's were a guileless blue, and yet, Lyssa felt a hint of uneasiness. She wondered if Ian experienced the same.

"Please come in," the woman offered and led the way up the steps to the front door.

Ian turned to Lyssa. He raised his eyebrows, questioning what she wished to do.

She had no choice. She'd traveled far to get here and she would not be put off now. Besides, her apprehension was probably due to being tired and finding herself at journey's end. Putting on her best smile, she moved forward with a confidence she didn't feel.

At the doorway, she paused in front of her newly discovered cousin. "I'm Isobel's daughter."

"So, one of you has finally come home, have you?" her cousin asked, the hint of a smile on her lips not quite reaching those disconcerting eyes.

"I suppose."

For the space of a heartbeat, the woman took Lyssa's measure. At last, her cousin said, "I'm Anice Davidson. Your uncle Alan's daughter."

"It is a pleasure to meet you at last, Cousin," Lyssa said politely.

Anice smiled and opened the door. "Please come in." She entered, expecting them to follow.

Inside, the house was not anything like Lyssa had anticipated. In her imagination, she pictured an old, established mansion with ancient furniture that had survived the generations.

There was no furniture in the front hall or a place to put it, since the room was completely taken over by hunting trophies. The heads of stags, red deer, whitetail, and even what appeared to be a reindeer covered every available inch of wall space. Stuffed grouse, quail, and pheasants lined the floor around the walls. The showpiece was a wildcat posed to be fighting a badger in an alcove by the stairs of what had been designed to be a stately room.

Lyssa was all too conscious of so many lifeless eyes staring down upon them. Attempting to defuse her unease, she commented, "Someone is quite a hunter."

Anice smiled. "All Davidson men are hunters."

Nodding her head in acknowledgement, Lyssa caught a glimpse of the next room. The red walls there were covered with swords and dirks. She was aware that Ian stood by the closed front door, his arms crossed. She knew he was no more comfortable than she was.

Footsteps came from a side hall off to the right and a portly manservant entered the room. He had a bald pate with a tuft of hair over each ear and a bulbous nose that commanded his face. "*Och*, Miss Davidson, I dinna hear you return." His accent was so thick, Lyssa could barely understand him.

"Birdy, please tell Ramsey we have visitors, and perhaps Cook will prepare a tray for our guests? They have traveled quite a distance."

The servant eyed both Lysse and Ian in a bold manner that Lyssa didn't find appropriate. She stared right back. Birdy's gaze dropped. "Aye, ma'am," he said, bowing and leaving the room by way of the hall.

"Shall we go into the sitting room?" Anice asked and led them into the weapon room without waiting for a response.

Lyssa glanced toward Ian. A muscle worked in his jaw and she could tell he was on guard. She didn't feel comfortable herself. The air in the house was as cool as the mossy dampness of a stream bank. She wondered if the windows had ever been opened to let in a fresh breeze. The whole atmosphere gave her goose bumps.

Anice sat on one of two grand leather settees facing each other in the middle of the room. There also were two large, high-backed leather-upholstered chairs positioned in front of the marble fireplace, their backs to the rest of the room. Anice motioned for Lyssa to sit on the settee opposite her, before looking up at Ian expectantly. "You have not introduced your companion, coz."

The familiarity of the name "coz" struck a jarring note with Lyssa. "This is Mr. Ian Campion of London," she said quietly. "He is—" She hesitated. How should she introduce him so as to not create the wrong impression with these new relatives?

"Her bodyguard," Ian interjected smoothly.

"A bodyguard?" Anice gave him a speculating glance. "I am certain you have been in good hands with such a brawny man to protect you," she purred with a slyness that would have served the Widow Potter well.

"He has seen me safe," Lyssa confirmed stiffly.

"Would you care to sit, Mr. Campion?" Anice asked, patting the place on the settee beside her.

"I'm content here," he replied dutifully, having taken a post by the entry between the weapon room and the front hall. Lyssa noted he was using his brogue and she didn't know why.

Anice's gaze slid to meet hers. "He's Irish."

"Yes. From Dublin."

Her cousin's gaze turned lazily knowing. "I've always liked the Irish."

Lyssa released her breath slowly, caught by her cousin's open sensuality. Ian didn't move, not even a muscle, and Anice's smile grew larger.

Fortunately, Lyssa was saved from making any reply by the appearance of her cousin, Ramsey Davidson.

He was of average stature with a lean, hungry face and slashing eyebrows. Whereas she and Anice were fair of skin and hair, he was the opposite. Dark hair, dark eyes, dark clothes . . . and a dark smile.

"Cousin," he said holding out his hand in greeting. Lyssa stood and offered her own. He gallantly kissed the back of it. "Welcome to Amleth Hall."

"I appreciate your welcome, sir," she murmured.

"Sir?" He laughed. "We are cousins. I'm your second cousin. My father was Osgood Davidson, your mother's uncle."

"It is a pleasure to finally meet you," she said dutifully.

Ramsey glanced round at Ian. "He is her bodyguard," Anice supplied. "Mr. Campion is Irish."

"Hmmm, Irish." Ramsey repeated, as if the words held no import. His whole attention was on Lyssa, and she felt a certain warmth rise to her cheeks under his full regard.

Birdy entered the room, carrying a tray of biscuits and, of all blessings, a teapot with steam rising from its stem that he set on a tea table beside Anice. "Would you care for a cup?" Anice offered.

"Gratefully," Lyssa answered, sitting.

Ramsey dropped to sit beside Anice. He crossed his legs, spreading his arms along the back of the settee. Lyssa was conscious that he watched her every move. Ian came to stand behind her. Anice served them.

"How interesting you travel with a bodyguard," Ramsey observed. "Did you bring other servants?"

Lyssa was in the act of taking a sip of her tea so Ian spoke for her. "We were waylaid by robbers. We had a maid with us but she was separated from our party."

Ramsey sat up. "How unfortunate. Did you report the matter to the local magistrate?"

Ian replied smoothly, "Yes. All is taken care of."

"Ah," Ramsey said, drawing out the word. "Very good. And we have you here safe and sound, Cousin."

Lyssa smiled and hid behind another sip of her tea, not displeased at Ian's story. There followed an awkward moment of silence. Ramsey broke it by saying, "You look very much like your mother, Lyssa."

"How do you know?" she wondered.

"From the painting. Did you not know about it?"

Immediately, Lyssa set down her teacup. "No. I mean, Father has portraits of Mother, but they were done after I was born." And after she'd become ill. The color in her mother's cheeks had all been artificial.

"We have the one our grandfather commissioned," Ramsey said. "He had the painting done to show potential suitors far and wide what a jewel the Davidsons had to offer. I admit it is a masterpiece. The family lore is Isobel received no fewer than five offers for her hand on the basis of the painting alone."

"I never knew this story," Lyssa said.

Ramsey leaned forward. "I'm not surprised your father didn't tell you. He must have thought it a grand jest, stealing her away from us the way he did."

There was a proprietary air in his comment. "My grandfather must have been disappointed," Lyssa said.

"He was outraged," Ramsey agreed, but without heat. "His temper lasted for weeks. The family coffers needed to be replenished, we needed her to marry for money, and your mother's choice of husbands did not honor her obligations."

"My father has done well for himself since," she said in her defense.

"Yes, he has." Ramsey smiled. "Welcome home, Cousin."

Lyssa didn't know quite how to take his remarks. As with Anice, there seemed to be a hidden meaning as if he played some game with her. She didn't know if she was particularly keen on him.

But then he asked, "Would you like to see the painting?"

Without hesitation, she said, "Yes, very much."

Ramsey stood and offered his hand. "Then come."

Lyssa placed her hand in his and came to her feet. Anice also rose and as they started from the room, Ian fell into place beside them. He had his knapsack slung over one shoulder and Lyssa sensed he would rather have his pistol out and ready.

Ramsey glanced at him. "Is he always this tiresome?"

"Yes," she said proudly and could almost feel Ian grin behind her.

Ramsey led her into a long gallery that took up the rear of the house. The walls had more hunting trophies and the paint was plain. These were family quarters. The windows overlooked Loch Linnhe. Through a window off to the left, she could see rooftops.

"Those are the stables," Ramsey said, noting where she'd been looking. "You've heard of the Davidson Stallion?"

"Yes."

"Wait until you see him. We've had nothing but winners out of our mares, but he is a prize."

"That's what I've heard."

"Have you?" he asked. He took her hand. "I'm

flattered my horse's fame has spread already to London. Or has your father kept a particularly sharp eye on this part of the family?" He gave her fingers a little squeeze.

Lyssa didn't know what to make of his words or his actions. She tried to move away, but her cousin kept his firm hold. She could not pull her hand away without insulting him. "My father admires fine bloodstock," she murmured and then changed the subject, "Is that Loch Linnhe?" She attempted to gesture with the hand he held. The movement was awkward but served to get Ramsey to release his hold.

He smiled good-naturedly. He knew what she'd been about. "Yes, it is. There is a cliff there. Not steep, but one should be cautious all the same."

"Why?" she asked. "Has someone gone off it?"

Anice answered, "Over the years we've lost a person or two."

Lyssa looked out at the smooth water beyond the cliff and did not feel comfortable.

"Come," Ramsey said and steered her toward a sitting room off the gallery. It was so small it only held a desk and two chairs. The walls were paneled and Lyssa could imagine the lady of the house using this room to make out her menus and list of chores for the week.

Above the desk hung the portrait.

The moment Lyssa set eyes on it, she could not speak. This was her mother as she'd never known her. This was the woman her father had fallen in love with, and Lyssa understood why.

Her mother's skin was the color of rich cream, her eyes a laughing, sparkling blue. Lyssa remembered how, before her mother had become so terribly ill, their house had been full of her laughter.

In the portrait, her mother's hair was a rich auburn. She sat beneath a spreading oak. Over her shoulder, she wore the Davidson plaid, much like Lyssa's own, and behind her stood a horse as silvery white as the moon. *Gealach*. Her grandfather had placed in this picture everything of value to his clan—its pride and its beauty.

The wave of homesickness caught Lyssa off guard. She leaned over the desk as if wanting to see beyond the artist's brushstrokes. In truth, she was moved to tears by how much she missed her mother.

Her trip was worth all the danger and hardship for this one moment. This was what she'd come looking for—a glimpse of her mother. Of her past. Of what might have been and was no more.

When her mother had died, she'd mourned as only a child can . . . but she hadn't realized truly all that she'd lost. Her father had moved on. She couldn't. There was no replacing her mother in her life. She'd lost the wisdom, the concern, the care . . . the understanding.

And no matter how long she lived, this void in her life would not be filled. Her mother's love was irreplaceable.

But that didn't mean she was betraying her mother's memory by not stepping forward with her own life.

Sinking into the chair at the desk, Lyssa folded her hands and let the tears flow. They rolled down her cheeks and she didn't bother to wipe them away.

She sensed Ramsey and Anice withdrawing as if embarrassed by her emotion. Ian moved closer and she welcomed his strength. If they were in private, she might have even reached for his hand.

"If you'd like, I'll give you the portrait," Ramsey offered.

"You would?" Lyssa said, looking up at him. "I would be ever so grateful. I would even pay for it."

Ramsey knelt beside her chair and Ian was forced back. "I could not accept money from you, beautiful cousin." He spoke in a low voice but she knew his words were heard by everyone . . . and there was the warmth of male interest in them.

She was too grateful to care. "Thank you. You cannot imagine what this means to me."

"We've all lost someone or something in our lives and this is a fitting gift." He stood. "Now, come. Dinner will be served in two hours and we still haven't taken you to your room to freshen up. I'm certain Birdy has seen to your luggage."

"I have no luggage," she confessed and then relying Ian's earlier lie she said, "It was stolen when we were attacked." She could have told the truth. She didn't.

Ramsey shook his head. "How fortunate you are to be alive."

"Yes," Lyssa agreed.

Turning to their cousin, he said, "Anice, do you have a dress that would fit Lyssa?"

"I'm certain I do. I shall have one or two sent to your room."

"Thank you, coz," Lyssa said and meant the words. Her earlier foreboding had evaporated. In fact, she thought she'd been rather silly. She took her cousins' hands and, in an effort to make amends, said, "I can't tell you how pleased I am to be here . . . and for this moment with the portrait." Tears threatened to overwhelm her again. She forced them back. "I'd forgotten so much. If you will excuse me, I would like to go to my room." She needed a moment alone to compose herself.

"Of course," Anice said and shepherded Lyssa out into the gallery, directing her toward a back staircase.

Ian started to follow but Ramsey stepped in his path. "I'll have Birdy take your bodyguard to the servants' quarters."

Lyssa stopped. "No."

"No?" Ramsey turned as if surprised she would countermand him.

"I mean, my father wants him close to me."

Ramsey's eyebrows rose speculatively.

Lyssa met his gaze squarely. "He is my body-guard, cousin. Nothing more, nothing less."

"I didn't mean to imply an impropriety," Ramsey answered, and heat rose to Lyssa cheeks.

"I'm certain you didn't."

For a second, she thought Ramsey was going to push the issue. Instead, he said, "Anice, have Birdy put the bodyguard in the White Room."

"Come," Anice said. "I'll show you both to your rooms." She started up the stairs and there was nothing left for Lyssa to do but follow, Ian at her heels.

The first floor where the bedrooms were located was a long stone corridor. The carpet down the center of the hall was practically threadbare. The walls were obviously thick and not a sound seemed to travel through the house. The whole effect was positively medieval.

Halfway down the hall, Anice stopped at a room and opened the door, motioning Lyssa through.

The room was done in shades of blue and burgundy in a style that had long since passed. The furniture was heavy and ornate and the bed curtains seemed to have been hanging for a century or more, because the dust was still there. Yet the sheets appeared to have been changed and there was hot water in the pitcher on the washstand and clean towels.

Lyssa nodded her pleasure. "This is very nice."

"I thought you would like it. This room was your mother's," Anice answered. "I hope you will be comfortable. I'll have my maid bring the dresses for you, and perhaps a pair of slippers? We seem to be of the same size."

"I would appreciate them," Lyssa answered. "And a bath, if it would not be too much trouble."

"Of course not," Anice answered.

Lyssa noticed that Ian was looking around the room as if expecting danger lurking in the corners. "Where is Mr. Campion's room from here?"

"The White Room is at the top of the front stairs," her cousin said. "He should be comfortable and close. If you'll follow me, Mr. Campion?" She went through the door.

Shouldering his ever present knapsack, he followed Anice out, but before he shut the door behind him, he whispered, "Be watchful."

Lyssa nodded. He left and she was alone in her mother's room. Lyssa tossed her plaid on the bedspread, crossed to the window, and opened the drapes. Her room overlooked the back lawn and Loch Linnhe. She didn't hesitate to try to open the windows; she wanted the fresh air.

They didn't open easily and she had to put her shoulder to the task, but she accomplished it. For a moment, she enjoyed the breeze while looking at the stables, surprised at how well she could see them from this angle. Stable lads were busy with their chores. There must have been ten horses being walked or exercised, but she did not see a gray stallion.

Closer to the house, she noticed Birdy talking to three burly tenants. She hoped they were discussing work to be done in the gardens. The yards could be quite charming with a bit of planning. Perhaps she could suggest some ideas to Ramsey over dinner—because she was going to stay for a while. Her earlier doubts had vanished. She *needed* to be here.

Her hand on the windowsill, she turned and surveyed the room, and felt a sense of belonging.

A knock sounded at the door. "Come in," she called, expecting Anice's maid.

Instead, Ian entered, his knapsack still over his shoulder. He carefully closed the door behind him. "We must get out. Now."

"Why?"

"Can't you feel it?" he said with surprise. "Something is not right. I don't trust your cousins. I don't like any of this."

And he also wanted to get her back to London to collect his money.

Lyssa crossed to the washbasin and poured warm water into the bowl. She picked the soap up and smelled it. It was a homemade variety, one not as good as the sort Ian's sister made. "I'm not going anywhere," she confessed, unable to look at him. "We've only arrived and I'm happy to be here."

"And I've learned that when the hairs at the

small of my neck are standing on end, danger is nearby."

She started washing her hands, her back to him. "Could you not be overreacting?"

He came round to face her. "Overreacting? They are the ones who are not reacting at all. No one seems surprised at your arrival—"

"Anice did."

"They didn't ask a few questions about your luggage and lack of servants—"

"We explained to them we were robbed and frankly, we look like we've been robbed."

"Nor did they wonder why Dunmore Harrell's daughter had to walk across Scotland?"

"What are you suggesting, that we run out the back door while everyone waits for us to come down for dinner?"

"Yes," he answered. "And the sooner, the better. Something is not right."

She dried her hands and laid down the towel. "I don't want to leave."

"You don't have a choice," he returned evenly. "We are going down those stairs and out the door. I'll find another way for us to reach London."

"I'm not going to London." There, she'd said it. She braced herself for the worse.

A muscle hardened in his jaw but he didn't act surprised. "You must go to London. Your father wants you there. Immediately."

"I'm not going," she affirmed quietly, well aware of what was at stake for him. But she couldn't do it.

She couldn't leave—not yet. "I wish I could, Ian, but I can't. I *belong* here."

"The hell you do." He took her by the arms and appeared ready to shake her he was so angry, but he didn't. Instead, he stared down into her eyes. "You have a marriage to go to, lass. A man you are promised to and I have a family waiting for the money I'm to earn. You will leave with me if I have to carry you, and you know me well enough, Lyssa, I don't make empty promises."

"Don't worry about money!" she flashed back. "I'm certain Ramsey will reward you handsomely."

"Ramsey?" Ian laughed. "Have you not looked around? There is no money here, and if they have any, it appears they spend it on the horses."

"You will get paid your money," she promised, reaching for her temper to ease her conscience. "I'll see that you receive every shilling. But I'm not returning to London. If my father wants me, he can come here himself."

Ian let go of her as if she had turned to fire. His eyes silvery bright, he said, "You planned this from the beginning, didn't you, Miss Harrell? All right. Very well. Have your evening with your family, but come the morrow, we leave."

"We will not," she vowed with equal heat.

He shook his head. "I'm not a man to cross, Miss Harrell, and you'd best remember the fact." He stormed over to the door, threw it open and almost ran over the maid who had arrived with An-ice's dresses.

Lyssa collapsed on a chair at the dressing table. Standing up to Ian was not easy . . . especially when she knew she was doing him wrong.

The mobcapped maid said in a timid voice, "Miss Davidson asked I bring you these." She held out two dresses, one blue and the other a soft green. She also had a pair of black slippers.

"Yes, thank you," Lyssa replied. "Please put them on the bed." She wished the girl had not caught Mr. Campion in her room. The worst part was, she was still so upset by the confrontation that her hands shook—something she did not want the maid to see.

So she put on her best smile and pretended to admire the dresses. And if he thought she would leave here on the morrow, he was wrong.

Ian was so angry he could break something. He charged into his room and threw his knapsack on the bed with such force it skidded across the mat-tress and fell off on the other side.

Damn Lyssa Harrell for cheating him.

He'd known it was coming. Last night, she'd been unusually quiet. He'd sensed something was at work in that red-haired head of hers. He should have paid attention to his instincts and not brought her here! He kicked shut the door.

Now what the devil as he supposed to do?

He felt damned betrayed. He'd thought of himself as her protector—he'd thought he'd meant something to her. He'd believed—

Ian broke off his thoughts and leaned back against the door. "You poor, stupid Irishman. You're a lovesick fool."

The moment he spoke the words aloud, he realized they were true. He had fallen in love with the most stubborn woman in the universe.

And his marching into her room moments ago? Had he truly sensed danger or was he acting out of jealousy?

He hadn't liked Ramsey Davidson the moment he laid eyes on him. The man was too poised, too glib—and his heels were as round as Ian's own. The man was done up. Anyone with half of a head's sense could see that by the state of the house and grounds.

At first, Lyssa had been as uneasy as he—until she'd been presented with the portrait of her mother. Then her whole response to the situation had changed.

Ian pushed away from the door and walked to the center of the room. His was not as finely furnished as Lyssa's was, but he wasn't interested in rugs and drapes.

Pacing a path across the room, he focused his thoughts on the portrait and the response it had provoked in Lyssa, one he was certain she could not have anticipated. If so, it would be up to him to keep her safe, even if he must physically remove her from this place.

As to the rest, his love for her was doomed. Pirate Harrell would never let some Irishman—especially one who didn't have two guineas to his name—marry his prized daughter. Furthermore, Lyssa had too much sense to saddle herself with a man like Ian.

A soft knock on the door disturbed him and his first thought was it had to be Lyssa. Perhaps she'd thought about what he'd said and had come to her senses, so without hesitation, he crossed to the door and threw it open.

Lyssa Harrell was not standing there.

Instead, there were three ugly Scottish brutes. Two stood no higher than his chest but the third was almost a head taller than himself.

And they weren't here to welcome him to the estate. Two held cudgels which they slapped in the palm of their hands. The big one carried a sack.

"Mr. Campion?" one of them said.

Ian backed into his room. He wasn't going anywhere peacefully, and the Scots followed him in, ready for a fight.

Damn, he hated being right.

Chapter Fourteen

🐎🐎 OBSERVING the trouble the maid had preparing a bath, Lyssa decided that the occupants of Amleth Hall did not bathe often.

The maid had carried up two buckets of tepid water, but there had not been a bathing tub in the room. So she'd gone in search of a tub and returned with something that was little more than a washtub.

Lyssa sent the maid for more water so she could wash her hair. She filled the bath herself, relieved to have a task to keep her busy. Anything to take her mind off the scene with Ian.

She rationalized she was not doing anything other than what she'd intended from the very beginning. She couldn't return, not after she'd just arrived. This deadline of her father's was completely arbitrary. She didn't want a betrothal ball; she didn't want a betrothal.

And she would see Ian was paid anyway.

Undressing, she took the tarot card from its safe

place in her belt and laid it on the top of the dresser drawers that had not been dusted very well. The poor card was the truly worse for wear, curved and warm from being tucked close to her body. Madame Linka may also be known as Bawdy House Betty, but every warning she'd issued had come to pass.

Lyssa sat in the tub of tepid water and felt the lowest of the low. She faced the truth—she did not like being at odds with Ian. He was the first person beyond her father whose opinion she respected.

The maid knocked on the door. This time the water was warmer, but not much. Lyssa soaped her hair and asked the maid to pour the fresh water over her head. She wished she could clean her conscience as easily.

She had to talk to Ian . . . and perhaps she *would* leave on the morrow—

Her thoughts broke off. The regard and respect of one rogue Irishman meant more to her than her own wishes, or even those of her family.

The revelation was stunning.

"Is something the matter, miss?" the maid asked.

Lyssa looked up, her dripping wet hair in her face. "No . . . nothing." *Dear God, she had fallen in love with him.*

She hunched over. *What was she going to do?* Her father would be livid, out of his mind with anger . . . and yet, she had no choice in the matter.

At some point, perhaps while he was saving her life or battling ruffians or forcing her to mingle with those different from herself or berating her for one thing or the other, she'd lost her heart. Like a naïve child, she'd not realized it at the time.

She should have. The signs were there—her jealousy, the asking for a kiss, the admiration and respect she'd grown to have for him . . .

And with a woman's understanding, she knew he'd cared for her, too. Why else attempt to warn her off? He was so good, so honorable—and she was a complete traitor.

Lyssa stood, pushing her wet hair from her eyes. "Please, a towel," she said to the maid. She was handed a square of linen that was hardly worth the name. "That will be all," she said, dismissing the girl. "I can dress myself."

"Yes, miss." The maid left the room.

The moment the door closed, Lyssa scrambled out of the tub. What was she going to do? Ian had been furious with her. She had to make amends. She had to speak to him. Now.

Love. The word shimmered in her mind.

Funny, but love wasn't anything like what she'd thought it would be. She'd assumed when she fell in love, it would be an all-knowing sense of purpose, as it had been for her parents.

Instead, a part of her wondered if she wasn't going a bit mad. Her father would forgive her running away, but he'd never forgive her for not marrying well, and she'd always meant to marry well. Never in her wildest romantic imaginings had she placed herself beside a poor man.

Ian had been right. She was a snob.

Still, she couldn't live without her Irishman. She didn't want to live without him.

Hurriedly, Lyssa dried herself. The towel was useless, especially when it came to her hair, so she used her green gypsy skirt to finish the job and hung it on a peg to dry. She'd become quite resourceful over the past week. She chose Anice's sage-colored dress to wear. The silvery green was a good color for her hair and she couldn't help but note that the material was of the finest quality. Not only that, the stitchery on the seams was most excellent, even if the cut was out of date—and she felt a moment's relief.

Ian's suspicions were wrong. Anice and Ramsey spent their money on something other than horses. They obviously had a taste for fashion.

She slipped the dress over her head. The high-waisted bodice and shoulders were edged in a lace of the same sage color. The print-on-print material had a good weight so it flowed around her ankles. She was a bit bustier than Anice, and her waist thinner. Looking in the mirror, she thought she probably looked better in the dress than Anice did—and knew this was what to wear while begging Ian's forgiveness.

Her hair was still damp. She left it down, slipped her feet into Anice's black kidskin slippers, and hurried to the door.

Cautiously, she opened it, not wanting to be caught running to Ian's room. She peered down both directions of the empty hallway, listening. No sound echoed through the house because of the thick walls. Nor did she hear the tread of footsteps on the stairs. She would have to chance running to Ian's room, and if anyone caught her in the hall, she would say she was going downstairs.

Part of her thought she was being silly; another part couldn't help but heed Ian's warnings.

Lyssa quietly dashed to his door and gave a quick knock.

No answer.

She leaned toward the door as if she could hear inside the room and knocked again, more forcibly.

Still, no answer.

Lyssa searched the hall. Could she have chosen the wrong room? She didn't think so ... and something was not right. The hairs on the back of her neck were standing up.

She opened the door. The spread, drapes, and walls were white. This had to be the right room, but it was empty, the air smelling slightly of vinegar.

Slipping inside, Lyssa shut the door. The only colors in the room were the faded greens and golds of a patterned Indian carpet. A path was worn from the door to the bed. Nothing looked like it had been touched. The emptiness of the room was overwhelming.

Ian was not here. But he had been here. She had become so attuned to him she could feel his presence, even the absence of it.

For a second, she feared he'd left without her, and just as quickly rejected the thought. Other men might, but not Ian. He was true to his word, and if he said he wasn't leaving without her, he wouldn't.

Moving to the middle of the room, she searched with her eyes, sensing there was something here she was missing. She wanted a clue or some reassurance that all was as it should be. Then she noticed the room had been dusted. Thoroughly. Even the bed drapes had been dusted.

And beside the dresser, she saw a place where the wall was discolored. Investigating, she realized someone had tried to clean a smear off the wall with vinegar but had been unsuccessful.

On the floor beside the wall, she discovered three drops of blood—still wet.

Lyssa fell to her knees, frightened. She touched the blood with the tip of her finger. Then she saw the edge of his knapsack strap hidden behind the bed curtains.

Ian didn't go anywhere without his knapsack.

Grabbing the strap, she pulled the leather bag out and came to her feet. Slowly, she walked the perimeter of the room, hunting for other clues as to what may have happened.

The water basin and pitcher were bone dry. She

knew her man. If he had a chance to shave, he would take it.

Against her chest, she could feel the shape of the pistol in the soft leather of the knapsack. She had to believe Ian was all right. He was a big man and a clever one. He could not be taken easily. For a moment, she tested her senses. She did not feel he was dead—certainly she would know if he was!—but he had to be in danger.

Lyssa sat on the edge of the bed. What would Ian do in these circumstances? How would he react?

He'd get out of the room before he was discovered.

She didn't hesitate but hopped up and ran to the door. Outside, the hall was still empty. Taking care to quietly shut the door to the White Room when she left, she raced for her room and didn't breathe again until she'd safely closed the door behind her.

Turning, she was startled to see Anice standing by the dresser, studying the tarot card.

Lyssa choked back a gasp of surprise. Finding her voice, she managed to ask, "What are you doing here?" while carefully lowering the heavy knapsack to the floor behind the door with one hand. She prayed her skirts would hide what she was doing.

Anice didn't offer apology or explanation. Nor did she seem to notice the knapsack. Instead, she looked at Lyssa with bright eyes and said, "What is this?" She held up the Knight of Swords.

"A tarot card."

"What is that?"

"A fortune-telling scheme."

Anice restudied the card and then laughed lightly. "So this card holds your future?"

"My fate. There is a difference," Lyssa corrected, before asking bluntly, "Is there something I can do for you?"

"I came to escort you down to dinner . . . but you weren't here. The maid should clean up your bath."

"I dismissed her before she had a chance. She can do it later."

"Yes." A cool smile curved her cousin's lips. "Where were you?"

Lyssa felt her heart beat slow down and replied with equal serenity, "I was looking for you. I thought you'd already gone downstairs."

Anice raised delicately arched eyebrows, appraising Lyssa's answer and she knew Ian's suspicions had been right. She did not trust anyone under this roof.

"Well, now that we've found each other," Anice said, "shall we go down to dinner?"

"After you, cousin," Lyssa answered, conscious of the knapsack lying close to her feet behind the open door. If Anice *had* noticed, she didn't say a word. Instead, she swept past Lyssa as if it were her due to go first.

Lyssa shut the door behind her, praying the knapsack would be all right. The maid would be up to clean the room. She prayed the lazy girl would not find its presence amiss.

Her heart in her throat, she forced a smile. "Thank you for letting me wear your dress."

Her cousin gave her a critical eye. "It looks well on you. But then, *you* are accustomed to beautiful clothes, aren't you?"

"I suppose."

"It must be enjoyable to have all the money you could wish for," Anice allowed, starting toward the front staircase.

Lyssa didn't answer. Instead, she paused in front of the door to the White Room. "Shouldn't we wait for Mr. Campion?"

"Oh, he's already downstairs," Anice said heading down the first set of treads. "Coming?"

Lyssa mouth went dry. *Oh, dear.* "Of course." On the way down, trailing in Anice's wake, she picked up the thread of their conversation. "You have a talented seamstress in Appin. This gown is exquisite."

"Do we?" Anice shook her head. "I must tell her. She will be flattered to have a fine London lady compliment her work."

There was no warmth in Anice's voice. She was responding mechanically, as if her mind was preoccupied.

Lyssa's apprehension grew even stronger as she reached the bottom stair to the entrance hall with its hundred pair or so of glass eyes unblinkingly watching her. Anice moved into the red room decorated with daggers.

A fire now burned in the hearth. As Lyssa entered, Ramsey rose from one of two deep chairs facing the hearth and turned to welcome Lyssa. He'd changed into a bottle-green jacket, polished boots and buff breeches. He appeared more English than any gentleman she knew in London, and that irony was not lost on her.

Her image about the proud Highland Laird Davidson was apparently a fantasy. She'd prefer the common folk any day.

"You appear somewhat rested, cousin," Ramsey said congenially. "Would you like a glass of sherry before dinner?" Anice already stood by a side table set up with sherry and the ever present whiskey in glass decanters.

"No, I'm fine, thank you," Lyssa said, aware that there was another man seated in the chair next to the one Ramsey had vacated. She took a step forward, hoping it was Ian—and knowing it wasn't. Ian would have risen. This man did not move. Because of the high back of the chair, she could not see his face.

On guard now, Lyssa moved back toward the door leading to the great hall, pretending interest in the hunting trophies. "Did you bag all of those, Ramsey?" she asked and then stopped at the door, not going farther because the manservant Birdy and a large, ruddy-faced man—one of the three she'd seen him talking to earlier—had entered the hall from a different direction.

She wondered what her chances were of grabbing a sword off the wall to protect herself, even as Ramsey said cheerily, "You flatter me, coz, but no. Hunting is the family tradition."

"My mother was never fond of hunting," Lyssa said, suddenly remembering. In fact, her mother would have nothing to do with it, and looking at the room of lifeless heads, she understood.

She turned, no longer in the mood to play games, especially when she sensed time was running short. "What have you done with Mr. Campion?"

Her directness gave Ramsey a moment's pause. He recovered. "Very well," he said as if coming to some conclusion in his mind. "My dear cousin, there is someone I want you to meet." He turned toward the occupied chair. A lean, balding gentleman unfolded himself from its deep recesses and faced Lyssa. The gentleman had cold, blue eyes and wore black riding gloves.

"It's a pleasure to meet you, Miss Harrell," he said sardonically.

The moment she heard the distinctive voice, her blood ran cold. "Fielder?"

"You have my name and recognize me?" He shook his head. "Amazing. You and Campion were much wilier than I had anticipated."

Lyssa threw aside all thoughts of her own safety. She took three angry strides into the room.

"What have you done with him? Where is Mr. Campion?"

It was Ramsey who answered. "Relax. He's fine . . . for now. His fate depends upon your cooperation."

Slowly, Lyssa turned on her cousin. She should feel fear, but what vibrated through her being was anger. "Do you know this man attempted to kill me?"

Ramsey didn't stall. "Yes. I also know he has been searching for you, desperate to find you. Of course, I have devised a plan that should serve us all very well. Shall we discuss it over dinner?"

"I'm not eating with him," Lyssa countered, "so if you have something to say, say it now. What sort of cooperation do you need for me in exchange for Ian's life?"

"Ian, is it?" Ramsey questioned and his eyes were alive with amusement. "So tell me, are the Irish as good as lovers as they like to claim they are?"

Lyssa ignored the barb. "What do you want me to cooperate with, *cousin*?"

"Our marriage," he answered, and toasted the air with his wineglass.

Chapter Fifteen

LYSSA's response was swift. "You can't be serious."

"But I am," Ramsey answered. "Anice thought of the idea. I need a wife and here you are, an heiress, no less. And one who clearly feels a connection with Amleth Hall. After all, it is in your blood and you have put everyone to considerable trouble to arrive here."

"But we're cousins."

"*Second* cousins," he corrected

She raised her chin as if considering the matter, her mind working frantically, her worry for Ian. "Well now, Ramsey, if I marry you, does that mean Mr. Fielder is going to kill me afterward?"

"You are a brave one," Ramsey said with admiration.

It was Anice who answered. "He'll have to. Otherwise, you could have the marriage set aside."

"What makes you think I would?" Lyssa said,

putting surprise in her voice to hide the trembling. "Your brother is a handsome man and I would have Amleth Hall, which is what I came here for."

"She's right," Ramsey said to his sister. "Why make matters messier?"

"Because I'll be out a hundred pounds if she lives," Mr. Fielder said, stepping between the cousins. "I'm being paid to see her done in."

"Careful, Mr. Fielder," Lyssa chided softly. "You are outnumbered here." Birdy and the other man had come to the doorway, apparently to wait further orders. "They'll be getting rid of you if you become too threatening."

"Sod off," Mr. Fielder said rudely and confronted his hosts, but Lyssa wasn't done with him.

"How did you know I was coming here anyway?"

The henchman smirked. "It wasn't hard to figure out, once we knew you were headed for Scotland. Finding the place was more difficult. This house is a bit out of the way."

"Yes, and few people know about my family's connection to it."

"Her ladyship did," Mr. Fielder said with satisfaction. "And all I had to do was use my wits. Neither you nor Campion is clever enough to outfox me."

There it was. Lyssa had the proof she needed. She'd been right. Her stepmother had hired killers to chase her.

But instead of feeling triumph, she was disheartened. Her father loved his duchess. Now that Lyssa understood what love meant, she knew the betrayal would cut deep . . . and she felt culpable. She had not been as pleasant as she should have been to her stepmother. There had been times when she'd childishly, willfully gone out of her way to make her stepmother not only uncomfortable but despised. Nor had her response to their marriage been mature. But would the woman wish to see her dead?

"Yes, you are very clever, Mr. Fielder," Lyssa agreed softly, mindful of the callous way he'd shot one of his own men, information she decided not to share with her cousins. Let them find out the hard way the danger of dealing with murderers.

Instead, she crossed to Ramsey and linked her arm with his. Purring into his ear in a manner she'd learned from the Widow Potter, she wondered, "Would you really have turned me over to Mr. Fielder, Ramsey?"

He drained his glass and shrugged. "I may do it yet. I have not made up my mind. You are pleasant on the eyes, cousin, but can I trust you?"

"Can I trust you?" she countered and rubbed her breast along his arm.

Ramsey's gaze heated up with interest and he leaned close as if he thought to brush her ear with his lips.

Anice was not pleased. She pulled Ramsey

aside and confronted Lyssa. "How much is your inheritance? What is your father truly worth?"

"I have it on good authority I'm worth my weight in gold," Lyssa replied, echoing Ian's assessment. "Is that enough for you?"

"More than enough," Anice answered. "Ramsey, give her to Fielder. Our purpose is to go to London. We can't take her with us. All she'd have to do is confess all to her father and you know he hates the Davidsons—"

"No, he doesn't," Lyssa interrupted.

"Oh, but he does," Anice returned. "There was no love lost between Dunmore Harrell and Grandfather, especially after Grandfather had him horsewhipped."

Lyssa had not heard this story—and knew this was a pain her father had kept to himself. With a dignity that would have made him proud, she said, "Horsewhipped for what? Daring to court my mother? To honor her with his love?"

"For daring to even look at her," Anice returned disdainfully. "He was a peasant. What your mother saw in him is beyond anyone's understanding."

"Obviously she saw more than everyone else," Lyssa flashed back, "for he made something of himself. Something fine and noble!"

"And for that reason, he will not hand money over to you, the Davidson heir," Anice said with satisfaction to Ramsey. "Marry her, but kill her."

Lyssa drew a deep breath. She should be frightened. Instead, she was angry. "And do you think my father would just turn over my fortune to you?" She shook her head. "He's no fool. You need me. Without me, he can ignore your claim."

"And why would you side with us against your father?" Ramsey asked, suspicious.

"For the money." Wasn't money in the excuse of everyone in the room? They would believe their own motives.

Ramsey hedged. "I don't know—"

"I do," Anice cut in. "Ramsey, you promised we would be off for London. There's nothing for us here. Nothing! This is Dunmore Harrell's daughter. Can you trust her?"

His cousin knew him better than Lyssa did. "You're right," he agreed somewhat reluctantly. His gaze shifted to Lyssa. "Too bad, coz. I rather fancied you."

Lyssa looked him right in the eye and said, "I wish you to hell." She'd removed all pretense and let him see exactly how she felt about him.

Ramsey took a step back, stunned by her revealed anger. Mr. Fielder started laughing, the sound soft at first and then growing louder until he was practically bent over.

"I told you she was a fire eater," he said to Ramsey. "You'd best let me do the deed tonight. We'll get rid of both of them."

"You can't do it tonight," Ramsey snapped.

"Not until we are married. The claim must be legal."

"Then I have weeks to live," Lyssa challenged, "if you are going to post the banns."

"No need to, cousin," he returned. "It's easier to marry in Scotland than England. Had no one told you that? We don't even need a special license. But I'll have a parson. I'll have no one say I didn't do this right."

"What makes you think I'll cooperate?"

"What makes you think the parson will care?" he answered. "Parson Dunn has had several— how shall we call them?—*indiscretions* for which he relies heavily on my regard. He'll do whatever I tell him."

"My father is a stubborn man," Lyssa said. "He won't trust you. You'll never see any money."

"Don't underestimate me," Ramsey shot back. "I can weave a good tale. We already have the beginning—Lyssa Harrell promises herself to me but is abducted by her Irish bodyguard, who turns out to have been her lover. It's a bit lurid but you've already run off on one man, so why not another?"

"You heard I was betrothed?"

"Of course," Ramsey said. "Our friend Fielder told us all."

Yes, her stepmother had set her up very well.

"Are you ready to go in to supper?" Ramsey asked.

"I don't dine with scum," Lyssa replied succinctly, her manner as polite and pleasant as a debutante's but speaking words her father would understand. She wasn't her father's daughter without a reason.

The insult rolled right off of Ramsey. He actually grinned at her. "How unfortunate. I suppose you shall marry hungry in the morning then. Birdy, you and Joseph escort Miss Harrell to her room. Stand guard and keep her safe. She is a very special guest of ours."

Birdy nodded and reached for Lyssa's arm. She pulled it away from him. "Don't touch me. I don't consort with murderers."

Her words upset Birdy, who took a step back and looked askance at Ramsey.

Her cousin laughed. "Don't be dramatic, Lyssa. Much of Scottish history is about one murderer or another. Fates are changed with the help of a knife blade . . . and you did want to see the *real* Scotland."

Lyssa turned on her heel and walked out of the room, not dignifying him with an answer. She might have tried going straight out the front door, but Birdy's muscular companion blocked her path. His face was expressionless as he motioned her up the stairs. She noticed what she should have seen from the beginning: he had a cut over a black eye and his nose was swollen. Bully for Ian.

"Now don't try anything," Birdy warned her before locking her in her room. He was nervous, as he should be. "Joseph and I will have an eye on the door."

Lyssa smiled her response. If he thought she was going to be a meek captive, he was wrong—especially since she still had the knapsack.

The bath had been removed and the window closed, but no one had noticed the leather bag by the door. The moment she was alone, she whisked the knapsack up and carried it to the desk by the window. The shadows outside were lengthening and there wasn't even a stub of a candle to use for later.

Spreading the contents of the knapsack on the desk, she picked up Ian's pistol and remembered him reloading it. She sat at the desk and hefted the gun's weight her hand, wondering if she had the nerve to use it. She'd have one shot, no more, no less.

Out the window, she caught sight of Birdy walking toward the stable yard. Two beefy men met him and they entered the main barn. The stables then fell quiet. Some ducks nested close to the pond. A dog chased a cat. A horse here and there stuck its head out of the paddock . . . but all was quiet—and Lyssa would have bet her soul Ian was someplace in the stable.

She knew her guess was right when Birdy and one of the men left, leaving another to stand guard. The man leaned against the wall and appeared bored beyond reason.

After putting everything back in Ian's knapsack, Lyssa continued to sit at her window post, weighing grim options. For the first time, she wished she had never left London. She deserved to pay a price for her foolishness, but what of Ian? What of the family who waited for him?

In truth, no one needed her. Not even her father anymore . . . and obviously not her stepmother.

Lyssa rested her arms on the desk and laid her head upon them. "Please, Mama, help me."

There was no answer.

And so Lyssa did the only thing she could do. She wept.

Lyssa woke with a start, lifting her head up off the desk.

She was immediately alert. The hour was late. She listened, uncertain why she was awake. No sound echoed through the heavy walls and yet, something had woken her.

She looked out the window toward the stable. The contrast of the full moon and black shadows gave the landscape an eerie light—and then she saw movement. The guard, the same one she'd seen earlier, still stood at the door. But then, yawning, he moved inside.

A current of cool air swirled around her and Lyssa caught the scent of roses. It had been the air that had woken her.

The window was closed.

"Mother?" The word came out of her mouth before she'd even realized.

Lyssa slowly rose to her feet, uncertain of her own runaway emotions. Was she so frightened she was imagining ghosts now?

And then an idea struck her. A daring, foolhardy notion. Almost as if pushed by unseen hands, she moved around the desk, unlocked the window, opened it, and looked out. Not even a breeze stirred the trees. She leaned over and investigated the wall her parents had once climbed down to escape this very room.

Of course.

The drop to the ground was daunting but in the silver moonlight, she saw that uneven stones jutted here and there down the house's wall . . . and again there was the fragrance of roses.

Facing the room, Lyssa announced triumphantly, "You're here!"

There was no answer. But she knew.

She was not alone . . . she had *never* been alone.

Her mother's presence filled her with hope. The fresh air of the draft slipped through her but this time, her heart was warm. She had no choice but to trust. She'd asked for a way and one had been presented. All that was left now was screwing up her courage.

Lyssa changed back into her "Gypsy" clothes, throwing her plaid over her shoulders to hide her white blouse. She didn't want anything from Anice and it felt good to be in her own clothing. Retrieving the leather tie she'd been using for her hair, she quickly braided the heavy mass as best she could and tied it off. Her curls sprung out this way and that, but she didn't care.

She started for the window but stopped. The tarot card lay in a pool of moonlight on the dresser as if beckoning her.

The Knight of Swords. She couldn't leave without him. Swooping the card up, she stored it in the knapsack she wore over her shoulders, checked outside to see if anyone was watching and then threw one leg out the window.

Surprisingly, the going wasn't that bad. The shoes that had been so stiff at the beginning of her journey were now perfect for this sort of exercise. She was only two stories up. The rocks made for good handholds and she didn't have any trouble finding a place to put her feet. All it took was courage.

The toughest part was that right below her window, there was an exterior door and next to the door, another window. She climbed along sideways, finally losing her foothold and finding herself dangling for a moment before dropping to the earth. She landed in some overgrown boxwoods that smelled like cat urine.

Stunned, she sat there a moment before clambering out of the bushes and onto her feet. Her stockings were ripped and she had a few scrapes but, thankfully nothing was broken.

The house was in darkness. Keeping to the shadows, Lyssa moved toward the stable, a plan forming in her mind. Not far from the stable door, hidden in the shadows of overhanging fir branches, she pulled the pistol out of the knapsack and approached the stable door.

The horses were inside and asleep. No nickered greeting marred her entrance. In the distance, by the pond, she could hear the croak of frogs and the incessant chirp of other night insects, but they were not disturbed by her.

The moonlight spilling in the stable door highlighted the guard's legs. He'd propped himself against the wall of the first stall and had fallen asleep.

No one else seemed to be about.

She stepped into his line of sight and held up her pistol. "Don't move."

The man jerked at the sound of her voice and raised a sleepy head. His eyes widened as he saw the gun. Lyssa pulled back the hammer of the pistol just as Ian had done and was satisfied with the solid sound of the gun being cocked.

"Don't hurt me," the guard pleaded.

"Then take me to your prisoner. Now."

She must have sounded as if she meant business because he hurried to do her bidding without challenge.

Ian was in one of the last stalls. Her eyes were growing adjusted to the dark, and she could see his wrists and legs were tied and a gag stuffed in his mouth. "Untie him," she ordered.

The guard dutifully did as she commanded, starting with Ian's wrists.

Ian was in pain. He moved stiffly, twisting and turning his wrists to get the blood circulating before removing the gag from his mouth. He had to go through the same process with his ankles. He staggered to his feet, using the stall wall for support.

The guard stepped back, but he wasn't quick enough. Ian's fist shot out and he caught the man right in the jaw. The guard flew backward against the other side of the stall where he unceremoniously slid to the ground, out cold.

Ian then turned to Lyssa.

"I'm so thankful you are safe—" she started, but her words were cut off by Ian's hard mouth covering hers. His arms, powerful and strong, wrapped around her and he kissed her right on the lips with a startling intensity.

Fear and worry vanished from Lyssa's mind. Who would have thought a kiss could be like this?

Yet it was over almost before it began.

"I knew you would come," he growled out, his voice hoarse. "Knew it." He took the pistol from her and lifted the knapsack off her back. He still wore his jacket and she noticed the sleeves were practically ripped off at the shoulder seams. "Let's get out of here," he said.

She expected them to run directly out the door, but he stopped by one of the stalls. "Hold this." He shoved the pistol back at her and disappeared into the darkest corner of the stable. When he reappeared, he carried a saddle and a bridle.

"What are we doing?" Lyssa asked anxiously.

"We're leaving," came his harsh response. His arm came around her waist, protective, familiar. His lips were close to her ear. "And we are not visiting any more of your relatives ever again."

His dry comment surprised a hiccup of relief out of her. "I'm so glad you are alive."

"So am I." He opened the door to the first stall and walked in. A second later he emerged leading a ghostly gray horse by its halter. The Davidson Stallion. Ian started saddling the animal.

"You can't!" Lyssa whispered.

"I can. Your bastard cousin owes me." His hands moved swiftly in the dark.

"But it's a stallion."

"And the finest, most temperate horse I've ever seen. I've been watching him for hours. I had nothing else to do. The vicar was right. This animal is a prize and he's mine in repayment for your cousin attempting to murder me."

"Fielder is here."

Ian paused. "So, that's what it is all about," he said as if finally fitting together the pieces of the puzzle.

"It was my stepmother," Lyssa said. "He said so."

Ian slipped the bit into the horse's mouth. "He called her by name?"

"No, but he mentioned 'her ladyship.'"

"If he was speaking of the Duchess, he would have said, 'her grace.'"

Lyssa made an impatient sound. "Why won't you believe me?"

Before he could answer, a groan came from the stall where the guard lay. "Hurry, Ian," she whispered.

A door creaked open. Lantern light appeared from beyond the tack room. "Douglas?" a man's voice called sleepily. "I thought I heard someone in the tack."

"Quick!" Lyssa urged.

Ian brought the stallion out into the aisle. In a blink, he swung up into the saddle. "Give me your hand."

The groom and his lantern appeared in the door of the tack room. "Hey there! What are you doing?" he shouted when he saw Ian up on the horse.

Ian took the pistol from her and aimed it at the groom. "Back off."

Immediately the man did exactly that.

Holding his other hand out to Lyssa, Ian ordered, "Give me your hand."

She reached for him. He lifted her as if she weighed no more than a feather, but as he was setting her in front of him, the guard fully came to his senses and started shouting. The groom dropped the lantern and raced to shut the stable doors.

"Hold on," Ian ordered as he put heels to horse. The stallion snorted and gave a prancing step before taking off, knocking over the groom in the process—and they were off even as a cry went up to stop them.

Chapter Sixteen

IAN leaned low over the horse, sheltering Lyssa with his body, his legs wrapped around hers, as they headed out of the stable yard toward freedom.

He paid no attention to the cries of alarm being shouted. He was off to London and no one was going to stop him. His arm around Lyssa's waist and his other hand holding reins and mane, he sent the animal flying like the wind.

Ramsey hadn't been making false claims about the stallion. He was true to his breeding, a mighty animal with the heart to run forever. His legs were strong, his lungs healthy, and he loved to race.

All Ian had to do was hold on and keep Lyssa safe.

His poor, brave Cailín. She was shaking but she needn't be afraid. He'd let no one harm her now. When he'd been tied up in the stables, he'd known she would come. He'd *willed* it—and she'd answered his call as clearly as if he had reached out and touched her. Something lay between them, something rare. And he would protect her with his life.

They came to a fork in the road and he guided the stallion east, but he didn't stay on the road long. Instead, he turned off, slowing the pace, and rode over newly plowed fields and across hedge fences, guided by the stars and his own dogged sense of self preservation.

His hand holding the pistol rested beneath Lyssa's breast. He could feel the pounding of her heart and knew she was frightened. He eased up so she could sit upright, resting back against his chest.

"That was faster than I ever traveled before in my life," she admitted. Her skirts were all the way up to the top of her thighs. He let his hand slip down to rest there. He couldn't help himself. Her garters and hose were bunched around her ankles and the tips of his fingers touched bare skin. Her red curls covered his shoulder and if he turned his head, he could kiss her ear—and Ian felt powerful.

Having this woman and this horse made all right with the world.

He was like the great Finn mac Cumhail, the legendary Irish warrior who fought against the forces of darkness and won. Like Finn, he'd taken what he'd wanted—and no one would wrest them from him. He was invincible. He was brave, courageous. At long last, a whole man. He had won.

And he was in love.

Ian kicked the stallion into a trot.

"Are they behind us?" she whispered.

His lips close to her ear, he soothed, "Don't worry, Cailín. I'll let no harm come to you."

"Ramsey was going to marry me for my money and then kill both of us. He was going to tell everyone we were runaway lovers. Ian, I was so afraid."

He slowed the horse, dropping the reins, and put both of his arms around her, wanting to hold her forever.

Her body went still. Slowly she turned to face him. Feeling the change in their body position, the stallion came to a stop in the middle of the plowed field.

The moon high in the sky was reflected in Lyssa's eyes. "You kissed me," she said, "when I cut your ropes."

Ian smiled, his heart fuller than he had ever anticipated. "I was so proud of you, Cailín."

"My mother sent me to you. I was in her room. I—I could feel her presence."

"Cailín," he said gently. "There is no such thing as ghosties. 'Twas myself calling you."

She stared at him a moment in disbelief. He nodded. "I pictured you in your room, waiting, and called your name in my mind."

"You were telling me you needed me."

"Aye."

"And is *that* why you kissed me?"

He dropped his gaze to her lips, to those very kissable lips. "Because I was thankful?"

She nodded, a troubled line between her brows.

"Don't be foolish." And to prove his words, he kissed her again.

Only this kiss was different from his earlier one. Then, he'd been exuberant that she had come, that she had heard him.

Now, he attempted to explain the depth of what he felt, an emotion he did not fully understand yet himself. Their lips fit together perfectly. Everything about them fit together perfectly.

She made a soft mew of surprise, pulled back. He refused to let her escape—and she capitulated, turning more fully in his arms to receive him.

Ian had kissed more than his share of women, but none was as sweet and tempting as this one.

Deep within there rose a need for fulfillment like nothing he'd experienced before. All his life he'd been in search of what she was offering, in search of what she alone could give, and now here she was offering herself with such sweetness—

The pounding of hooves across the ground were his only warning. A heartbeat later, a party of four men and horses charged into the field. Ramsey Davidson was at their lead followed closely by another man in a low brimmed hat.

"It's Fielder," Lyssa said, identifying the second man.

Ian kicked the stallion and the chase was on. He drove the horse toward a midnight dark line of trees. He trusted this horse. He was smart and surefooted and Ian sensed he wanted to escape Davidson as much as they did.

Bracing her against him, Ian half-cocked the pistol, preparing to fire if necessary.

They reached the woods. Through the dark forest they ran. The stallion chose his own path, weaving in and out through the trees. Behind them, Ian heard their pursuers fall behind. At least two riders were unseated, their bodies crashing to the ground.

Someone fired off a pistol shot. It went wide and Ian grinned. Only a fool would waste a shot in a chase like this. He would beat them. He had no doubt.

They came out into another pasture. The stallion's hooves threw up clods of newly turned earth. A hedgerow loomed ahead and without breaking stride, the horse jumped—

A second shot was fired.

Midair, the stallion squealed, kicking out and twisting in alarm. His front hooves hit the ground. He stumbled, coming down to his knees.

The horse had been hit.

He struggled to his feet and then, with a frightened squeal, reared in fear. Ian had to make a choice between Lyssa and the pistol which he let fall to the ground. Anger the likes he'd never felt before surged through him.

Ramsey Davidson shouted, the sound a screech in the night, "Damn you, Fielder, you shot my horse!"

Ian slid off, bringing Lyssa with him. "Run," he ordered. "Head for the trees."

"What about you?"

"I have a score to settle." He gave her a push in the direction he wanted her to go and turned to face his attackers.

However, Davidson was no longer interested in him. He'd reined his horse in and confronted Fielder, "You shot my horse, you fool!"

"I wanted to stop them and I have!" Fielder flashed back. He was almost upon the hedgerow where Ian stood waiting. A man on foot could have an advantage over a rider, if he was cagey. Ian pulled the knife out of his knapsack and dropped the leather bag to the ground.

Fielder's teeth flashed in a grin of anticipation as he approached the hedge, but then a shot rang out. Fielder stiffened just as his horse started the jump. His eyes widened in surprise and he went tumbling off the back, his hat flying through the air.

Davidson had shot Fielder.

Ian stepped out of the way of the riderless horse. The animal had jumped in fear to escape what he didn't understand and now galloped over to the stallion for protection.

Lyssa gave a small scream and Ian didn't need to look in her direction to know that she had, once again, not followed his orders.

Davidson rode up and looked down on the man lying in the tilled soil. Fielder groaned. Davidson pulled a second pistol from his saddle horse's holsters and shot the man again.

The gun spent, he shoved it back in its holster. "Bloody bastard." He looked up at Ian, standing on the other side of the hedge. "We're not done yet," he promised and pulled a sword from the scabbard at his waist. He kicked his horse.

Now, Davidson was fighting Ian's sort of battle, one he'd learned against the French. Ian dashed out into the field, not wanting to be trapped by the hedgerow. He turned to confront his attacker.

Davidson rode like a Hussar, the sword high in the air. He cleared the hedgerow and bore down on Ian. The moon glinted off the dangerous blade. As Davidson drew by, he swiped the air with the sword. Ian ducked, hearing the blade whistle past, inches from his shoulder.

Lyssa made a move as if to come join him. "Stay back," Ian yelled. "If you must do something, run!"

This time, she obeyed him, obviously realizing he couldn't worry about Davidson and her at the same time. She took off running.

Her cousin had brought his horse up short, ready to make another pass at Ian when he noticed her racing toward the trees. He looked to Ian, then back to Lyssa—and grinned.

"Davidson, come get me!" Ian shouted, wanting to distract the bastard from Lyssa, but it was too late.

With a cocky salute of his sword in Ian's direction, Davidson urged his horse after Lyssa.

Now, Ian was afraid. He shouted a warning and ran for Fielder's horse.

The animal spooked but Ian caught the saddle in time and pulled himself up even while racing after Davidson.

Again, the dangerous sword was raised. Davidson was so intent on his prey, he didn't noticed Ian riding up hard behind him. Ian slid the knife into his boot. He drove the horse hard, pushing it alongside Davidson's animal and then he jumped, hitting Davidson with the full force of his body.

Both of them went flying through the air. Their bodies hit the soft earth heavily and they rolled over and over each other until at last they stopped.

Ian scrambled to his feet, his heart beating in his ears, his fists raised, ready to strike—but Davidson did not move. He lay on his back, partially buried in the newly turned earth, his head at an odd angle.

Cautious, Ian lowered his fist. Lyssa stood a distance away, watching as he waved his hand back and forth in front of Davidson's sightless eyes.

Ramsey Davidson had broken his neck. He'd fallen off at such an angle, he'd hit the ground head first and met his Maker.

Ian was glad to be done with him.

He released his breath and fell back to the ground, spent. "It's over," he said.

Lyssa slowly moved forward. "Did you kill him?"

"He killed himself." Ian got to his feet and turned his attention to the stallion, who stood not far away, the whites of his eyes showing in fear. He could smell death.

Davidson's horse had run toward home, the stirrups bouncing off his sides. Fielder's animal stopped, pawed the earth and waited.

"Come here, boy," Ian said, approaching the stallion, with his hand open.

The stallion wasn't trusting.

He whispered in Irish, "*Ná bí buartha* ('Don't worry')."

Pricking up his ears, the stallion listened. Ian touched the velvet of his nose. "*Ná bí buartha*," he repeated. The stallion lowered his head, a gesture of submission.

"You are so beautiful," Ian praised and trailing his hand along the horse's body so the animal knew where he was, he searched for where it had been shot.

"Is he all right?" Lyssa asked, coming to Ian's side.

Ian didn't answer. He found the wound on the stallion's right flank. The bullet had grazed the horse and passed on. He leaned his head against the horse's rump and said a word of thanksgiving.

"Will your salve help?"

"We can try it." He picked up the reins, lifted them up over the stallion's head and handed them to her. "Hold him while I get my knapsack." He also took a moment to find his pistol.

Moving swiftly, he soothed the salve over the stallion's wound, caught Fielder's horse, a chestnut, and mounted. "Come, let's get out of here."

"Ian, we can't go off and leave my cousin and Mr. Fielder lying here."

"We have no choice. Who knows who will be chasing us next, and I don't want to be here waiting to see if they accept our explanations." He held out his hand and she took it without further argument.

Ponying the stallion, they started riding across the field. It was another sign of the stallion's temperament that he didn't balk at the arrangement. The beast was a jewel, a royal jewel.

Ian headed them south—toward London. They didn't talk. Lyssa was very still and he feared she was having a hard time accepting the sudden turn of events.

When they came to a shallow stream, Ian urged the horses into it and followed its course for as long as he could. He had no illusions. A cry would be put out once the bodies were discovered. He could be held in suspicion of Fielder and Davidson's deaths. Lyssa and the evidence would show him blameless . . . but there was still the tricky matter of a price on his head. He had no desire to tweak the nose of the local authorities, not when he was so close to gaining everything he'd ever wanted.

Lyssa stayed in his arms, so tired she eventually fell asleep sitting up, her head against his chest. Her precious plaid was still wrapped around her shoulders. Dark clouds rolled in on the horizon, blocking the moon. Ian kept on.

The night sky grew lighter. He had no idea where they were or how far they'd come. Close to dawn, he finally sensed they were safe. Lyssa had roused several times during the night. She was awake but too quiet for his comfort.

He wished he knew what she was thinking. He feared the worst. He had seen many men go through this same phase after battle. He'd wondered why even hardened soldiers were always surprised to discover death was no more than a stone's throw away. It seemed to him he'd always lived with death right at his shoulder.

Lyssa, however, was different. She needed a safe place in order to come to terms with what had happened.

And he prayed she didn't blame him.

In the dim light of a murky dawn, he spotted an abandoned shepherd's bothy. They had traveled from the main roads, taking paths only shepherds and hunters would know.

The bothy was built beside a hill and was made of jumbled boulders piled one on top of another. The door hung loose on one leather hinge. There was a drink trough by the entrance full of brackish water. Dry, gray thatch covered the roof.

Ian hopped down and reached to help Lyssa off the chestnut. In the distance, he heard the rumble of thunder and the air felt heavy. Their horse took a skittish step and Lyssa fell into his arms.

Carrying her into the bothy, he put her down gently. The room was swept clean and dry. The hard stone floor would have to do.

She opened her eyes, disoriented.

"Wait for me," he said quietly.

She nodded.

Outside, both horses were already grazing. Ian unsaddled them, hobbling both with the reins. Neither gave him a worry. The chestnut turned out to be a gelding and of good quality. Ian felt repaid for the horses Fielder had stolen from him in the beginning.

The first huge drops of rain hit the ground just as he ducked inside, saddles and bridles in hand.

Lyssa still sat where he'd placed her.

"A storm's coming," he said.

The frown formed between her brow. She tilted

her head as if she might have heard his voice but wasn't certain.

He moved to stand in front of her. "Are you all right?"

Her frown deepened. Her jaw tightened. She reached up and yanked at the plaid, pulling it off and tossing it aside, her actions speaking louder than words what she was feeling.

Ian picked the tartan up and spread it on the ground, using a saddle for a pillow. "Here, lie down. You need the rest."

She didn't move. "They'd both be still alive if I hadn't arrived. If I hadn't ever started on this foolish, ill-fated adventure."

He hunched down until he was eye level with her, his hands resting on his knees. "Either that or your cousins would have tried to murder someone else. I have no illusions about Fielder. We weren't his first victims." *But we had become his last.* Ian felt no remorse over seeing the man dead. Life was like that.

Outside, the skies suddenly opened and the rain came down in gray sheets, separating them from the rest of the world.

"Perhaps we should go to the magistrate," she said, not looking at him. "We stole horses."

Ian shook his head. "Lyssa, we'll go to your father first. He will take care of everything from London. It will be better to explain ourselves there than here, where Davidson may have friends."

"But you were right," she said. "From the very

beginning, you told me I was a fool for running away."

"I—" he started but she cut him off.

"I've destroyed everything. I've opened the door for my stepmother's hatred and almost cost you your life."

He reached for her but she edged away, crossing her arms tight against her chest. "It's my fault," she said. "And I was actually happier before. Even marrying Robert couldn't be worse than the way I am feeling now, seeing those men die—"

Ian moved in, wrapping his arms around her. He held her tight, his chin on top of her head. She felt stiff and cold. He tried to warm her with his body heat, to take the pain she was feeling upon himself.

"Don't do this to yourself," he begged her. "There are things that go on in this life that no one understands. Perhaps running away was a mistake or perhaps you were meant to be here and everything happened exactly as it should have. I don't pretend to understand the world, Cailín. All I know is that you can't go back. The past is done. It's out of your hands now."

"Don't say that," she whispered. "Please don't say that."

"It's gone," he pressed sadly.

She moved, forcing him to loosen his hold. From her belt she pulled a card. Ian had to lean back to see it properly. It was a picture of a rider on horseback swinging a sword. "What is it?" he asked without recognition.

"The Knight of Swords. It's a tarot card, Ian. Used to tell one's fate. I've carried it with me ever since Madame Linka told my fortune and I met you."

"You don't believe such nonsense, do you?"

"I don't know."

"I do. No one can tell the future."

She raised tortured eyes to him. "Then why has it all come true?"

"Lyssa—" He wanted to reason with her but he didn't know how. This was not his spirited Cailín but a woman who had just learned her limitations, who had discovered fear.

And then, she broke down, crumpling the card in her fingers. She would have collapsed on the ground, her body racked with heart-stopping sobs, if he hadn't been holding her tight.

Ian was at a loss. "Please, Lyssa. It's not your fault," he said. But she was retreating to a place he couldn't go . . . a place that frightened her.

He couldn't stand idly by. Not without a fight to bring her back.

So, he did what he could do, what he wanted to do. He kissed her. Savagely, possessively, completely.

And to his surprise, and everlasting joy, she kissed him back.

Chapter Seventeen

To Lyssa, Ian's kiss was a lifeline. He understood her when she didn't understand herself.

He was her fate.

The crumpled tarot card fell from her fingers as she put her arms around his neck and kissed him with everything she was worth. The touch of his tongue against hers signaled that all had changed between them. There were no more walls, and she could have cried in thanksgiving.

The rest of the world faded.

Fears, doubts, mistakes—nothing mattered. In his arms, she was safe.

In his arms, *she belonged* . . . and that was a powerful, heady discovery for a woman who'd feared ever finding her place in the world.

Neither of them held back. Breeding, inexperience, social standing—none of that mattered. Outside, the rain came down harder. Lyssa didn't care. The only reality that existed for her was the feel of this man's body against hers.

She met him kiss for kiss, arched to be even closer to him. He leaned her back upon the plaid. His knee rode up her leg and instinctively, she moved toward him, eager for what she didn't yet understand.

His response was to devour her with his mouth. And deep within Lyssa, the sweet ache of need built. She wanted more, needed *more*.

Their lips never parting, they began pulling at clothing, searching with blind fingers for fastenings and secret openings. The first moment his hands covered her bare breasts, Lyssa gasped, her heightened senses electrified by his touch. When he leaned down to cover one hard nipple with his mouth, she cried out his name in shock, a cry that ended in a moan of pure pleasure.

Her legs parted with a will of their own. She buried her fingers in his hair, never wanting him to stop—and yet hungry for something deeper, more fulfilling.

Ian knew what she wanted. He sucked hard as if marking her, and her breath caught in her throat, the pull of his tongue traveling down to her very core.

She'd long ago kicked off her skirt. Her petticoats and chemise were around her waist. His jacket with the torn sleeves had been practically ripped off him and she hadn't helped the damage any in her enthusiasm to undress him. His shirt was up under his arms. He still wore his boots and leather breeches, but she'd undone the buttons—and it was there, the male part of him, the one wags swore had more power over men's heads than their hearts and brains did. It was bold and insistent. Lyssa could feel him against her thigh. She ran her hand down over his hip above his breeches, but shied from going closer to *it*.

However, if her mind was skittish, the rest of her body didn't seem afraid at all, and let him settle himself between her legs.

Ian closed his lips over her other breast, and she could feel the stroke of his tongue there, at the most intimate part of her. The head of *it* caressed her and Lyssa thought she would go through the ceiling from the sensation.

She pulled at his shirt and ran her palms down his naked back. Hot, wet, anxious . . .

He slid down, positioning himself.

Oh, dear God.

Ian looked up. His lips were swollen and his glazed eyes had turned the color of dark pewter.

Who was this man? The Ian she knew always had control. This man was raw, open . . . vulnerable.

"Lyssa." He whispered her name like a benediction and thrust deep inside her with one smooth movement.

For a second, she couldn't think, couldn't breath.

He was inside her.

And he felt *so* good. *So* right.

There was no pain. A small discomfort but nothing to compare to the satisfaction of being joined with him. Of being one. *Oh, Sweet Lord!*

She tilted her head back, reveling in the feel of him. Accepting him. There was a low growl of triumph in the back of his throat, and he took what she offered. Kissing her neck, his whiskers tickling her skin, he moved deeper still.

Here was the meaning of life. Her reason for being.

Her body was no longer her own, but his. Her senses were filled with him, with the texture of his skin, with the warm male scent of him, with the feel of every muscle, every sinew.

And Ian knew it.

His hands cupped her buttocks and he thrust deep, pulled back and went deeper still, claiming every fiber of her. Nor did Lyssa suppress her joyful response. Their joining took on a life of its own. She hugged him close, and met him move for move.

Together they strived toward what she did not quite understand—yet. But he knew and drove on, knowing exactly what she wanted.

Her heart beat in her ears. His skin was hot and slick against hers. He pressed deeper still, the heat of him pushing her toward some pinnacle, sharp, precise—

Her world exploded.

One heartbeat she was whole and sane, and in the next, she felt she'd shattered, her senses a million stars.

So this was why poets sang and wise men sacrificed. This was behind all those romantic novels, the element she hadn't quite been able to fathom. *This* was worth a hundred books, a thousand poems.

She wondered if she still lived and yet, had never felt more alive in her life, especially at the moment he released his seed deep within her.

Time stopped. The life force moved from him and into her—and she was complete. Whole. One.

He eased down on her with a satisfied sound of his own fulfillment—a lover's highest praise.

The weight of his body on hers felt good. His head rested in the curve of her neck, one hand possessively on her hip, the other buried in the tangle of her hair.

Lyssa dared not move. The sound of the rain mingled with the beat of his heart, a beat her own matched.

"Are you all right?" he whispered.

Still unable to speak, she wrapped her arms around him. He smiled against his skin.

"Yes, me, too," he answered and gathering her close, rolled off her. Pulling the edge of the plaid around their hips, he kissed her forehead lightly, once, twice.

Nestled in his arms, her body satiated, Lyssa fell asleep.

Ian held the woman in his arms close. After years of wandering, his life now had substance.

Love did exist.

He should be tired, and yet he'd never felt more awake or more aware of his senses.

The rain let up, becoming little more than mist. Fog rose from the ground, even daring to roll inside the stone bothy, and he knew it would be a dreary day. Not one good for traveling, but perfect for making love.

He no longer worried about pursuers. What was left of the Davidson clan might not be too keen with the prospect of him sharing his side of the story with the magistrate. But even if they were, they'd have a search on their hands. The rain would wash away all traces of their tracks. If he wished, they could disappear completely.

Even Pirate Harrell wouldn't be able to find her—

Ian was stunned by the direction of his thoughts.

Reality was not pleasant.

Suddenly, he came face-to-face with the enormity of what had happened. He'd just bedded Pirate Harrell's daughter. He'd plowed into her, taking all that she'd offered and then some. He'd reamed her good. Her innocence was his, as was any babe that might even now be growing in her belly.

He thought of Janet and Fiona waiting for him. Of the money he desperately needed. Harrell would kill him instead of paying him . . . and Ian didn't know if he cared.

Lyssa was his and, now that he had her, he would never let go. Ever.

Lyssa woke to find herself tucked in by Ian's side. He was sleeping, his chest moving with quiet regularity. Propping herself on one arm, she studied him. The shadow of his beard gave him a dangerous look and she decided she'd never known a more handsome man. He appeared exactly the way the Knight of Swords should look. However, she no longer feared him. *Or his sword*, she added to herself with a smile.

She'd crossed the threshold and had no regrets.

Ian's eyes opened. "Hello."

Lyssa smiled, full of happiness. "Hello," she whispered.

He moved his leg, curling his toes and tickling the bottom of her foot. "How do you feel?"

In love. "Perfect."

"Perfect?" Humor lit his lazy gaze.

"Puuurrrfect," she repeated and he rolled over on top of her. His lips brushed the top of her hair. She curled her arms into his chest. "Ian?"

"Mmmmmm?" He kissed her temple. Outside, the rain had renewed. They'd not be traveling anywhere this day.

"Are we going to do it again?"

His lips pressed against her forehead stopped

moving. "Would you like to?" he asked, and she felt him aroused and strong.

Her answer was to reach down and boldly brush the length of *it*, no longer timid. And this time, making love was even better than the first.

There didn't seem to be a need to get dressed, so they didn't.

The furnitureless bothy became their own Garden of Eden. It could have been furnished with the richest stuff, and Lyssa would not have been happier.

They spent the rest of the day listening to the rain and making love until Lyssa ached in places she didn't know could ache, and still she yearned for more.

When they weren't making love, they talked, their topics covering anything and everything. He confessed his worry for his nephew Liam. She made him laugh with stories of what a disaster she'd been in Society. He'd kissed her nose and assured her that if he'd been present he would have swept her off her feet.

Of course, Lyssa was no fool. She noticed Ian did not mention the future and she tried not to let her fear show. There was only the here and now. Nor did they speak words of love . . . but she knew. She knew. Even though she hadn't the courage to say them first.

They didn't leave the next day either. The rain

had stopped but the sky was still threatening, or so they convinced themselves, and that seemed to be as good a reason as any to stay where they were.

Ian found a stream close by. From his magic knapsack he pulled hook and line and caught fresh fish for their lunch and supper. The filets, cooked over an open flame, were delicious after a diet of dried beef and catch-as-catch-can.

That evening, she went with him to tend the horses. Ian wore nothing but his leather breeches and she left off stockings and shoes. The tall grass tickled the bottoms of her feet, making her laugh. She'd never been so happy.

The stallion's bullet wound was healing nicely thanks to Ian's salve. "What's in this?" she asked, giving the tin a sniff.

"Lobelia flowers." He ran his hand down the horse's flank.

"Anything else?"

"Goose grease." He straightened, brushing off the horse hair that had stuck to his fingers. "Simple enough, hmmm? I received the recipe from a Portuguese woman known for her abilities as a healer. In the army, we all went to her before we'd go to any military quack."

Lyssa pressed the lid on the salve tin. "And how did you manage to wheedle it out of her?" Her imagination could jump to obvious conclusions.

He threw his arm around her neck, pulled her close, and whispered in her ear, "I saved her son from a bullet." He took the tin and dropped it back into his open knapsack on the ground. "The lad was where he shouldn't be and almost took it from a French sniper."

"Oh." Lyssa shifted her gaze away from him. "So, I'm not the first life you've saved?"

"You're the most important one," he answered, brushing a possessive kiss against her temple. "Here. What shall we name our stallion?"

Our stallion. Lyssa leaned her back against Ian's chest. "I don't know. It must be a grand name, but not something Gaelic."

" 'Davidson's Pride' won't work?" he teased and she elbowed him in the ribs.

"What about Fortune? Irish Fortune."

His arms came around her and he rested his chin on her head. "I didn't know there was such a thing."

"There is," she confirmed, covering the hands he pressed against her stomach with her own. "I'm discovering a good Irishman creates his. And the truth be known, I have a weakness for self-made men."

There, she'd made the first tentative step forward to what was in her heart. She held her breath, waiting for his response.

"I want to believe," he said softly.

"I do, too," she confessed

His arms around her tightened. He held her close, then said, "Lyssa, we must return to London."

She felt her heart drop.

"I must face your father," he said.

"*We* must face him," she corrected.

"Of course."

"He won't be happy."

"No."

Lyssa turned in his arms. She knew what he was saying. "Ian, what if he refuses us?"

"Then I'll tell him the truth. That I debauched his daughter, stole her innocence, and will marry her in a heartbeat whether she likes it or not . . . although I would like his blessing."

Joy surged through her. She threw her arms around him. "You love me!"

"Was there any doubt?"

She shook her head, even while admitting, "I couldn't be certain."

"My sweet, wonderful Cailín. I think I've loved you ever since you crashed that ironstone pitcher across the innkeeper's head."

"That was terrible of me."

"Despicable," he agreed, smiling, and her happiness knew no boundaries.

Putting her hand on his chest, right over his heart, she asked, "You will really ask my father for my hand?"

"Aye. That is, if you'll have me."

"Oh, Ian, such a stupid question."

"It's not, Lyssa, I have nothing—"

She cut him off with a kiss. "You have me," she whispered. "You'll always have me."

"And can you live with the fact your father may not give us his blessing?" he asked, doubt in his voice.

"Yes," she replied with conviction.

But Ian didn't laugh this time. Instead his expression grew thoughtful. "Now, is this before or after we accuse his wife of attempting to murder you?"

"I don't even care about that anymore," she told him. And then she took the leap of faith. "Ian, I love you."

Simple words, and yet they made all the difference to her world.

And to his. "You are everything to me," he whispered to her, his voice fierce. "Everything." He pulled back, holding her hands in his. "Lyssa Harrell, will you promise to be my wife, to love me, to be faithful to me all the days of my life?"

"Is this our church then?" she asked.

"Are we not before God?"

"Oh, yes," she agreed, her chest tightening with emotion. "And, yes, I will have you Ian Campion. I will love you and honor you—" She paused, and then an imp of mischief caused her to add, "And *obey* you."

"I doubt that," he said, half laughing. "And I don't care, Lyssa, for I shall be strong enough and courageous enough to take care of you all my days. Even if I have nothing to offer right now."

"You have me," she corrected.

With a glad, wild Irish whoop, he picked her up

in his arms and swung her around. He twirled until they were both laughing uncontrollably and they tumbled to the ground in each other's arms.

Suddenly, they both went quiet. This was a sacred moment, one Lyssa wanted to capture and remember all her life. She never wanted to forget anything, not even the exact color of the blue sky behind white and silver clouds, or the feel of the light breeze on her cheek. And she wanted to burn in her mind forever the look of love in Ian's eyes.

He kissed her . . . and she knew he was feeling the same. This moment was magic. It was the sealing of their troth. Their promise of commitment.

She held her hand up, palm out. He laced his fingers in hers and she drew him down upon the cool green grass.

They made love there, beneath the Scottish skies where God and all His kingdom served as witness. The act between them took on a different dimension than at anytime before. There was no lust—but love. Each kiss, each caress, each touch went beyond the mere physical. They were pledging their lives to each other.

And when Ian entered her, Lyssa silently offered thanks to God. She belonged in his arms. Could never leave them. He held her heart.

Later, her head on his chest, her legs entwined in his, Lyssa knew this was how it should be.

She only prayed her father would agree, but she did not speak doubts to Ian. She knew him well enough to know he harbored his own. She also believed they were both stubborn enough to live their lives as they pleased.

The next morning they left for London. Lyssa rode the chestnut. She was a good rider. Not as good in the saddle as Ian, but she could ride hard and well.

They would make the city in less than three days.

She didn't know what the future held, but she trusted Ian enough to place her fate in his hands.

Chapter Eighteen

THEY reached London late in the afternoon.

Ian had been considering each of his options and decided it was best they not meet Harrell in his own home.

"You don't trust my father there?" Lyssa asked.

"We have much to say to him. Neutral territory is best."

She lowered her gaze to the reins in her hands. The frown line he was beginning to anticipate every time she worried formed between her eyes. He leaned over and covered her hand with his for reassurance. "All will be well," he promised. "After all, you are already mine." Every night on the road he'd held her in his arms. And last night, he'd dreamed she carried his child. Nothing could take her away from him now.

Her gaze met his. She nodded. "Must we tell him about my stepmother?"

"What do you wish?"

She pressed her lips together. "I wish that we did not, and yet, what choice is there? I'm happy to remove myself from her sphere but what happens if some day in the future—?" She didn't finish the thought. "His life could be in danger."

Ian nodded. Of course, he had no illusions as to what Pirate Harrell's response would be to an accusation against his wife. Harrell didn't strike him as someone who would appreciate having his judgment questioned. And no matter how much Lyssa talked in the positive, he also knew Harrell would not accept him.

The test of Lyssa's love would be if, when confronted by her father, she still choose Ian. He believed in his heart she would.

And yet life had played far too many dirty tricks to not consider the possibility of betrayal.

"Where do you propose we ask him to meet?" she said.

"I have a friend who owns an inn down by the wharves. It's a respectable place although not in the best of neighborhoods."

"Let's go there then."

"All right."

He started to urge Fortune on, but Lyssa reached out and placed her hand on her arm. "Ian, no matter what, I shall stay with you."

Bringing her hand up to his lips, he kissed it and she smiled. *Yes, yes, yes*, he wanted to believe.

They arrived at the Scrolled Serpent an hour later. He and Roddy, the inn owner, went way back to his days in Ireland. His friend was happy to let them have a private room and wise enough not to ask too many questions. The room was located on the ground floor next to public room and had a window overlooking the street, perfect for Ian's purposes.

While Lyssa wrote the letter telling her father she was home and begging him to come meet her *alone*, Ian stabled the horses. He had no money, so he offered the stable manager his pistol until payment could be made, knowing full well the gun might be pawned or sold before he returned.

That was just as well. In the future, he planned not to need it again.

Walking down the narrow alley back to the Serpent, he realized he was a changed man from the one who had left London mere weeks before. He stopped, looking around at his surroundings. Soon this would all be in his past. Before, he'd been a man who trusted no one. Now, he searched for the good and meaningful in life. The dream he'd had of finding freedom, of building a new home for his family was now in his grasp—and all because of Lyssa.

He found her sitting by the window, waiting for him while enjoying a cup of tea. Dropping his knapsack on the floor, he took the chair opposite hers at the table and asked, "Do we need to send the note?"

"We need the money my father promised you for finding me," she answered, a practical wife already. "Besides, it's already gone. Roddy had his son take it. We have only to wait now."

Wait. He didn't know if he could. As if reading his mind, she reached over and squeezed his hand. "It won't be long now."

"It could be hours."

"Ian, not with my father."

She was right. Within the hour, Harrell's fine carriage rolled up to the inn door.

Lyssa caught sight of it out the window and sat up straight. The carriage door opened and Parker climbed down. "He didn't come alone," she said, her voice tight. Ian didn't answer. Parker's appearance could mean anything.

They watched as Harrell climbed out of the coach and then turned. He held out his hand for his wife.

"He brought her," Lyssa said as if betrayed.

The former duchess moved slowly because of her advanced stage of pregnancy. She seemed calm, but her expression was one of worry. Ian couldn't judge whether her concern was for her stepdaughter—or because she was about to be found out.

Grossett followed her out of the carriage but instead of moving on, he held out his hand and another woman came out of the coach. She was some twenty years older than Mrs. Harrell and dressed expensively, although her clothing appeared gaudy next to Mrs. Harrell's simple elegance. She and Grossett bore an uncomfortable resemblance in their bulldog jowls and squinty eyes.

Lyssa looked to Ian. "That is Robert's mother. A more unpleasant person you could never hope to meet, and she despises me. I don't know why she is here. Ian, I'm afraid."

"Don't be," he ordered. "I'll not let any harm come to you, and we might as well face them all. Come, let's get this over with." He stood, inviting her to do the same. Together they faced the door, her hand in his.

There was a moment of silence where the footfalls and sounds from the rest of the inn masked the opening of the front door, and then she said, "I wonder if Father will notice that I've changed?"

"That you are well loved?" he asked.

She laughed, not mistaking his meaning, but then sobered. "I feel I left London a child and I now return a woman. I've grown up so much, Ian. Let us pray Father can see beyond my worn clothes and wild hair and see what it is I have." She gave his hand a squeeze for meaning.

Her words mirrored his own recent revelation. But before he could speak, Harrell's voice came from out in the hall, demanding Roddy take him to his daughter.

The door opened without a knock and Lyssa pulled her hand from Ian's. Her fists clenched . . . and Ian took a step back, trying to understand.

Pirate Harrell marched into the room. He was an imposing figured dressed in his black superfine down to his polished boots.

For a second, he and Lyssa faced off. "Father," she said, acknowledging him.

"Daughter," Harrell answered. His green gaze, so much like his daughter's, swept her person from head to toe.

The tension stretched taut—and then Lyssa broke it by stepping forward. "I am so sorry."

Her words seemed to linger in the air for a second before her father reached for her. They fell into each other's arms, and he hugged her as if he'd never let her go.

And Ian feared the worst.

The others crowded in, Roddy shutting the door behind them. Grossett appeared as pompous as ever with his expensive hat and artfully combed hair. Ian was too conscious of their contrasts, of the fact he wore no coat, having left his off because of the torn sleeves. His fortunes seemed to have been halved over the past weeks while everyone else had prospered.

Mrs. Harrell glided over to her husband and stepdaughter while Parker made arrangements for more chairs and drink.

She still didn't strike Ian as a murderess.

At last, Harrell and Lyssa parted. "I was so afraid for you."

"I was safe, Papa," she said.

"How was I to know that?" he demanded. "I feared the worst, you know! I thought you might have been kidnapped."

"But there was no ransom," she answered.

"Who helped you? Who was behind this!"

"Me. I did it all myself," she confessed.

Her words were a shock to her father. "But why? Why would you endanger yourself in such a manner?"

"Because I had to go to Amleth Hall," she told softly. "I had to."

Harrell made an exasperated sound. "For what purpose? And why could you not have asked me instead going off on some wild escapade?"

Her gaze grew sad. "I did ask you, and you ignored me. You were busy."

"Lyssa, when have I refused you anything?" he countered.

Her gaze strayed to her stepmother. Ian braced himself, but instead, Lyssa said, "It was something you didn't want to do. I've met the Davidsons. I understand why you would wish to never see them again. And, I think, too, there would be sad memories."

Her father sat in the chair Parker had arranged, bringing her down to sit in the one beside his. "You could have talked to me. I would have made arrangements and given you protection."

"I know that now . . . but at the time—" She released her breath and admitted, "At the time, I was not thinking clearly."

"Absolutely right. I've had Runners out looking for you."

"I was camping with Gypsies," she confessed.

"Gypsies!" The word exploded out of her father. The others in the room were as shocked as he.

Lyssa plunged on, saying all, "But they weren't really Gypsies or else I might have been in terrible trouble. Mr. Campion made me understand my foolishness."

"If they weren't Gypsies, who were they—?" Harrell turned horrified eyes to his wife. "She ran off with strange people?"

Mrs. Harrell leaned across her husband to place her hand on Lyssa's arm. "You were all right, weren't you?"

Lyssa's gaze dropped to her stepmother's gloved hand. Then, for the first time since her father had entered the room, she looked to Ian. In her eyes was a plea for guidance.

He stepped forward. "She was safe and unharmed in any fashion when I found her."

"Then there is nothing to worry about, Dunmore," Mrs. Harrell said. "We have Lyssa home safe and that is all that matters, isn't it, my lord?" She addressed this last to Grossett."

"Yes, it is," the bull-nosed viscount agreed. He still stood by the door. His gaze met Ian's, and narrowed. He moved forward territorially, but his mother reached to hold him back. He ignored her. Putting his hands on the back of Lyssa's chair, he said, "We've very glad to have you back, my dear."

Ian heard the unspoken challenge. Grossett didn't really believe *nothing* had happened to the woman he planned to marry and his narrowed eyes told Ian so.

Harrell didn't miss a thing. His sharp gaze went from one man to the other before settling shrewdly on his daughter. He stood. "Well, Campion," he said, "you were true to your word and I am grateful to you for fetching my Lyssa back. I never would have thought she'd head toward Scotland. Fancy that, because it does make sense. Perhaps I should have talked to my daughter more about her past. Then she wouldn't have romanticized it. Here, Parker, pay the man so he can be on his way."

Considering Ian dismissed, he turned back to his daughter. "You've had quite an adventure, Lyssa, although you don't look too much the worse for wear." He ran a critical eye over her person and added, "Well, you could be cleaned up some. And this costume you have on? Where the devil was your maid?"

"Missing," Ian answered for her. Parker had taken a purse of coins from his jacket and held it out to Ian, but he didn't take it. Instead, he said, "I found your daughter a day over the Scottish border about ten days ago—"

"Ten days ago?" Harrell asked. "Why did it take you so long to return her?" There was a father's steel in his voice.

"Because I discovered I'd been trailed by a party of men who attempted to kill your daughter by shooting at her twice, setting the wagon she was in on fire, and chasing us through the woods. Later, one of those same men nearly did us in at Amleth Hall."

Ian watched Mrs. Harrell's face as he spoke. She registered shock and then concern. He could have sworn all of this was news to her.

"The man leading the villains was named Fielder," Lyssa said, finding her voice. She stood. "He knew a great deal about us, Papa. Mr. Campion protected me and we decided it was best we continue on to Amleth Hall with the hopes the Davidsons would help us."

"They are the devil's own kin," Harrell said.

"I know that now, Papa," she agreed quietly. "Ramsey, my cousin, gave Fielder shelter. His plan was to marry me for my fortune and then let Fielder kill me and Mr. Campion."

"Dear God," Harrell said. "Who would have wanted to murder you?"

Lyssa pressed her lips together. The frown line formed between her eyes and Ian took another step forward, ready to say all—but she held up her hand to stave him off, a signal that this was hers.

"My stepmother," she said. There was no victory in her voice, only sadness.

"Frances?" Harrell said in disbelief.

"Not I!" she quickly objected, rising to her feet. "Lyssa, I would not hurt you!"

Lyssa shook her head. "I don't accuse you lightly. I heard the truth of those words from Fielder's mouth."

"But why would I do such a thing, Lyssa?" her stepmother demanded.

"I don't know," Lyssa admitted. "Not any longer. I thought at first you would do it for your child so he would inherit all. Or perhaps you were jealous of my father and I. Whatever, I don't know anymore."

Mrs. Harrell turned to her husband. "Dunmore, I had nothing to do with a plot to kill Lyssa. I have no reason to."

And Ian believed her. Harrell wasn't certain. The information was too new, too fresh for him to accept or deny.

Lyssa appeared heartsick over the whole matter. Only Grossett seemed ill at ease. He glanced at his mother, who met his gaze with a level one of her own.

"But I didn't do anything!" Mrs. Harrell protested. "Bring this Fielder here so I can confront him."

"I can't," Ian answered. He looked to Grossett's mother and said, "He's dead."

Now her expression changed—and Ian knew his hunch was correct. "You wouldn't know a man named Fielder, would you, Viscount Grossett?"

His verbal jab scored a hit. Grossett paled and turned to his mother. Ian waited for them to deny any knowledge. He was surprised when, sweat forming on his brow, the viscount said quietly, "A balding man. Tall. Thin. He has a dark voice."

"That's him," Lyssa answered.

Grossett said, "Mother, you wouldn't . . . ?"

"I *would*," she replied and her chin came up as if daring him to criticize her.

"What is going on here?" Harrell demanded.

Neither the viscount nor his mother spoke, so Ian said, "I believe his lordship's mother may have attempted to murder your daughter."

"Why?" Grossett asked his mother, the single word filled with pain. "Why would you do such a thing?"

"I couldn't let you betray your heritage for money," she said simply as if her statement explained all.

"Betray?" Grossett asked. "Mother, have you gone mad? She was our only way out. I can't pay your gambling debts any longer. We're done up."

"I can still get vouchers," Lady Grossett snapped. "All the clubs accept *mine*. But doors will be shut if you marry her."

"No one was pressing you to pay because they were milking me dry!" her son exploded. "You have ruined me with your gambling. There is nothing left, Mother, *nothing left at all*."

"There is our pride!"

"Harrell has pride! He married a duchess!" The words shot out of the viscount as if he'd had this argument before.

"A duchess?" Lady Grossett snorted. "She sold herself to him for merchant money. Nor is she accepted in the best circles, either. Not anymore. People gossip behind her back, and I will not let that happen to us!"

Harrell waved his hands in the air in exasperation. "Will someone tell me what the devil is happening here? And who are you," he demanded of Lady Grossett, "to insult my wife?"

"I would do *anything* to save my son from the likes of you," Lady Grossett returned with ringing tones. "I never approved of this match and have done everything I must to see it broken!"

Her son appeared ready to weep. "Mother, you are ruining us all." He looked to Harrell. "You must ignore her. She's not been well lately. For quite some time actually—"

"Don't humble yourself to him," his mother said disdainfully. "You are Grossett!"

Her son's answer was a frustrated groan. He pleaded now, "Don't send for the magistrate. I'll have her taken away, far from London. She'll not bother Lyssa ever during our marriage."

"You'd still marry her?" his mother demanded even while Harrell frowned.

"I will not let you have my daughter."

Harrell's words were the ones Ian wanted to hear. But Grossett fought back. "Please, I care deeply for Lyssa."

"You care for her money," Harrell said, "and that would have been acceptable, my lord, since I covet your title. But even we *merchants* draw a line at murder."

The lines of Grossett's face hardened. "Oh, no, you will not take her from me!"

"Robert—!" his mother started, but he cut her off.

"Shut up! Shut up, shut up, shut up! I'm the head of this family. *I* make the decisions." He ran a distracted hand through his thinning hair before grasping at a new argument. "Who else do you think will marry your daughter now, Harrell?" he said. "She's been running around Scotland with some Irish bounty hunter completely unchaperoned. Look at her."

Every eye in the room turned to Lyssa.

"She's been had," Grossett accused. "Had by the worst sort who could touch her."

Ian stepped forward, doubled his fist and wiped the smirk off of Grossett's face with one well-placed punch to the mouth.

The bastard dropped like a rock.

Chapter Nineteen

THERE wasn't a sound in the room, until Lady Grossett took one look at her son on the floor and began screaming.

The ever-present Parker did not miss a beat. He opened the door, shoved her ladyship out, and slammed the door firmly.

"Thank you, Parker," Harrell said dryly.

"No problem, sir."

Grossett groaned. "What about him?" Harrell asked.

"If Mr. Campion would help?" Parker suggested.

"I can," Ian said. He picked the viscount up by his coat. Parker opened the door, surprising Lady Grossett in mid-scream. Ian unceremoniously dumped her son at her feet. The door was shut again.

"I suppose we should see her home," Mrs. Harrell said.

"Must we?" her husband asked.

"Yes," she answered regretfully. "We let them ride with us."

"Parker—?"

"I'll have our footman hail a hack, sir." The secretary left the room.

Lyssa, Harrell, the duchess, and Ian were alone. Ian knew the time had come.

As if sensing he was getting ready to speak, Harrell said quickly, "A job well done again, Campion—thank you very much—you are dismissed—"

"I'd like your daughter's hand in marriage."

Ian's words seemed to suck the air out of the room. The duchess arched her brows in surprise; Lyssa tensed. Harrell pretended he hadn't heard him. He turned to his wife. "Are you ready, Frances? Lyssa? We must go."

"No, Papa," Lyssa said, coming to where Ian stood by the door. "I'm not going. Not until you answer Mr. Campion, and I'll warn you now, there is only one answer I want."

Now her father could not pretend. He met Ian's eye. "I'd rather see her in hell than married to the likes of you."

Lyssa staggered as if he'd struck her. The duchess was as surprised. She took a step forward, but Harrell warned her back with an imperial wave. "I know what you are, Campion. You have nothing to give my daughter."

"I don't want anything, Father, save your blessing!"

"You'll not have it," was his even reply. "Now, enough of this nonsense, let us leave."

"I'm not going with you," Lyssa said clearly and firmly—and Ian could have kissed her.

Harrell frowned. "Did I not offer you enough money?" he suggested rhetorically. "Very well, I'll double what I was paying you."

"I don't want money," Ian said quietly.

"Oh, yes, you do," Harrell answered. "You think you've caught the prize. Well, you haven't . . . and let me advise you to leave now."

"No." Ian didn't want to make Harrell angry and, yet, he could not live without Lyssa. "I didn't even take the payment your man wanted to give me earlier. It's not about the money, Mr. Harrell. I love her."

There was a moment of silence and then Harrell started laughing as if a great jest had been told.

"Dunmore . . ." his wife pleaded.

He shook his head. "I could either laugh or applaud. They say the Irish are the best actors. I never believed it until now." He looked at his daughter. "I understand, Lyssa. He's played you well, but enough. Get your money from Parker, Campion, and leave my daughter alone." There was a father's steel behind his voice.

"Father, it isn't him. It's me, too," Lyssa pressed. "He saved my life."

"I understand, and you feel grateful," her father agreed. "But marriage is not the way to show your appreciation. He's using you, Lyssa. He wants your money."

"He hasn't taken any money!" she countered with exasperation.

"Of course not. He wants your inheritance, or are you willing to give that up, too?"

Here was the threat of disinheritance.

Lyssa took a moment, but then said calmly, "I do want my inheritance. And I want your blessing. But I *will* marry this man with or without your permission."

"This man is a scoundrel," her father countered. "A bounder. A bloody Irishman!"

"This man could be the father of the babe I might already be carrying."

Lyssa had struck a deadly blow. Harrell went pale, but then, his features hardened and Ian pulled Lyssa close to his protection. Mrs. Harrell moved forward to stand between the two parties, her expression uncertain and afraid.

"So you did it," Harrell said quietly to Ian. "The thought crossed my mind that you might. After all, you are an ambitious man."

"I'm also an honorable one," Ian said and, ignoring Harrell's snort of disbelief, said, "Claiming your daughter was not my intention."

"It wasn't?" Harrell mocked. "You truly expect me to believe you?"

Lyssa made an impatient sound. "Oh, Father, don't pretend to be so noble. You were willing to sell me for a title."

"I was using your dowry to buy you security!" Harrell lashed out. "I wanted you safe and with all the trappings of respect I could give you and your children. And what do you do? You bed a bloody nobody. He has nothing, Lyssa. There are those who would even spit on his name."

"He's the man I love," she returned, angry tears in her eyes, and Ian had had enough.

He took her hand. "Come, let's leave." He didn't even want the payment promised because he knew anything he received, Harrell would twist for his own purposes.

And bless her, Lyssa was willing to come with him. Her love was true. Ian opened the door and they would have left save for Harrell's saying, "Wait!"

He stopped. He did not want to part with her father as enemies.

Pirate Harrell said, "I need to talk to you alone, Campion. Lyssa, you and Frances go out to the coach."

"I'm staying here," Lyssa said.

"No," her father answered. "Campion and I need to speak honestly with each other. If when I'm done, he is still determined to take you from me, then I'll let you go with my blessing."

"You would?" Lyssa questioned.

"I would."

She hesitated in indecision. Ian said, "Go. It will be fine."

The worried line appeared on her brow, and he smiled. "Wouldn't we rather have his blessing?"

"Yes," she agreed fervently.

"Then, let me hear what he has to say. Perhaps I can convince him I have your best interests at heart."

She turned back to her father. "I love you, Papa, and I love him." Her statement was simple and powerful. She opened the door and left. The duchess followed silently behind after one worried glance at her husband.

Harrell waited until the door was shut behind them. He moved to the window and watched until the women had arrived to stand by the coach. He closed the curtain.

"You have a nephew?"

The question surprised Ian. Before he could answer, Harrell said, "Liam is his name. Smart lad. Young, able, a bit wild."

"He can be all those things," Ian returned tightly.

Harrell hummed an agreement. "He was also in with a bad crowd when we first met, was he not?"

"You'd not harm a child."

"I will do what I must to protect my family," Harrell replied plainly. "Parker had a good conversation with Liam. He learned quite a bit. Oh, don't worry, your nephew is safe in the cottage in Chelsea where you stashed them. You see, Campion, I do admire you. You protect your family and I have no doubt you would do everything you could for Lyssa."

"I love her."

"I'm certain you do."

"But?" Ian prompted.

"I've already said the but. You are a wanted man."

Ian went very still.

"Liam thinks it is very exciting," Harrell confided.

"Liam doesn't know what he is talking about," Ian contradicted.

"He does on this matter." Harrell sat on the edge of the table in front of the window. "I had Parker check the matter through. We could even collect the bounty for you."

"It doesn't make any difference what you do," Ian said, choosing his words carefully. "Lyssa is mine."

"Yes," Harrell agreed, his expression losing its false pleasantness. "I'm not pleased you took her but it isn't a matter that can't be overcome."

"By what means? Another Grossett?"

"By many other means." Harrell stood. "Here's what I'm offering. You leave Lyssa and I will pay you handsomely—"

"I don't want the money."

"You are the only man in London who doesn't then. But this isn't about only you. There are your sisters and their children to think about."

"Are you blackmailing me?"

"Yes! And let me assure you, Mr. Campion, you are very blackmailable." His features set, Harrell continued, "We both know your sisters and their children would starve without you, or even worse. Instead, I'm offering you passage to wherever you *and your family* want to go, and more money than your poor Irish brain could ever have thought possible."

"And if I don't take your offer?" Ian asked.

"I'll destroy you. I'll turn you in to the authorities. You might even be hanged. It depends on how irritated we are with the Irish right now and whether the gin crowd needs a show. At best, you'll be transported. Six months in the belly of a merchantman bound for Australia, being treated little better than a slave. Your family can go with you. After all, they harbored you."

There it was, the true threat.

"So what will it be, Campion? How far are you willing to go with this little 'love' charade?"

Anger settled cold and hard within Ian. Here it was, one more bloody injustice, and he had no choice. "She'll hate you for this."

"I can live with that," Harrell answered. "I can't live with her married to you."

"Because I'm Irish?"

"Because you don't have enough and never will."

Ian shook his head. "You had nothing at one time."

"You're not me," was the short response.

And that was it. Ian knew he had no choice. He could not see Maeve or the boys braving the brutal trip to Australia for his sake. The adults might make the trip, but not the littlest ones. And his sisters could not part with their children. They would not leave them behind.

He came to a hard decision. "You're wrong, you know," he told Harrell. "I'm more like you than is comfortable. Where do I get the money?"

Lyssa watched her father walk out of the inn followed by Parker, and knew Ian had left.

Her father climbed into the coach, taking the seat across from her and her stepmother. He knocked on the roof, a signal for the driver to go.

The duchess took her hand in silent commiseration.

"He couldn't be gone," Lyssa said calmly, "not without you doing something terrible."

"I didn't do anything 'terrible,'" her father answered without looking at her. "We both decided his leaving was what was best for you."

"He wouldn't leave me," she repeated.

"He did," her father said.

Her heart wanted to deny the truth of his words, while her mind knew he did not lie. Her father was too calm, too satisfied. Parker was quiet, his expression unusually somber.

Lyssa's first urge was to scream, to rant and to rave—but then she sensed they braced themselves for just that possibility.

Instead, she took pride and courage in hand. "What if I'm carrying his baby?"

"Then we shall see what could be done," her father said.

"Dunmore," the duchess said. "Give her something."

Her father didn't pretend to not understand. He pinned Lyssa with his sharp green eyes so much like her own. "He loved you," he said.

And to Lyssa's surprise, that was enough.

She also sensed her father was not completely pleased by his own actions. Perhaps because she did not react the way he may have anticipated. She was stronger now. More certain of herself. More of a woman.

If she did carry Ian's child, she'd not let anyone take him from her. She would have to find a way to protect the child. After all, the world all seemed to come down to money—and what value was there to being worth one's weight in gold if one couldn't throw that weight around when necessary?

They were almost home when she said, "I saw Mama's portrait. The one her father had done and had sent out to prospective suitors."

A muscle tightened in her father's jaw and there was a sadness in his eyes. "She was very beautiful, wasn't she?"

Lyssa noticed he didn't tack on a caveat such as "She was beautiful when she was *young*." To her father and to herself, her mother would always be beautiful. But the freshness of youth and good health had been a wonderful thing to see upon her mother's face.

"As lovely as my stepmother," Lyssa agreed, the words coming from her heart, and she knew she'd surprised the duchess. Pleasantly surprised her. "But with the illness, I'd forgotten so much about Mama."

"Yes," her father echoed and turned his face to look out the window at the passing scenery.

She listened to the wheels turn against the cobblestones. "I won't forget him, Father."

"I know," was the answer. "I know.

Lyssa's homecoming was not comfortable. What she'd once taken for granted now seemed ostentatious. She knew she would grow accustomed to it again . . . she didn't want to, but it would happen.

Her first night in a feather bed, she could not sleep. She tossed and turned, her body aching for Ian.

Finally she wrapped herself in her raggedy plaid and laid on the carpeted floor. Sleep didn't come until she pretended she was in Ian's arms.

For the next two days, the duchess did her best to try and distract her. Lyssa felt guilty for not having realized before how generous and kind her stepmother was.

She saw her father at midday and then for supper. They were both quiet, having little to say to each other.

After supper on the evening of the second day, he sought her out in the sunroom, where she had wandered to be alone for a moment. Night had fallen and the room was dark save for the glow of her single candle.

"Lyssa?"

She turned toward him in the chair she was sitting in. "Yes, Papa."

"I have a gift for you."

She unwrapped the package and found a book of poems by Lord Byron.

"Thank you," she said.

"I know you need something to occupy your mind. After all, your other books were destroyed in that fire and Lord Byron was one of your favorites."

She nodded without enthusiasm and opened the book. The words leapt out to her from the page and she read aloud,

I would I were a careless child
Still dwelling in my highland cave
Or roaming through the dusky wild
Or bounding o'er the dark blue wave—

Her voice broke as tears stung her eyes. She shut the book. She took a moment to compose herself before asking, "Has he left London for good yet?"

She didn't expect him to truly answer her, so his reply caught off guard. "He left on the first tide. Parker and I didn't give him much time."

No, she had assumed they wouldn't. "Parker can be very efficient. Where did you send him?"

"To a place of his choosing."

"Maryland?" she guessed.

Her father frowned. "How did you know?"

"It is where we both would have gone." She hugged the book to her chest.

Coming around to sit on the footstool in front of her, her father placed his hands gently on her arms. "The ship is gone, Lyssa. He can't come back. He and I agreed." He paused and then said, "I know I may seem harsh to you, but someday you will understand."

"I might." She shook her head. "Would mother have?"

"Unfair, Lyssa."

"No, Papa, I'm being honest. At least tell me you paid him well?"

Her father snorted. "I paid him his weight in gold," he said and for the first time since Ian's leaving she wanted to smile.

"Good. He earned it." She kissed him on the cheek. "Thank you, Papa." She rose, forcing him to sit back, and started for the door.

His voice stopped her. "Lyssa, I am sorry."

"No, you aren't," she replied without heat. "But perhaps all parents think they know what is best."

She didn't wait for his response but left to go to her lonely room.

The Davidson tartan was folded neatly at the

foot of the bed. She pulled the pins from her hair to set it free and put on her nightdress. Wrapping her plaid around her, she sat in a reading chair by the window. Candlelight was not the best to read by, but she had no choice. She needed to read the rest of the poem and savor its haunting words.

Someday she'd feel complete again. But right now, it was as if she'd lost half her soul, half her conscience, half her reason for being.

So she could be excused if when she saw Ian's face framed in the branches of the tree some two feet outside her dark window, her first thought was she must be dreaming—until he reached to knock on the glass pane and almost fell out of the tree.

Chapter Twenty

"LYSSA, open the window. Let me in."

It *was* Ian. She hadn't made him up out of dashed dreams and lost hopes.

Lyssa bounced out of the chair and raised the sash. "Ian." She said his name like a blessing.

"Aye, and I'm not good at climbing. Nor do I like heights." He reached for her window ledge. The branch shook under his weight. "And this bloody branch wasn't made to hold my weight."

"Be careful," she warned.

"I'm trying," he promised just as a crack sounded. He leaped the distance and practically fell into her arms, taking both of them to the carpeted floor.

Lyssa hugged him close and drew in a deep breath, reveling in the scent of warm male and fresh air—Ian's scent. "What are you doing here?" she asked happily. "You are supposed to be on your way across an ocean."

He brushed her nose with his. "I can't leave without you."

Struggling to make sense of everything, Lyssa asked, "What of your sisters and their children?" Ian had started nibbling the tender skin beneath her chin. She placed a hand on each side of his face and made him look at her. "That's how my father made you do his bidding, isn't it? He threatened your family."

"It is—"

"I thought as much. His behavior goes beyond being misguided or bullying. To threaten your sisters and their children is reprehensible. No wonder he's been acting so guilty."

"Well, it's good to know he has a conscience," Ian observed dryly.

"He'll have more than a conscience when I'm through with him," she flashed back, her temper rising. She would have scrambled to her feet and gone in search of him, except Ian rolled her over on top of him and held her still.

"Lyssa, listen to me. Fiona and Janet are on the ship and they're safe. And you and I must hurry if we are to catch up with them." He sat up so that her legs cradled his ribs. He kissed her nose. "So are you coming, Lyssa? Are you ready for an adventure the likes of which you will never have again?"

"You want me to go with you?" she repeated dumbly, scarcely believing her good fortune.

"I told you I wouldn't leave without you," he said somberly. "I would never leave you behind."

And he kissed her. Fully, completely, thoroughly.

He drew back. "You're crying?"

Lyssa put her arms around his neck, buried her face in his shoulder, and sobbed. She needed at least a good minute of this before she confessed, "I didn't know if I could live without ever kissing you again. I felt as if something inside of me was broken and would never be repaired. And now, here you are and you feel so good and smell so good and kiss so—"

Ian kissed her again, gently, brushing her curls back from her face. When the kiss broke off, he whispered, "I want to kiss you like that every morning and every night for the rest of our lives."

She could have melted right on the spot.

However, Ian had other plans. "Quick, let's get going, because if your father finds me here, we'll both be done up."

He didn't have to tell her twice. She scrambled to her feet and started changing into a simple day dress. "What I need are breeches," she said, her head in her wardrobe as she fetched her well-broken shoes. "If I had breeches, I could climb, I could ride."

"You'd be a Mistress of Running Away," he agreed.

"I'm serious."

He held up his hands. "I don't doubt one word you've said. I've learned my lesson."

She stopped in the act of putting her foot in her shoe. "I love you," she said fiercely.

Pride shone in his eyes. "And I love you. Now come, let's hurry."

"Can I take anything else?"

"Whatever you think we can carry down the tree."

Lyssa pulled up short. "We're going to climb down the tree? On the branch your weight just broke?"

"I don't have another plan," he admitted candidly. "Between packing my sisters and the children and getting them and the horses on the ship, I've been a bit busy."

In two steps she stood before him. She gave him a hard buss on the mouth. "I'm pleased you could think of me."

"I could think of little else," he answered, and her heart soared. Ian was here and all would be right in the world. They would make it out this night. Anything was possible.

Lyssa stuffed three dresses in a small portmanteau, grabbed her hairbrush, a length of ribbon, tooth powder, and scented soap and she was ready to go—until her eye fell on the book her father had given earlier. It was a slender volume and would not take up much room.

"Another book, Lyssa?" he asked quietly.

"My father gave it to me to start my new collection."

"I hope it isn't Homer's *Odyssey*." Ian took the book from her hand and opened it to the title page. "Byron. I should have known." He closed the book and handed it back to her.

"Oh, but you should read this poem," she said and would have reopened the book to share it with him, except for his common sense.

"Lyssa, we can read on the ship. In fact, we can do a good number of interesting things on the ship—like invent our own poetry."

For a second, the images his suggestion conjured caught her spellbound, until he prompted, "Pack the book, Lyssa."

With a shake of her head, she came to her senses, tucked the book in the bag and pronounced herself ready just as a soft knock sounded on the door.

Both Lyssa and Ian froze.

"Lyssa, are you asleep yet?" came her stepmother's voice.

Lyssa could not answer. She'd lost her voice and perhaps because she did not say anything, the door slowly opened.

"Lyssa?" The duchess looked to the bed, and seeing it empty lifted her gaze until she saw Lyssa standing beside Ian. "Lyssa," she whispered in horror. "What are you doing?"

"I'm leaving." She touched Ian's arm. "He's

come for me and I must go. Tell Father I will be fine."

"I don't know . . . ?"

"Please, Frances. I won't be happy unless I'm with him." This was the first time Lyssa had used her stepmother's Christian name. She'd asked Lyssa to use it years ago when she and Lyssa's father had married, but Lyssa had stubbornly refused. Now Lyssa was embarrassed by her childish behavior.

The use of her name worked like a talisman on the duchess. She moved into the room, cradling the weight of her pregnant stomach with one arm. "Have you thought this through?"

"I knew what I wanted before I stepped foot back in London," Lyssa answered. "He's everything to me."

"I'll take care of her," Ian promised. "She'll be safe." Frances frowned. "Please, we belong together," he said.

It was his final plea that softened her. "Yes, you do," she agreed softly. "And I haven't seen anything. I wasn't even here."

She backed away, ready to leave, but the door suddenly flew open, Lyssa's father stood there.

Lyssa gave a frightened cry, but Ian seemed completely unafraid.

"What the devil are you doing here?" her father said. "You should be on a ship for America!"

"I could never leave without her."

"We had a bargain." Her father opened the door so the light from the hallway lanterns flowed into the room.

"No, you gave orders," Ian corrected. "And I did leave on the tide, but I found I forgot something very important to me and I've returned to claim her."

"I'll not let you have her."

Lyssa dared to defy him. "What will you do, Father, have him horsewhipped?"

Her soft words gave her father a start. He stared at her as if truly seeing her for the first time and realizing she was all grown up. "Where did you hear about that?"

"Ramsey Davidson bragged about it, Father. He laughed as he told the story, but I know that one incident was enough to drive you to best them."

"It was," he agreed. "I made something of myself and for your mother and what are they?"

"Nothing," Lyssa said quietly.

"You're right, lass," and for the first time in a long while, she heard the hint of a proud brogue in his voice.

But then, his expression changed. His eyes narrowed. "Don't compare us, Lyssa. I'm nothing like this Irish upstart." Before she realized what could happen, he charged Ian, his fists doubled. His actions were so out of character, both Lyssa and her stepmother were caught off guard.

To his credit, Ian moved back. He could have

settled the matter with one blow. She'd witnessed him doing it more than once. Instead, he allowed Lyssa and Frances the time to put themselves between the two men.

"Dunmore, stop this," Frances ordered sharply and to Lyssa's surprise, her father listened, perhaps because of the baby she carried, perhaps because of something else.

"You're taking leave of your senses," she told him. "It's done. Lyssa is going and you will not stop her."

Her father looked to his wife. "But we'll not see her again."

The tone of his voice revealed a depth of pain Lyssa had not imagined. Her victory turned bittersweet.

Frances took her husband's hands. "She's no longer yours, darling. It's the way of the world and the way it must be. You have the child and it needs you, but then it must go and create its own life. You can't keep her forever . . . and she loves him. Loves him enough to defy all wisdom and convention. Just like I love you."

"She's my last link to Isobel."

"I know," Frances said with the understanding only a woman who truly loves her husband can give. "But Isobel would want it this way, too."

Slowly, her father moved to where Lyssa stood with Ian's arms around her and she realized with startling clarity that he'd been younger than she was now when he'd run away with her mother.

"He's Catholic." His accusation had no bluster, but a quiet sense of resignation.

"He doesn't practice," she said.

Her father's frown deepened. "But someday, when you have children, he will want his church."

"I love him, Father. I respect him. We will find some agreement, some middle ground. Certainly, if two people care as much for each other as we do, God can only be pleased."

For a second, her father appeared ready to protest again, but then Frances said, "Dunmore, it is time."

In his sad acceptance of what was to be, her father appeared to age right before her eyes. Frances touched him on the shoulder and he covered her hand with his. Now Lyssa was glad her step-mother was in their lives. She would protect and care for Lyssa's father.

"Don't let any harm come to her," her father said to Ian.

"None will," Ian swore.

"Then go," he said with a curt motion of his head.

Lyssa was not about to leave him like this. She left Ian's arms and crossed to her father to hug him one last time. He smelled of lemon oil and spice. His shoulders were still strong and she knew he would be fine . . . but it didn't make the parting easier. "I shall think of you every day. And we shall see each other again. I will want to see my half brother." She kissed his cheek and then kissed Frances, too. "Thank you," she murmured before facing the man she loved. "Let's use the door. I have no desire to climb on that tree branch you cracked."

Her change of subject seemed to spark life in her father. "He came in the window?"

Lyssa nodded. "It was a very dramatic entrance."

"Well, leave it to the Irish," her father said, but there was no longer anger in his words.

Ian picked up her portmanteau and held out his hand. Lyssa placed hers in his and together, they left the room. She didn't even need to look back.

As they went down the stairs, he said, "There is a sloop waiting for us. We should reach the ship by tomorrow morning."

She nodded, stepped down to the landing and found Parker waiting there. For a moment, their three gazes met. Lyssa spoke first. "Good-bye, Parker. Please take care of Papa and my step-mother."

"I will, Miss Harrell." He looked to Ian. "Obviously, I'm not the only one who knows how to make swift arrangements."

"No, you're not," Ian agreed and reached to open the front door.

"Good luck, Mr. Campion," Parker said and Ian grinned.

They were free.

The sloop was waiting exactly as Ian had said it would. As they set sail, Lyssa and Ian stood at the prow, his arms around her waist, watching night-darkened London drift away. The wind through her hair was exciting and after days of sadness her spirits soared.

He held up his hand. In his finger was a card folded and worn from being carried from one end of the kingdom to another. The Knight of Swords. She was surprised he had it, having assumed she had lost it during their sojourn in the bothy.

"Are you ready for an adventure?" he whispered.

"Yes," she agreed, taking the card from him.

"Then follow me," he said and he led her to his private quarters . . . and it was a very fine adventure indeed.

Epilogue

Ian thought he'd go to pieces the night he and Lyssa's first child was born.

It was storming, a powerful lightning and thunderstorm that shook the earth. One of many things they'd liked about their new country were the magnificent storms, and of course, the baby would choose the occasion of one to make its first appearance in the world.

Fiona and Janet took matters in hand, giving Liam strict orders to keep his uncle occupied. "No matter what, don't let him enter the birthing room," Janet had said.

"I won't," Liam had promised and was true to his word. He blocked the door with the tenacity of a Beefeater.

The lad had taken to his new surroundings. Of course, the horses helped. After all, they were in his blood, and where he used to use his speed to serve as lookout for others or to filch an occasional fob chain for himself, he now dreamed of racing.

Irish Fortune had just won his first race, bringing in a good purse. Ian knew Liam hoped to go along when he took Fortune to New Jersey next month for another race.

Racing in the United States was not as disciplined as in Britain, or the stakes as high, but Ian thought they could do well, and after all, horse breeding was horse breeding. Given a few more wins, Fortune would be in demand.

Ian had even started reading the law again and hoped to soon be called before the Maryland bar. Here, he could practice all aspects of law.

Maeve and Johnny were adjusting well, too. But then children always adapted easily.

For a time, Ian had worried about Fiona and Janet. They suffered occasional bouts of homesickness although that might soon change. Their neighbor, a fine young farmer named Mr. Cartwright, had begun courting Fiona, and several gentlemen in the area had asked to pay their respects to Janet. She said she wasn't ready yet, but the time was coming.

At that moment, from the other side of the door, Lyssa shouted his name, the sound ending with a soft moan that tore at Ian's heart.

He stopped his pacing outside her door. They'd just finished the house and it smelled of new lumber and paint. Johnny and Maeve had been sitting on the staircase, waiting with the rest of them. Maeve now rose and ran over to Ian to give him a commiserating hug.

"She doesn't sound happy with you," Liam said.

Ian sank down into a chair, pulling Maeve into his lap. "I don't think she is."

"She isn't," Janet cheerily confirmed as she ran out of the room, having overheard what they'd said. She patted her children on their heads, disappeared a moment into her own room, and then came back carrying clean rags.

"Will she be all right?" Ian asked.

"Once this baby is born," Janet promised and disappeared back into the room again, shutting the door firmly behind her.

Ian buried his face in his hands just as Lyssa cried out again and again, this time with more urgency. He didn't think he could stand listening to her in such pain. Dear God, he'd never touch her again, not if it could cause her so much misery.

Liam put a manly hand on his uncle's shoulder and even Johnny, his expression serious, moved to hook an arm around Ian's shoulders.

"Don't you wish this was over?" Maeve asked. She ran her hand along Ian's jaw and then drew back. "You're scratchy. Will you scratch the baby?"

Ian rubbed his hand across his face and agreed. He'd shave. That's what he could do. And mayhap when he was done, the baby would be born.

As it was, he took no more than one step, when he heard the sound of a baby's cry—and no sound had ever been sweeter.

Finally Janet opened the door and Ian flew through, anxious to see his wife and be reassured she was fine.

In the feathered recesses of the bed he'd built for them with his own hands, Lyssa gave him a tired, satisfied smile. Her curls were every which way and, in spite of her white embroidered nightdress, she looked like she'd been in a fight.

He didn't think he'd ever seen her more beautiful.

"Did you see him?" Lyssa asked.

"Him?" Ian turned just as Fiona walked over and placed a red-faced, angry-with-the-world infant in his arms.

"Congratulations, brother."

Liam and Johnny hollered liked wild men and danced around the room. They'd wanted a boy. Maeve didn't even pout, but pushed forward to see the baby.

Stunned at the wee marvel in his arms, Ian sat on the edge of the bed. Lyssa reached up and pulled him to her side so she could see her baby's face.

"Isn't he a miracle?" she whispered, touching his tiny fingers.

"Perfect," Ian agreed. Holding his son was a revelation . . . and he discovered that settled deep within him now was the peace that had eluded him since his exile from Dublin.

His life had come full circle.

He glanced up at the crucifix on the bedpost

that had been in his family for generations. Lyssa had placed it there the day he'd finished building the bed. He still didn't practice, but it reminded him of his heritage, of his family. He knew that someday he would make his peace with the Church. He must. He had to give his son tradition.

Lyssa reached up and ran her fingers lightly across the baby's downy head. "His name?" she asked.

"Daniel. If you agree," he added diplomatically. "It was my father's name. Daniel Dunmore Campion."

Her smile was all the approval he needed. "Daniel," she repeated. "A good, strong name. And what would you give me for such a fine baby?" Lyssa whispered, her voice full of pride.

"Your weight in gold," he answered. "Your weight in gold."

Acknowledgments

$\mathcal{W}$HAT is the allure of the Irish hero?

There is something strong, passionate, poetically romantic, and incredibly charming about these men. Of course, those of us who are married to them have the opportunity to see a different side.

Thank God for the gift of laughter!

I enjoyed creating the character of Ian Campion. I received help from many sources along the way and would be remiss if I did not express my appreciation.

First, my gratitude goes to my editor, Lucia Macro, who has honed the use of that four-letter word "more" to a fine art as any top editor should.

Her push set me off on a wonderful journey in search for answers to Ian's background via my good friend Erin McGlynn. Her Irish connections opened many doors for me, including those of Dr. Rory O'Hanlon, TD, Ceann Comhairle of Dáil Éireann; and Colette Fleming, Private Secretary to the Ceann Comhairle. Collette's enthusiastic help led me to Brendan O'Donoghue, Director of the National Library of Ireland and also its Keeper of Collections, Dónall Ó Luanaigh. For those of my readers who enjoy Irish history, Mr. Ó Luanaigh gave me a fine reading list you may find of interest. I shall post it on my website (*www.cathymaxwell.com*).

I am also indebted to Breege McGrath, Executive Officer, Communications Office, and Mary McGetrick, both of Trinity College Dublin. Their aid in answering my initial questions was invaluable.

The "key" to what I needed came, surprisingly, from close to home. My neighbors Daniel and Tricia Ennis have helped me before and did so again. I discovered why the name Daniel O'Connell came so readily to Danny's lips when I learned a monument stands to O'Connell in Ennis. Seems only right Danny should know his name well. Thank you.

I also benefited from the input of fellow writers Mary Jo Putney, Mary Burton, and Pamela Gagné. I am wealthy in my friends.

And finally, I'm pleased to salute my new local resource, Fred Lamb, Antique Arms Consultant, here in beautiful Ashland, Virginia. Fred showed extraordinary patience while answering *all* my questions. (I'll be out to fire that musket soon, Fred. Just one more deadline to get out of the way.)

If there are any errors in my interpretation of information given to me by those above, the fault is mine alone.

Cathy Maxwell
Midlothian, Virginia
September 12, 2002

OH! THE SCANDAL!

A runaway heiress, a letter that was never meant to be sent . . .
A celebrity in disguise, a womanizing duke . . .
There are *such* goings on in the Avon Romance Superleaders. . . .
It's as shocking as the headlines you read in the gossip columns!

But there is much more than mere scandal; there is love—sometimes unexpected, sometimes unpredictable . . . and always *passionate! These new love stories are created by the best and brightest voices—Cathy Maxwell, Patti Berg, Eloisa James—and there is one of the most beloved romances ever, as created by Laura Kinsale.*

So don't miss the scandal, the sizzle . . . and the chance to read about some truly handsome men!

WAYWARD HEIRESS BOLTS TO SCOTLAND FACES RUIN IN EYES OF SOCIETY!

"I'm furious!" states her father. "I've arranged a perfectly good match for her, and the ungrateful chit repays me by doing this!"

In *New York Times* bestselling author Cathy Maxwell's *Adventures of a Scottish Heiress*, Miss Harrell takes one look at her proposed husband and runs as fast as she can—to Scotland and the protection of her mother's family. But before she reaches the border she's tracked down by Ian Campion—a powerful soldier-turned-mercenary hired by her father to haul her home. But before he can get her back to London, the two begin a romantic adventure they never expected . . .

It was Abrams who broke the somberness of the moment. "Let us not be too grim, eh?" he said. He rose, offering his wife a hand up as he did so. "The future can wait until the morrow. Tonight, I need my sleep."

Madame nodded. "You are right, my son, and very wise. Come, Viveka. You will dream tonight and, in the morning, tell me every detail. Then perhaps we shall know more."

"I don't know if I'll be able to sleep," Lyssa answered.

"Keep the card close," Duci advised. "Your Knight will protect you."

She said the words in earnest and yet they sounded strange, because, for a moment, it had been the Knight that had frightened Lyssa. Her uncertainties dissipating, Lyssa laughed at her own gullibility. Neither Reverend Billows nor her father would be pleased.

Madame rose. The Gypsy gathered the cards while her

husband put away the folding chair and the reading table. No one seemed to notice that Lyssa still had the Knight of Swords. She stole a look at it and then turned to secretly tuck it into her bodice—

And that is when *he* appeared.

He stepped out of the darkness into the waning firelight, as if appearing out of nowhere.

For a second, Lyssa thought her eyes deceived her. No man could be so tall, so broad of shoulders. Smoke from the fire swirled around his hard-muscled legs. His dark hair was overlong and he wore a coat the color of cobalt with a scarf wrapped around his neck in a careless fashion that would have done any dandy proud. His leather breeches had seen better days and molded themselves to his thighs like gloves. A pistol was stuck in his belt and his eyes beneath the brim of his hat were those of a man who had seen too much.

Here was her Knight come to life.

He spoke. "Miss Harrell?" His voice rumbled from a source deep within. It was the voice of command.

Lyssa lifted her chin, all too aware that her knees were shaking. "What do you want?"

The stranger smiled, the expression one of grim satisfaction. "I'm from your father. He wants you home."

Ian was well pleased with himself. His entrance had been perfect—especially his waiting until *after* the card-reading mumbo jumbo. At the sight of him, the self-styled "Gypsies" turned tail and scattered off into the woods. They knew the game was over. But best of all, the headstrong Miss Harrell stared up at him as if he were the devil incarnate.

Good.

This task was turning out to be easier than he'd anticipated.

With a coin slipped here and there in the dark corners of London, he'd learned of a wealthy young woman who had hired some "Gypsies" to transport her to Scotland. Supposedly, the heiress was to stay hidden in the wagon, but after a time, she had felt safe enough to show herself along the road and thus became very easy to track. More than one person, upon seeing the miniature, told Ian that the young lady's red hair was a hard thing to forget—especially among dark-haired Gypsies.

Now he understood why they had felt that way. Here in the glowing embers of the fire, the rich, vibrant dark red of Miss Harrell's hair with its hint of gold gleamed with a life of its own. She wore it pulled back and loose in a riotous tumble of curls that fell well past her shoulders. It was a wonder she could go anyplace in Britain without being recognized.

And her clothing would catch anyone's eye. It was as if she were an opera dancer dressed for the role of "Gypsy" . . . except the cut and cloth of her costume was of the finest stuff. The green superfine wool of her full gypsy skirt swayed with her every movement. Her fashionably low white muslin blouse was cinched at the waist with a black laced belt and served to emphasize the full swell of her breasts. She must have had some sense of modesty, because she demurely topped off the outfit with a shawl of plaid that she wore proudly over one shoulder.

It was a wonder she didn't have hoops in her ears.

Her awestruck silence was short-lived. She tossed back her curls, ignored his hand, and announced, "I'm not going with you."

"Yes, you are," Ian countered reasonably. "Your father is paying me a great deal of money to see you home safe, and see you home safe I will. Now come along. Your maid is waiting at an inn down the road with decent clothes for you to wear."

Her straight brows, so much like her father's, snapped together in angry suspicion. "You're Irish."

Ian's insides tightened. Bloody little snob. But he kept his patience. "Aye, I am," he said, letting the brogue he usually took pains to avoid grow heavier. "One of them and proud of it."

She straightened to her full height. She was taller than he had anticipated and regal in her bearing. Pride radiated from every pore. A fitting daughter to Pirate Harrell. "I don't believe you are from my father. *He* would *never* hire an Irishman."

"Well, he hired *me*," Ian replied flatly, dropping the exaggerated brogue. He rested a hand on the strap of the knapsack flung over one shoulder. "The others couldn't find you. I have. Now, are you going to cooperate with me, Miss Harrell, or shall we do this the hard way? In case you are wondering, your father wants you home by any means *I* deem necessary."

Her eyes flashed golden in the firelight like two jewels. "You wouldn't lay a finger on me."

"I said 'by any means I deem necessary.' If I must hog-tie and carry you out of here, I shall."

Obviously, no one had ever spoken this plainly to Miss Harrell before in her life. Her expression was the same one he imagined she'd use if he'd stomped on her toes. The color rose to her cheeks with her temper. "You will not. Abrams and my other Gypsy friends will come to my rescue. Won't you, Abrams?" she asked, lifting her voice so that it would carry in the night.

But there was no reply save for the crackling of green wood in the fire and the rustle of the wind in the trees.

"Abrams won't," Ian corrected kindly, "because, first, he knows he's not a match for me. I have a bit of a reputation for being handy with my fists, Miss Harrell, and that allows me to do as I please. And secondly, because he's no more a Gypsy than I am. Are you, Charley?" he called to "Abrams."

"Who is Charley?" Miss Harrell demanded.

"Charley Poet, a swindler if ever there was one. You probably think Duci is his wife?"

"She is."

Ian shook his head. "She's his sister. And your fortune-teller is his aunt, 'Mother' Betty, once the owner of a London bawdy house until gambling did her in."

"That's a lie!" a female voice called out to him. "The house was stolen from me!"

"Is that the truth, Betty?" Ian challenged. "Come out of hiding and we'll discuss the matter."

There was no answer.

The color had drained from Miss Harrell's face, but still she held on to her convictions. "I don't believe you. I've been traveling with these people and they are exactly what they say they are—Gypsies. They even speak Romany."

"Charley," Ian said. "Get out here."

A beat of silence and then sheepishly, Charley appeared at the edge of the woods. He was slight of frame, and with a scarf around his head Ian supposed he could pass for a Gypsy. "Tell Miss Harrell the truth," Ian said with exaggerated patience.

THE D——OF J——TO DUEL AT DAWN
NOTORIOUS NOBLEMAN TO
CHOOSE HIS WEAPON
AND DEFEND HIS HONOR

**Friends are concerned that this "brilliant" and
"dangerous" man may tempt fate once too often.**

~~~~~

Who could ever forget the first time they opened the pages
of *New York Times* bestselling author Laura Kinsale's *Flowers
from the Storm*? It's one of the greatest love stories of all
time.

If you haven't yet experienced its powerful magic—and
the exquisite love story of London's most scandalous rake-
hell and the tender woman who saves him—you are in for an
experience you'll never forget.

❦

"How long ago did you lose your sight, Mr. Timms?" he
asked.

Maddy stiffened a little in her chair, surprised by such a
pointed personal question. But her papa only said mildly,
"Many years. Almost . . . fifteen, would it be, Maddy?"

"Eighteen, Papa," she said quietly.

Jervaulx sat relaxed, resting his elbow on the chair arm,
his jaw propped on his fist. "You haven't seen your daughter
since she was a child, then," he murmured. "May I describe
her to you?"

She was unprepared for such a suggestion, or for the light
of interest that dawned in her father's face. "Wilt thou? Wilt
thou indeed?"

Jervaulx gazed at Maddy. As she felt her face growing hot,
his smile turned into that unprincipled grin, and he said, "It

would be my pleasure." He tilted his head, studying her. "We've made her blush already, I fear—a very delicate blush, the color of . . . clouds, I think. The way the mist turns pink at dawn—do you remember what I mean?"

"Yes," her father said seriously.

"Her face is . . . dignified, but not quite stern. Softer than that, but she has a certain way of turning up her chin that might give a man pause. She's taller than you are, but not unbecomingly tall. It's that chin, I think, and a very upright, quiet way she holds herself. It gives her presence. But she only comes to my nose, so . . . she must be a good five inches under six foot one," he said judiciously. "She appears to me to be healthy, not too stout nor thin. In excellent frame."

"Rather like a good milk cow!" Maddy exclaimed.

"And there goes the chin up," Jervaulx said. "She's perhaps a little more the color of a light claret, now that I've provoked her. All the way from her throat to her cheeks—even a little lower than her throat, but she's perfectly pale and soft below that, as far as I can see."

Maddy clapped her hand over the V neck of her gown, suddenly feeling that it must be entirely too low-cut. "Papa—" She looked to her father, but he had his face turned downward and a peculiar smile on his lips.

"Her hair," Jervaulx said, "is tarnished gold where the candlelight touches it, and where it doesn't . . . richer—more like the light through a dark ale as you pour it. She has it braided and coiled around her head. I believe she thinks that it's a plain style, but she doesn't realize the effect. It shows the curve of her neck and her throat, and makes a man think of taking it down and letting it spread out over his hands."

"Thou art unseemly," her father chided in a mild tone.

"My apologies, Mr. Timms. I can hardly help myself. She has a pensive, a very pretty mouth, that doesn't smile overly often." He took a sip of wine. "But then again—let's be fair. I've definitely seen her smile at you, but she hasn't favored me at all. This serious mouth might have been insipid, but instead it goes with the wonderful long lashes that haven't got that silly debutante curl. They're straight, but they're so long and angled down that they shadow her eyes and turn the hazel to gold, and she seems as if she's looking out through them at me. No . . ." He shook his head sadly. "Miss Timms, I regret to tell you that it isn't a spinster effect at all. I've never had a spinster look out beneath her lashes at me the way you do."

WHERE IN THE WORLD IS JULIET BRIDGER? CULT MOVIE STAR-TURNED-NOVELIST LEAVES PARTY SAYING SHE IS "SICK AND TIRED OF CAVIAR!"

"One minute she was enjoying the party,"
said her personal assistant, Nicole, "the next
she was driving off wearing her designer gown."

In Patti Berg's *And Then He Kissed Me* blonde bombshell Juliet Bridger has had it—too many cocktail parties, too many phone calls from her jailbird ex, too many nasty items in the gossip columns. So she disguises her identity and runs . . . straight into the arms of Cole Sheridan, a small town vet with troubles of his own . . .

He moved to the passenger door, rested on his haunches, and peered at the woman through the window. "What's the problem? Out of gas? Engine trouble?"

"I have absolutely no idea." She scooted as far away from the window as humanly possible, as if she thought he might punch his fist through the glass, latch on to her, and drag her out through the jagged shards—then eat her alive. "If you don't mind, I'd appreciate it if you'd go away."

Ungrateful female.

"You gonna fix the car yourself?"

"That's highly unlikely."

"You expecting a miracle? A heavenly light to shine down on this junk heap and make it start?"

"I expect no such thing." She sighed heavily. "Look, you could be the nicest guy on the face of the earth; then again, you could be Ted Bundy's clone."

"I'm neither," Cole bit out, her frostiness and his annoyance getting the better of him.

"Okay, so you're not nice; so you're not a mass murderer, but my dad taught me not to talk to strangers and, believe you me, I've watched enough episodes of *Unsolved Mysteries* and *America's Most Wanted* to understand not to accept help from people I know nothing about. Therefore"—she took a deep breath and let it rush out—"I wish you'd go away."

That would be the smart thing to do. Get the hell home before Nanny #13 walked off the job, but he couldn't leave the woman in the middle of nowhere, alone and stranded. Not in this heat.

"Look, lady, this hasn't been the best of days. My frame of mind sucks, and I'm in a hurry. Trust me, killing you doesn't fit into my schedule."

"All it takes is one quick jab with a knife or an itchy trigger finger and I could be history."

"I haven't got a knife, haven't got a gun, and I'm almost out of patience. If you're out of gas, just say so. You can sit right there, safe and sound behind locked doors, while I siphon some gas out of my truck and put it in your tank."

"The car's not out of gas. It simply backfired and died."

"Considering the lack of attention you've given the thing, I'm not surprised."

Even through her rhinestone glasses, he could see her eyes narrow. "I just bought the *thing* three days ago and before you tell me I got screwed, I already figured that out. Now since you're in a hurry and I'm not"—she attempted to shoo him away with a brush of her hand—"I'll wait for the cops to come by and help me."

Damn fool woman. "This isn't the main road and it isn't traveled all that often. If I leave, you could sit here for a day or two before someone else passes by."

She glared at his unkempt hair, at the stubble on his face, at his white T-shirt covered with God knows what. "I'll take my chances."

"You always this stubborn?"

"I'm cautious."

"Foolish is more—"

"Do you have a cell phone?" she interrupted, holding her thumb to her ear, her little finger to her mouth, as if he were some country bumpkin who needed sign language to understand the word "phone."

"Yeah. Why?"

"Perhaps you could call a tow truck."

"This isn't the big city; it's the middle of nowhere. There's one tow truck in town and it could be hours before Joe can get away from his gas station to help you."

"I'll wait."

"It's gonna be one hundred two degrees by noon. You sit in your car for a couple of hours you just might die."

"I get out of my car, I might die anyway."

He didn't have time for this. "Fine. Suit yourself."

Cole shoved away from the MG. Getting as far away from the crazy woman as he possibly could was the smartest thing to do. As bad as this day had been, he was sure it would get far worse if he stuck around her any longer.

He was just opening the door to his truck when she honked her horn. The squeaky beep sounded like a chicken blowing its nose, and the ghastly noise rang out four times before he turned. The confounded woman wiggled her index finger at him from behind her bug-spattered windshield, beckoning him back.

Shit.

Cole glanced at his watch. He glared at the woman, then, shaking his head, he strolled back toward the car and stared down at the face peering through the window. His jaw had tightened but he managed to bark, "What?"

She smiled. It had to be the prettiest smile he'd seen in his whole miserable life—but it was also the phoniest. "You will call a tow truck, won't you?"

Leave it to a woman to use her feminine wiles to get what she wanted. Leave it to a woman to be a pain in the butt.

LOVE LETTER GOES ASTRAY.
MEMBERS OF THE *TON* ARE AGHAST
AT SUCH IMPROPER DISPLAY OF AFFECTION.

"I never thought Henrietta could inspire such passion,"
said her bosom pal, Lady Esme Rawlings. "Especially from
a man like Simon Darby. He's so cool on the outside, but
clearly there are unseen fires burning there."

~~~

In Eloisa James' *Fool for Love*, Lady Esme Rawlings thinks she
can manage her friends' romances, so she concocts a plan to
have a love letter—proported to be written by the inscrutable
Simon Darby—"accidentally" read aloud at a dinner party.
Now, the only way the reputation of her friend Lady Henrietta can be saved is to marry Mr. Darby . . . quickly.

❦

Slope played his part to perfection. Esme waited until after
the soup had come and gone, and the fish had been eaten. She
kept a sharp eye to make certain that Helene and Rees weren't
going to explode in a cloud of black smoke, because then she
would have to improvise a bit, but besides the fact that Helene
was going to get a stiff neck from looking so quickly away
from her husband, they were both behaving well.

The roast arrived and Esme sent Slope for more wine. She
wanted to make certain that her part of the table was holding
enough liquor to respond instinctively. Mr. Barret-Ducrorq
was ruddy in the face and saying bombastic things about the
Regent, so she thought he was well primed. Henrietta was
pale but hadn't fled the room, and Darby showed every sign
of being utterly desirous of Henrietta. Esme smiled a little to
herself.

Just as she requested, Slope entered holding a silver salver.

Speaking just loud enough to catch the attention of the entire table, he said, "Please excuse me, my lady, but I discovered this letter. It is marked urgent, and feeling some concern that I might have inadvertently delayed the delivery of an important missive, I thought I would convey it immediately."

A little overdone, to Esme's mind. Obviously, Slope was an amateur thespian. She took the note and slit it open.

"Oh, but Slope!" she cried. "This letter is not addressed to me!"

"There was no name on the envelope," Slope said, "so I naturally assumed it was addressed to you, my lady. Shall I redirect the missive?" He hovered at her side.

She had better take over the reins of the performance. Her butler was threatening to upstage her.

"That will be quite all right, Slope," she said. Then she looked up with a glimmering smile. "It doesn't seem to be addressed to anyone. Which means we can read it." She gave a girlish giggle. "I *adore* reading private epistles!"

Only Rees looked utterly bored and kept eating his roast beef.

" 'I do not go for weariness of thee,' " Esme said in a dulcet tone. " 'Nor in the hope the world can show a fitter love for me.' It's a love poem, isn't that sweet?"

"John Donne," Darby said, "and missing the first two words. The poem begins, 'Sweetest love, I do not go for weariness of thee.' "

Esme had trouble restraining her glee. She could not have imagined a comment more indicative of Darby's own authorship. He actually knew the poem in question! She didn't dare look at Henrietta. It was hard enough pretending that she was the slowest reader in all Limpley Stoke.

" 'Never will I find anyone I adore as much as you. Although fate has cruelly separated us, I shall treasure the memory of you in my heart.' "

"I do not believe that this epistle should be read out loud,"

Mrs. Cable said, "if it truly is an epistle. Perhaps it's just a poem?"

"Do go ahead," Rees said. He appeared to have developed an active dislike of Mrs. Cable. "I'd like to hear the whole thing. Unless perhaps the missive was addressed to *you*, Mrs. Cable?"

She bridled. "I believe not."

"If not, why on earth would you care whether a piece of lackluster poetry was read aloud?"

She pressed her lips together.

Esme continued dreamily, " 'I would throw away the stars and the moon only to spend one more night—' " She gasped, broke off, and folded up the note, praying that she wasn't overacting.

"Well?" Mrs. Cable said.

"Aren't you going to finish?" Mr. Barret-Ducrorq said in his beery voice. "I was just thinking perhaps I should read some of this John Donne myself. Although not if his work is unfit for the ladies, of course," he added quickly.

"I believe not," Esme said, letting the letter fall gently to her left, in front of Mr. Barret-Ducrorq.

"I'll do it for you!" he said jovially. "Let's see. 'I would throw away the stars and the moon only to spend one more night in your arms.' " He paused. "Sizzling poetry, this Donne. I quite like it."

"That is no longer John Donne speaking," Darby remarked. "The author is now extemporizing."

"Hmmm." Mr. Barret-Ducrorq said.

"Did that letter refer to a night *in your arms*?" Mrs. Cable asked, quite as if she didn't know exactly what she heard.

"I fear so," Esme said with a sigh.

"Then we shall hear no more of this letter," Mrs. Cable said stoutly, cutting off Mr. Barret-Ducrorq as he was about to read another line.

"Ah, hum, exactly, exactly," he agreed.

Esme looked at Carola, who turned to Mr. Barret-Ducrorq and sweetly plucked the sheet from his stubby fingers. "I think this sounds precisely like the kind of note that my dear, dear husband would send me," she said, her tone as smooth as honey and her eyes resolutely fixed on the page, rather than on her husband. "In fact, I'm quite certain that he wrote me this note and it simply went astray."

Esme could see that Mrs. Cable was about to burst out of her stays. Henrietta was deadly pale but hadn't run from the room. Tuppy Perwinkle was torn between laughter and dismay. Darby looked mildly interested and Rees not interested at all.

Helene raised her head. She had spent most of the meal staring at her plate. "Do read your husband's letter, Carola," she said. "I think it's always so interesting to learn that there are husbands who acknowledge their wife's existence."

Esme winced, but Rees just shoveled another forkful of beef into his mouth.

Carola obediently read, " 'I shall never meet another woman with starlit hair like your own, my dearest Henri—' " She broke off.

All eyes turned to Henrietta.

"I'm sorry! It just slipped out!" Carola squealed. "I truly thought the letter must be from my husband."

Henrietta maintained an admirable calm, although a hectic rose-colored flush had replaced the chilly white of her skin.

To her enormous satisfaction, Esme saw that Darby was looking absolutely livid.

Mrs. Cable said, "Who signed that letter?"

Carola didn't say anything.

Mrs. Cable repeated, "*Who* signed that letter?"

There was an icy moment of silence.

Esme said gently, "I'm afraid it's too late for prevarication, Carola. We must look to dearest Henrietta's future now."

Mrs. Cable nodded violently.

"It is signed Simon," Carola said obediently. She looked straight at him. "Simon Darby, of course. It's a quite poetic letter, Mr. Darby. I particularly like the ending, if you'll forgive me for saying so. After all, we have already read the letter."

"Read it," Lady Holkham said in an implacable voice.

" 'Without you, I will never marry. Since you cannot marry me, darling Henrietta, I shall never marry. Children mean nothing to me; I have a superfluity as it is. All I want is you. For this life and beyond.' " Carola sighed. "How romantic!"

Then Henrietta did something that Esme had not anticipated, and which was absolutely the best of all possible actions.

She slid slowly to the right and collapsed directly into Darby's arms.